MURDER
IN MANHATTAN

BOOKS BY VERITY BRIGHT

The Lady Eleanor Swift Mystery Series

MURDER
IN MANHATTAN

VERITY BRIGHT

bookouture

Published by Bookouture in 2023

An imprint of Storyfire Ltd.
Carmelite House
50 Victoria Embankment
London EC4Y 0DZ

www.bookouture.com

ISBN: 978-1-83790-551-5
eBook ISBN: 978-1-83790-550-8

Dedicated to Hovis, my ridiculously cute and silly doggie, who watched over my Lady Swift series from the very first word I ever wrote.

1

___

'My lady, time is but the one luxury unavailable to you,' a measured voice intoned from the doorway.

Lady Eleanor Swift hurriedly stopped her young maid's fruitless efforts to tame her wilful red curls. At the sound of clattering dog's paws on the gleaming art nouveau tiled floor, she swished the train of her moss silk gown out of harm's way and accepted her bulldog's scrabbling greeting.

'Hello, Gladstone, old chum. You could have warned me a respectful telling-off was right on your heels.' Her green-eyed gaze swivelled to her butler's reflection she could now see in the three-quarter length mirror. His traditionally morning-suited form appearing even more striking, framed as it was by the modern asymmetrical black and white geometric patterned surround. He stepped over to her, the barest flick of one gloved finger sending her maid scampering to the far end of the expansive drawing room.

'Bit of a contradiction on your part there, Clifford,' Eleanor said. 'I distinctly remember you wittering my ears off with an in-depth discourse on the science of time being relative to one's frame of mind, according to Isaac Newton. And you wouldn't argue with him about such things, would you?'

'Indubitably not, my lady. Perhaps mostly, however, because it was the equally famed physicist Albert Einstein who purported such, some one hundred and eighty years after Isaac Newton died. Nevertheless, I believe the latter would agree that you have now strained the boundaries of time itself from beyond tardy into distressingly late. If you will forgive the observation.'

'Tsk! Very remiss of you, Clifford.' She waved her beloved late uncle's pocket watch. 'If you'd mentioned before how quickly time charged along here in New York in relation to sleepy Little Buckford in England, I'd have started getting ready earlier.'

'The pace is a trifle... vigorous,' he said drily. 'But "earlier", as in the day we arrived, perchance? That being a full week ago. Time enough, surely, to dress for a simple society affair, particularly in light of the unseasonal heatwave we are experiencing.'

'I don't imagine any society affair in this city is "simple". And "vigorous"! New York is positively frenetic. Just listen to that.' She shuffled in stockinged feet over to the two arched double-width windows which allowed the cacophony of horns, shouts and cries below to flood in. 'Exhilaratingly frenetic, wouldn't you say, Polly?'

Her maid stopped tickling the bulldog's ears and inched her gaze up to meet Clifford's. Receiving his nod that she had permission to speak, she jiggled from foot to foot, every inch the delightfully gangly girl Eleanor secretly hoped she would never grow out of being. 'Your ladyship, if as frene... frete... that word means like a litter of squirrels skipping round your tummy all the day, then, oh lummy, yes!' She tried to curtsey while speaking which only resulted in her stumbling sideways into Clifford's waiting gloved hands.

'Thank you, Polly,' he said wearily. 'That will be all for now.'

As her maid skipped away, Gladstone collapsed back onto the rug.

Eleanor peered up at her butler. 'I know that secretly Polly's clumsiness makes you despair, Clifford, but she means well.'

His lips pursed. 'Meaning well and performing one's duties well need not be exclusive of each other.'

'I agree. And thank you for all your sterling efforts to contain the ladies' exuberance at being in America. Having come all this way, we're here for at least the next month or two, so I realise it might be quite a task keeping our precious daily schedule on track.'

He tapped his ears as if he'd misheard. '"*Our* precious schedule"? Could it be that the lady of the house has actually begun to appreciate the importance of such?'

She smiled impishly. 'Not a bit. I'm having far too much fun just being alive in this amazing city to even think about doing the right thing at the right time. Not that you've noticed, of course.'

His silence said everything.

'Oh, come on, Clifford. You could put away your leather-bound tome of rules and give yourself permission to ease up just an inch. Especially with the heatwave you've quietly admitted even you are feeling. Let a little starch out of your underthings, perhaps?' Ignoring his sharp tut at her mention of what he always termed 'unmentionables', she continued. 'The six of us are supposed to be on holiday, after all. Especially after the journey here turned out to be anything but restful with all those hideous... other matters.' She shuddered at the memory of the double murder investigation they'd been involved in on their cross-Atlantic cruise. The one that had resulted in their needing to exonerate her policeman beau from both killings. The thought of his far too handsome looks and athletic frame made her shoulders rise with glee and then instantly fall at his having had to return to England the day before. Heart-wrenchingly too soon after he had only just proposed to her.

'Quite,' Clifford said. 'And yet ironically, the part you played in solving those hideous matters aboard is the very reason you now need a timekeeper more than ever. For you have become quite the highly sought-after celebrity. After, that is, you were hailed as "The Heroine of the High Seas" in the *New York Times*, no less.' He whipped his own pocket watch from his suit jacket and flicked the case open, holding it up in the mirror for her to see.

She peered at it before flapping a dismissive hand. 'Oh, I've got acres of time. Three quarters of an hour at least.'

'You are reading the hands in reverse, my lady. You are, in fact, already seventeen minutes late in setting off.'

'Well, whichever. And anyway, Hugh deserves as much credit for solving those ghastly murders as I do. And you, too. It was a team effort.' Hugh, or Chief Inspector Seldon, was Eleanor's long-running beau. And now her fiancé, having proposed on their last night afloat. She shrugged, twirling the ring on her left hand. 'And Gladstone, not me, is the *real* celebrity. Everywhere we've been, New York seems to have fallen in love with his wilful temperament, funny wrinkled jowls and over-stout belly. Isn't that so?' she called to her bulldog.

'Nice try,' Clifford said. 'However, changing the subject is no salve for minutes squandered from getting ready.'

She floundered for a plausible reply but merely blurted out the truth. 'I'm sure you've guessed why, you toad, but I'm big enough to confess.' She grimaced. 'I've spent too much of my life straggling through deserts and over mountains to know how to act at these wretched formal social affairs. And I'm all the more out of my depth now we're in New York. It couldn't be further from Little Buckford and Henley Hall where you and the ladies have made me believe I might actually belong.' She sighed. 'Dash it, I'm bound to make a complete hash of the whole evening and commit at least a handful of unforgivable faux pas.'

'Most assuredly, my lady.'

She laughed at his good-natured teasing, ever grateful her late uncle's bequest to her had included not only his estate but also his former batman, butler, confidant and best friend all rolled into one.

A gentle knock came at the door.

'Come in, Mrs Butters,' he called.

Eleanor's diminutive and soft-curved housekeeper flustered in, her grey curls bouncing around her motherly face, which, unusually, showed a hint of anxiety.

'Ah! Mr Clifford. 'Tis, umm, just—'

He held out a gloved hand without a word.

She grimaced and handed him a small, stoppered bottle from her apron. With an apologetic smile to Eleanor, she started towards the door, only to bump into Mrs Trotman, Eleanor's cook, hurrying in. Seeing Clifford, Mrs Trotman spun in a perfect arc, calling, 'Wrong room, 'pologies,' and beat her friend back out into the corridor.

Eleanor laughed. 'What was that all about?'

He placed what he had taken from the housekeeper into her hand. 'The almond oil relaxant for your hair, I believe, my lady.'

She frowned. 'But Polly...' She stared at the similar-looking bottle already on the bureau.

Clifford sighed. 'Polly was combing sterilising solution into your hair. If I might be so bold as to suggest one hastens to finish the final embellishments to your... almost elegant outfit. Or gets "a wiggle on", as I believe is the local expression. And also the latest repeated hilarity in the kitchen among the ladies.' He shook his head. 'To the detriment of several pieces of tableware already, in Polly's case. And, therefore, the household accounts. For which, my sincere apologies.'

Eleanor hid a smile at the image of her four female staff all wiggling and giggling their way about their duties. 'No apologies needed, Clifford. Since you were your ever-ferocious Jack Russell over those very accounts, we have managed to rent a rather sumptuous apartment for a bargain price. Even if it isn't in one of the most prestigious districts. However, it could not be any more beautifully appointed, or more perfect for our needs, or more exquisite a building itself.'

The palatial main sitting room with wrap-around balcony might have been designed to be the apartment's centrepiece, but she equally loved the vogueishly modern, but cosy, reception rooms and library. The three en-suite bedrooms were all delightful and the staff quarters generous. Her own personal suite included a private sitting room filled with art deco artworks, gold and marble bathroom, and a bedroom big enough to hold a party in.

She eyed him sideways. 'But it does mean with all that extra distance to tonight's uptown and very prestigious address, I'm going to be fearfully late. Especially as my butler has lost me many valuable minutes in squabbling.'

His lips quirked. 'Touché, my lady.' He bowed from the shoulders and headed towards the door.

'Hang on, you monster!' she cried after him. 'What do you mean "almost elegant outfit"? Clifford?'

2

In front of the lift, the increasingly impatient tap of Eleanor's satin evening heels reverberated around the polished ocean of marble tiles. Clifford had been infuriatingly right, as ever. There was still the teeming morass of vibrant life to navigate that she'd learned on day one roared ceaselessly beyond the nine floors of elegant tranquillity. And she should have left at least twenty minutes earlier to allow for it.

She gently restrained her over-keen bulldog, whose paws scrabbled on the tiles as he pulled on his lead.

Clifford eyed his pocket watch. 'Bravo, my lady. If you were to arrive twenty-eight minutes late, which seems inevitable at this juncture, one could almost regard it as on time, given your past tardiness.'

She caught his teasing look, which made her smile and her shoulders relax. 'Very droll!' She gestured down at her gown. 'I'd like to see you try furnishing yourself in all these acres of fiddlesome garb in less time.'

He stroked an imaginary beard. 'Hmm. On reflection, if I might respectfully decline the gauntlet you have thrown down.' He put away his watch and pulled out his notebook.

'Gauntlets have no place in an elegant lady's wardrobe, silly.' She tried to peer over his arm to see what he'd written, but he deftly closed the notebook. 'Have you really documented how often I've been late?'

He slipped the notebook back into his inside pocket. 'I couldn't say, my lady. Now, perhaps you might profit from this enforced interlude with another run over who you will likely meet this evening? Followed by a brief reminder of suitable topics of conversation?'

She threw her arms out. 'That would be helpful if only I could remember a single name or suggested subject matter when facing the swarm of society lions. All of them baying for a piece of me as the novelty of a titled English lady.'

'It might help to know that lions do not swarm. Or bay. Nor attend society functions. Even in New York.'

'Maybe not. But that's exactly how it feels.'

She groaned at the whirr of the lift mechanism as it rose and stopped yet again at any floor except hers.

Is the entire building colluding against you arriving at this function on time, Ellie?

'Stairs!'

Her butler shook his head and gave a surprisingly accurate impression of her tottering on her heels and falling headlong down them.

'My lady, patience needs be your other companion to Master Gladstone and myself this evening.'

'But the infernal lift can't need to operate this slowly! It's not like we'd turn inside out if it moved just a little faster.'

'True. However, the lift's gear-reduction drive mechanism feeds the two leading steel ropes the full length of the hoistway onto the drum. Were the lift to ascend any faster, the grooved sheaves would likely fail or the counterweight jam. Instead, it will arrive shortly and transport you safely to street level in stately style. And with your head still attached to your shoulders if' – he held up a finger as she reached towards the lift door – 'you wait for it to appear, rather than hang inelegantly and dangerously out into the shaft.'

She laughed. 'Which, in truth, you're secretly thinking would save you the trouble of boiling my head each time one of my trifling foibles irritates the very starch from your cuffs. Seriously, though, Clifford, how do you even know what kind of gubbins makes this thing operate?'

'An appreciation of engineering. Nothing more.'

'Nonsense.' Despite her exasperation, she was in awe of his relentless pursuit to increase his already encyclopaedic knowledge of just about everything. 'You devour learning such things as avidly as I do sausages. Oops!' She shook her head at Gladstone's eager-eyed look on hearing his favourite 's' word. 'Sorry, old chum. Breakfast was a horrible number of hours ago, I know, but you'll still have to wait until tomorrow morning.'

Her bulldog woofed woefully in disbelief.

'That creature of yours should be outside in the street where it belongs!' a husky female voice called in a strong New York drawl blanketed with much upper-class affectation.

Eleanor turned to see a woman in her early sixties glowering her way towards them. She seemed to be struggling without the aid of her gold-banded walking stick, which she was using to point at Gladstone. The disapproving rustle of her voluminous violet taffeta skirt added a further austerity to her persona as much as the tight lacings of her matching bodice jacket. Up close, however, the radiant and vivacious beauty that had once been was still visible through the mask of unkind wrinkles and sagging cheeks.

Eleanor slapped on her best winning smile. 'Forgive me. We haven't been introduced?'

The woman snorted. 'No need. You are that English "lady", happy to have her name and photograph splashed all over the gutter press!'

Eleanor held the hard stare boring into her skull. 'Well, as you obviously know who I am, it would be wonderful to know your name too, as clearly we are neighbours?'

Clifford cleared his throat. 'This, my lady, is Mrs Henry Theodore D. Melchum.'

'Ah, lovely to meet you.' Eleanor wondered if any wife in New York ever used their own first name rather than her husband's. 'Evidently you've met my butler already?'

This drew a purse-lipped look that could have passed for a ruched handbag. 'Well, whatever next! I would do no such thing as consort with a servant. As if! And I thought old money knew how to behave. How wrong one can be proved.'

The woman reminded Eleanor of Lady Saxonby, a friend of her late uncle's back in England. Before Eleanor had departed on her cruise to New York, Lady Saxonby had berated her similarly. She'd also insisted that New York was full of 'swindlers, thieves and murderers'. As Eleanor had dealt with all three on the transatlantic crossing, she figured there couldn't be any left in New York itself. But, apparently, there were plenty of waspish, entitled old women!

Before she could reply, however, she spotted that Gladstone seemed very animated. 'What is it, boy? Oh!'

With a swish of violet taffeta, a slender creamy-white cat with the silkiest of coats stepped out from under Mrs Melchum's skirts. It hissed at the bulldog who shot behind Eleanor's legs with a whimper. With a toss of its aristocratic head, the cat minced haughtily towards the lift which had finally arrived. Clifford opened the door, only to have the cat march over his shoes and position itself in the centre of the circular scrollwork cage. Gladstone peered around Eleanor's legs to risk a low growl, which earned him a sharp rap of Mrs Melchum's cane only half an inch from his front paws.

'After nineteen years here, Catamina is a well-respected

lady resident of this building. Like her owner,' she added pointedly.

'She's very pretty,' Eleanor said. 'Like all Siamese cats.'

'No!' Mrs Melchum snapped. 'Catamina is not like any other Siamese. But only a true aficionado would recognise that.' She bustled into the lift, standing to one side of her evidently beloved feline. 'And as for that!' Mrs Melchum pointed her cane at Gladstone again. 'A mis-proportioned beast like that has no place in a building of this calibre. If Catamina refuses to eat for the next week, it will be entirely his fault.'

'Her choosing,' Eleanor said firmly. 'Siamese are notoriously fussy eaters. Even as a non-aficionado, I know that.' She left out that as a young child she'd spent a week with her parents as the guest of the King of Siam playing with his precious felines who ruled the palace.

'Lady Swift, I believe you will find the streets are lined with other, more suitable, apartment buildings. I wish you a happy and rapid relocation!'

Eleanor bit back a smile as Clifford closed the scrollwork lift door on Mrs Melchum and her cat. Double-checking it was secured, he bowed.

'Rather than offend Miss Catamina with Master Gladstone's boorish presence, her ladyship will graciously take the stairs.'

As they hurried down the last of the ornate landings, Eleanor shook her head. 'Whatever can have bitten that old woman so hard, do you imagine?'

'I believe, my lady, it might be life itself. If you will forgive my rendering an opinion.'

She shook her head. 'Go on, Mr Ever-Even-Handed, what makes you say that?'

'Suffice to say, Mr Henry Theodore D. Melchum passed twenty years ago today, I happened to note.'

She smiled. 'Ah, "happened to note" as in you looked him

up. In the hope, no doubt, you could therefore excuse her unpleasant demeanour and soothe my irritation at the inevitable fireworks you predicted might erupt between us when we met?'

'It isn't my place to comment, my lady.' He winked. 'But, yes.'

Her brow furrowed. 'You know though, Clifford, I think you're right. There's a story behind that woman. And I don't think it had a happy ending.'

3

'Well, you're all the berries tonight, Lady Swift,' a cheery voice greeted her as the gilded double-front doors opened. 'And Gladstone in a spotted bow tie, too! Howdy, little guy.'

'Evening, Marty.' She smiled at the doorman as he playwrestled with a delighted Gladstone. He was around forty, she guessed, his fair skin setting off his dark eyes and near-black wavy hair that poked from his smart gold-braided cap. 'Mind you, "the berries"? I've no idea what that means.' She looked over at Clifford, who arched a mystified brow in reply.

'All it means is, it's gotta be a good evenin' guaranteed if you trip out looking so fancy in your nines.'

'Ah,' Clifford said. '"Leave dressed in one's finest", my lady.'

'That's it, Mr Clifford.' The doorman gave him a cheeky grin. 'You gonna accompany the lady for the sake of New York, seein' as her *fiancé* ain't here to do the honours? Is that the score?'

Eleanor didn't miss how much this tickled her butler's mischievous funny bone. 'Indeed. It's likely the short straw, Marty. But someone has to shoulder the responsibility now

Chief Inspector Seldon is no longer here to ensure her ladyship conducts herself in an orderly fashion.'

The doorman's chuckle made her smile. 'Then good luck to you out there, sir. It's a crazy jungle for trying to tame an excitable doll in.' He turned and slipped his thumb and forefinger in his mouth and let out a piercing whistle.

'It's certainly close to sweltering with this heatwave.' She fanned her face with the pristine handkerchief Clifford had passed her as they descended the last of the steps.

'In April! But you know that's New York in a bag. Always expect the unexpected.'

She pointed to his shiny-buttoned uniform coat. 'Surely in this heat you're allowed to remove that, aren't you?'

He rolled his eyes. 'Trust me, it's easier to stick it out.' He nodded to Clifford, who, despite Eleanor's pleas, still sported his equally heavy black wool overcoat. 'The ladies sure got the long straw on breezin' outta the wardrobe when the weather's playin' nice, say, Mr Clifford?'

She waved a hand. 'Don't encourage him any further, Marty. I've already lost a quarter of an hour squabbling with him. And then another with Mrs Melchum, and now I'm late.'

Okay, technically you were already late, Ellie.

Marty grimaced and lowered his voice. 'You want I should call you the doctor to dress the lacerations from your run-in with Mrs Melchum?' As she laughed, a taxi pulled up at the entrance. 'Iver Driver!' he hollered through cupped hands. 'You got Lady Luck again tonight.'

'Lady Luck?'

'I ain't bein' rude, Lady Swift, just sayin' even New York could do with the kind of magic I think you got hidin' up them pretty-frilled sleeves. Especially after what my eyes didn't believe they was readin' about you in the papers.' He opened the now familiar taxi door bearing the lettering 15C FIRST ¼ MILE; 5C EACH ADDITIONAL ¼ MILE. 'Where to?'

'Mr Ogden P. Dellaney's house.' She stepped into the taxi. 'That's—'

'Ain't no need to tell Iver the address,' Marty said, looking at her strangely. 'Everyone knows where that is.'

'Oh? Do you know of him, then?'

'Of him, sure. And him in the flesh, too. I... I used to work for him.'

'What a coincidence. Well, he kindly sent me an invitation to his charity evening.'

Marty hoisted the scrabbling Gladstone up into the cab with a grunt. 'Just remember not to take any wooden nickels there tonight, huh?' The door clicked shut, leaving Eleanor and Clifford staring blankly at each other.

'Evening back there, folks,' the driver called over his shoulder in a gravelly voice.

'Hello, Iver,' she said, shaking herself out of her confusion at Marty's parting words.

She thought, not for the first time, that Iver seemed the opposite of Marty the doorman's effervescent optimism. A good ten years older, she reckoned, with a cloth cap on his thickly grey-haired dome, his eyes looked out from under heavy brows with a pronounced world-weariness. Yet, despite his relentless airing of his somewhat contentious, and doom-laden, opinions, there was something that had made her warm to him on their first trip. Pride of place on his dashboard was a battered, unframed photograph of his wife. With every other sentence, he deferred to her, saying, 'But no one knows better on that than my Sadie when it really comes to it.'

'It's entirely Clifford's fault,' she said impishly, avoiding her butler's gaze. 'But I'm hopelessly late. I don't suppose—'

'I could tally hop and not spare the dogs? Or whatever lah-lah is the saying in England? You're in New York, lady! Time ain't never on your side out in the streets. Look about ya. We got Detroit cars everywhere now, like we used to only have scuffed boots a handful of years back. We taxis gotta fight the idiot business suits at the wheels. The buses gotta fight the trucks. The horse traps gotta fight the fools still strolling in the road as if the world ain't changed.' He grunted. 'And all of us gotta fight the stupid traffic cops and their darned whistles.'

She grimaced. 'I do realise that. But it's a really important event.'

'Like everyone else don't think the same about where they're going!'

Despite his protestations, however, it appeared he had taken her pleas to heart as he zigzagged around every obstacle. Clifford scooped Gladstone up to press the bulldog against his legs, shifting him first one way and then the other to protect the perfect crease in his suit trousers.

'Move it, buddy!' Iver yelled at the driver of a horse-drawn cart which had stopped in the middle of the road to retrieve his evidently inadequately lashed barrels which now lay across the taxi's path.

Once they'd picked up speed again, Iver scraped past a bus chock-full of passengers, many precariously balanced on the running boards. Clifford swallowed hard.

'My lady, I can assure you that arriving disgracefully late in New York society is still less of a faux pas than arriving disgracefully dead.'

'Oh, stop fussing,' she said, clinging onto anything within reach. *Perhaps you did lay it on a bit thick about being late, Ellie.* 'I survived decapitation by lift already tonight, so think of me as our lucky charm. Whoa!' She nodded gratefully as his arm shot out to stop her catapulting out of her seat. 'Besides, we came here for an adventure.'

'No. We came for a holiday, as we discussed most clearly. *Ho-li-day.*'

'That too. But it's exhilarating, admit it.'

Before he could reply, the taxi screeched to a halt.

'What'd I tell ya?' Iver grumbled, slapping his steering wheel. 'Now we got the broadsides holdin' everythin' up.'

'Broadsides?' Eleanor glanced at Clifford. 'Do you have a New York dictionary secreted about your impeccable butlering togs, by any chance?'

'Remissly not, my lady. Apologies.'

'Protest marchers,' Iver called back. 'These numb-headed doodles need to be Southside on the steps of City Hall, not stealing time offa folks heading up towards Broadway.'

'What are they protesting about?'

'Nothin' that's gonna change by wasting boot leather and painted words.'

Once past the protest, Iver slid their taxi right, only to slow down again. Eleanor leaned over the back of her seat to peer through his windscreen. 'What's the hold-up now? I can't see any more protestors.'

'There ain't no hold-up, 'cept where we are, lady. It don't do to knock down anyone as lives in this kinda neighbourhood. Nor ruffle the hem of their wife's petticoat as you pass. Or so much as breathe outta line. Trust me, you gotta behave right here, or else.'

Clifford's reassuring look as her nerves resurfaced was rather wasted as Iver drew the taxi to a halt and announced, 'Rather you than me.'

'Oh my!' she said, breathlessly. Spanning not only as far down the tree-lined avenue as she could see but also continuing around the corner was a mansion of unimaginable magnitude.

'Clifford! That's like several Henley Halls stuck together but in the middle of the city.'

Iver nodded. 'They bought the whole block and knocked it into one house. Eighty-four rooms, they say it's got. What's he do with them all, that's what my Sadie wants to know? But ain't likely we're gonna ever get invited in.'

Clifford opened her door and after she had stepped out,

Iver sped away. Nine expansive semicircular steps led up to an even more expansive terrace. At the top, Eleanor took a deep breath at the huge front door overseen by a giant stone eagle.

'Ready, my lady?' Clifford whispered as he slipped Gladstone's lead into her hand.

She smiled up at him. 'If the lions are.'

As the door opened, he melted away to find the staff entrance. She turned to the imposingly tall doorman dressed in such over-braided livery she wondered if she had interrupted him from starring in a pantomime. 'Ah, good evening. I am Lady Swift.' She gestured at the house. 'It must be marvellous to work in such exquisite, yet modern surroundings.'

She couldn't tell if his silence suggested that was a theory he did not subscribe to or if the poor fellow had actually lost his tongue.

'Myers! The instructions were clear,' an imperious voice called. A square-faced, middle-aged man appeared dressed in what she imagined Clifford would term a 'flashy' evening suit. He swung a gold and diamond pocket watch on the chain attached to his velvet waistcoat.

'Lady Swift! Welcome.' His piercing dark eyes looked her over with a little too much intensity.

'Mr Dellaney. Sincere apologies for being just a touch behind time.' She'd only met him for a moment at another society event, but he'd invited her to his next do and everyone had assured her that you never refused such an invite. She nodded at her bulldog. 'And this is Gladstone.'

He frowned at the dog and then looked at her again. 'We're mostly in the Grand Salon. I'll be joining you there shortly. In the meantime... Myers!' His bark made her jump. 'If I needed a doorstop, I'd have had one designed and cast. Show Lady Swift the way to the Grand Salon. Now!'

As she followed the doorman, she rolled her shoulders back. *Into the lion's den then, Ellie.*

4

'Oh, quite,' Eleanor said distractedly for the umpteenth time as she waved her untouched glass of fizz and flaky pastry lobster canapé, the latter much to Gladstone's delight as he eagerly snuffled up the crumbs. Her head was swimming with the blur of faces and already forgotten names. And with the very different way the upper echelons of Manhattan society behaved. Far from the English aristocracy's habit of playing down their wealth and position when together, here they positively revelled in it.

'Quite, what?' a penetrating female voice interrupted her thoughts.

Eleanor winced at the arc of expectant faces staring back at her. She'd been in the middle of a conversation with a group of ladies. However, nothing among the sea of pearl and diamond chokers and elaborate jewel-pinned tresses hinted at which of these sophisticated society women had spoken last. Then her eyes fell on one lady whose intense stare felt as though it was trying to climb into her soul. There was no mistaking that those eyes were a set she had yet to be introduced to. They were so intensely copper brown even the lights from the myriad suspended electrified candelabras added nothing to their natural luminosity. The accompanying mahogany curls set off her striking heart-shaped face all the more. She wore a beautifully tailored dress with a plunging fur-trimmed diamond of a décolletage. Yet despite being almost ten years older than her, Eleanor guessed, this woman exuded a vivacity like she'd never encountered.

'Good evening,' Eleanor said. 'We were just discussing how I could possibly fit in all the wonderful sights and activities New York has to offer in the time I have left here.'

The woman shrugged one perfect shoulder. 'A topic which you obviously are far from enthralled by.'

'Gracious! Quite the opposite.' Eleanor smiled apologetically around the group. 'In fact, I wish I had brought a notebook to capture all the suggestions so kindly offered. I shall feel such the blunt brick back in England if I've missed some.'

'Quite,' the woman said again pointedly. 'It seems you've even more to learn than I suspected. Come.'

Eleanor flinched in surprise as the woman slid her arm through hers and steered them both off to a quieter corner, Gladstone lumbering excitedly alongside. Despite her confusion, Eleanor threw on her best smile.

'I'm Eleanor Swift.'

'Lady Eleanor Swift, I know. What a ring that has to it.' The woman scowled at the nearest of the serving staff, who hurried away. She turned back to Eleanor. 'Not that you do, however. Have a ring, I mean.'

'Oh, I do, actually.' Her shoulders rose as she held out her left hand. 'My beau proposed the night before we arrived in New York.'

The woman examined it, wrinkling her nose in disdain. 'Pointless. No divorce court in the world is going to grant you a single dollar bill or one chipped corner of a brownstone on the strength of an engagement. Especially with *that* ring.'

Eleanor stiffened. It had been all her policeman beau had been able to afford, and it meant the world to her. 'Forgive the directness of my question, but who are you, by the way?'

She turned at the smooth male voice which answered from behind. 'Oh, there's no "by the way" about Mrs Lavinia Vanderdale. If you have any ambitions in this city, this is the lady you need to know.'

'Why, Atticus dear!' Eleanor's new companion purred as she ran a set of manicured nails down his velvet jacket sleeve. 'You're so charming. And so right, of course.'

The man in his late thirties gave a bright and easy laugh. He was one of the few clean-shaven guests she'd seen that evening. Sporting flatteringly trimmed champagne-blond hair, he had an air of well-travelled confidence that none of the other men she'd been introduced to matched.

He smiled warmly at Eleanor, his hand outstretched. 'Atticus J. Wyatt. It sure is an honour to meet you, Lady Swift. And your handsome furry friend, too.' He ran gentle hands around the instantly besotted Gladstone's wrinkled jowls. 'How is New York treating you so far?'

Eleanor's acute ear detected the delightful twang of a Southern accent.

'Splendidly. It's just an impossible decision as to what to go and see or do next.'

'Well, there sure is a hand willing to help.'

Eleanor's eyes flicked to the woman she now at least knew the name of.

Wyatt laughed. 'Oh no, not Lavinia. New York herself.'

Not for the first time, Eleanor was taken aback by how the residents held their city in such exalted regard. It seemed it was universally believed to exert a power and irrefutable will of its own.

'And how will I recognise that hand when it intervenes, Mr Wyatt?'

'Because every sunset will be late and dawn early, Lady Swift. And all the hours in between will have unfolded the way you wished for. And do call me Atticus.'

'And please call me Eleanor. But what if I haven't made any wishes?'

'Then you might as well slide on down to Virginia instead and simply enjoy that the trees grow real straight.'

Eleanor's bemusement evidently showed.

Mrs Vanderdale rolled her eyes. 'Honestly, Atticus, that's just riddles to simple English ears.'

Eleanor smoothed her expression at the pointed barb. 'It's true. Gladstone hasn't a clue what that means.'

Wyatt chuckled. 'My apologies, Gladstone, sir. What I meant is that New York is a place where life doesn't simply happen. Every minute has to be planned. And lived.'

'Which,' Mrs Vanderdale said mockingly, 'is why dear old Atticus can't bring himself to scurry back down South even though he misses so much about it. Not that he'll confess to that.'

'Whereabouts in the South?' Eleanor said.

'Beautiful, boundless, bountiful Texas.'

She whispered behind her hand. 'Actually, Atticus, sorry to break it to you, but that had all the hallmarks of a confession about missing your homeland.'

He rapped his knuckles against his forehead as he laughed. 'Am I that transparent?'

'Yes, Atticus dear.' Lavinia spun him by the shoulders. 'Now scoop up your tonic water, there's a good boy, and leave us ladies to talk about what really matters over Ogden's medicinal cocktails.'

After promising to send Eleanor an invitation to one of his dinner evenings, and the whispered advice not to upset Mrs Vanderdale, Wyatt did as he was told. He then strolled barely ten feet before he was surrounded by eager evening suits, all vying for his attention.

Eleanor held her hands up. 'So, Mrs Vanderdale, tell me, what is it that really matters?'

'Only one thing, naturally. But all in good time. Now go easy with Atticus. He's a widower.'

All the more mystified, Eleanor merely nodded.

Despite their own obvious wealth displayed in an astonishing array of jewels gracing their necks, wrists and foreheads, the group of women she now found herself steered towards all deferred to Mrs Vanderdale. Apparently, her last husband had been in construction and on his death had left her a very wealthy widow and a force to be reckoned with in high society. Collectively twittered assents followed her every word as they discussed who had bought what property that week and who had been seen with whom.

'You know, Lady Swift,' one of the indistinguishable beauties cooed as Eleanor devoured some surprisingly moreish breaded cheese balls in the hope it would stop her stomach from gurgling. 'You're every bit as I pictured.'

'Oh, me too,' another warbled. 'So lucky that Ogden invited you.'

The first of the two nodded along with the rest of the group, minus Mrs Vanderdale, Eleanor noted, who seemed amused by the exchange.

'We'd have been simply eaten up with curiosity otherwise,' the second ended with a smile.

'Well,' Eleanor said, floundering to know how to answer through her mouthful of cheese. 'I hope in person I haven't disappointed your curiosity?'

'Does it come with the title?' another woman jumped in.

'A bulldog?' Eleanor quipped to lighten her discomfort at feeling every inch the zoo exhibit. 'No. Well, yes, actually. I inherited him too.'

Behind her, she heard Wyatt's easy laugh as he passed with another man. He caught her eye, showing he was tickled by her words. Not so, her group of female inquisitors, it appeared. They stared back at her in confusion.

'Bull what? Oh, that sturdy fellow!' one of them said, gesturing at Gladstone. 'No, what she meant was, that reserved air you've got working for you. Like proper royalty.'

Despite herself, Eleanor couldn't help laughing. 'What! Me?' She shook her head. 'Sorry, ladies. Please don't think me rude, it's just that I wish my butler had been here to hear that!'

As if by magic, Clifford slid into her eyeline holding a silver tray bearing a single filled cocktail glass. 'Your special request, my lady.' He melted away as enigmatically as he had appeared.

Bolstered by his reassuring, if brief, presence, she smiled around the now more animated faces.

'Your butler?' one of them asked. 'English? A truly proper one? Like in those Regency novels?'

She cast about and, spotting Clifford was still within earshot, raised her voice. 'Exactly like that. Infuriatingly proper and the epitome of the eighteen-hundreds.' She spread her hands. 'And I couldn't imagine even a day without him.'

'Is that so?' she caught Mrs Vanderdale mutter as she stared over at him. Turning back to Eleanor, she nodded. 'Yes, you must.'

'Sorry? Must what?'

'Grace us with a visit to my club.' The assembled company gasped. 'The Ladies' Liberty Club. Membership is exclusively by my invitation only. But you may visit as a guest, of course.'

'Too kind. I'd love to.'

A gong sounded and a footman's voice floated over their heads. 'Ladies and gentlemen, the charity event is starting.'

Dellaney appeared on a raised dais and launched into a lengthy speech. Mostly concerned, it seemed to Eleanor, with boasting about his and, less so, other socialites' list of charitable works and donations. Several guests followed him to similarly praise mostly themselves before a round of applause returned the evening to the more pressing matter of high society gossip.

Now entirely devoid of anything to say and fearful her range of interested expressions was tiring, Eleanor excused herself and went off in search of the ladies' restroom. Before she could reach it, however, Dellaney berating one of his staff in the corridor drew her up short.

'You've no business being here, Temples! Get back to the cars,' he snarled to the abashed man regaled in a smart navy, brass-buttoned overcoat and matching cap.

'I would, Mr Dellaney, sir. And right away,' the man stuttered. 'But—'

'Not now!'

'But one of your cars, sir. It's not in the garage. I parked it there myself this after—' The member of staff Eleanor now assumed to be Dellaney's chauffeur jerked to a halt at the thunderous face before him.

'Are you deaf! I said NOT. NOW!' Dellaney spun on his heel and headed towards Eleanor, who was pretending to examine the objets d'art on the top shelf beside her. She waved at him.

'I hope you don't mind me admiring your collection? It's simply exquisite.'

His expression switched from anger to that of a smug toad lording it over the riverbank. 'Oh, just a few trifles.' He flapped a dismissive hand at the vast array of crystal, gold and marble ornaments. 'My wife likes how they shine.'

'Your wife? Gracious, how rude of me. I haven't met her to say thank you for the evening.'

'Oh, she'll be about somewhere,' he said disinterestedly. 'If you'll pardon me for a short while, Lady Swift, the garden calls, but I'll find you straight after. And that's an Ogden P. promise.'

She nodded. 'Enjoy your cigar.'

She shook her head at her host's departing back. Given the size and opulence of his mansion, she could only imagine the vast fleet of cars and why one missing would be of little consequence.

Still, Ellie, you can't blame the chauffeur for pointing it out.

'She's not about somewhere,' a nasal voice slurred in her ear. 'She's right here, don't you know?'

5

Eleanor turned to see an elaborately coiffured blonde woman dripping in jewels and fighting the mink stole draped unevenly over one shoulder.

'Good evening.' She tried not to reach out a hand as the woman swayed. 'Are you—'

'Why yes!' the woman cried theatrically. 'I'm Mrs Ogden P. Dellaney for my sins, as they say.'

Eleanor smiled at her hostess. 'What a pleasure to meet you. And to spend an evening in your beautiful home. Thank you. Oh, but I'm Eleanor Swift.'

'The English lady. I guessed. How did they treat you?' She jerked her head at the door into the Grand Salon.

'Your guests? Oh, delightfully...' She tailed off at Mrs Dellaney's strong headshake, which made her wobble on her perilously high heels. 'Would... would you like a seat?'

'No, I would like another drink.' Mrs Dellaney hiccuped and then giggled. 'The only smart thing my husband ever did was buy up an entire liquor store before this prohibition nonsense.'

'Ah.' Now Eleanor understood what Mrs Vanderdale meant

by 'Ogden's medicinal cocktails'. 'I've been enjoying the tonic
water, actually.' She had taken a leaf from Mr Wyatt's self-
professed teetotal book. The cocktail Clifford had furnished her
with was merely made to look like the genuine article.

'A word of advice,' Mrs Dellaney hissed conspiratorially.
'You need to learn how to lie better if you're going to survive
New York.'

Eleanor feigned a laugh. 'I'm only here for a few weeks.
Besides, I haven't—'

'Oh, come on, Lady... Lady...'

'Swift.'

'That. Ogden's vultures weren't delightful. The men left
you feeling like a curio they picked up from the sidewalk. And
the women, pfff! They'll be dropping your name at every event
for the next six months to boost their own standing because they
met a real, titled lady.'

Eleanor felt she needed to defend her host. After all, she'd
enjoyed his hospitality all evening. 'Well, I've been splendidly
looked after, actually. Especially by Mr Wyatt and Mrs
Vanderdale. It's lovely they are such good friends—'

Mrs Dellaney snorted. 'You've a lot to learn. The only thing
that isn't fake about this town is how fake it is. Let me tell you,
Atticus is about as teetotal as a wagon bent under the weight of
brandy barrels. And as for Mrs Glorious Queen Vanderdale
and him. If the war they're always waging is being friends, I'll
take enemies any day.'

Eleanor shrugged. 'Does that mean I won't see you at the
Ladies' Liberty Club? Mrs Vanderdale invited me.'

'Poor you,' Mrs Dellaney called over her shoulder as she
tottered down the corridor. 'If I were you, I'd lay in a ditch and
hope a truck ran over me instead.'

After her rather unsettling chat with Mrs Dellaney, Eleanor
rejoined the other guests and, to her surprise, actually started to
enjoy herself. She found fathoming the meaning of 'New York

speak' enchanting, to the extent that she had to restrain herself from imitating the bewitching drawl.

However, the crayfish tail, spicy prawn, and herby turkey rissoles she'd happily tucked into were now fighting in her stomach. She blamed the ubiquitous rich and vibrantly orange cheese they had all featured in one form or another. Either way, she had already decided to call it a night and seek out Clifford when Wyatt bid her goodbye.

'Your pyjamas calling you too, Mr Wyatt?'

His brows rose as much as his mouth curved into a broad smile. 'Now that's not a question I can honestly say I have ever been asked, Lady Swift.'

In her peripheral vision, she caught Clifford pinching the bridge of his nose in despair as he waited with her silver shawl.

She shrugged. 'Oh, it's an English expression.'

Wyatt laughed. 'I'll remember that. And thank you kindly for your stimulating conversation this evening.' He eased down to Gladstone's level and cupped the bulldog's wrinkled chin. 'And you for your entertainment too, sir.' He rose to offer Eleanor his hand, she thought, but instead held out a saliva-covered billiard ball. 'I believe your furry friend rather fancied a souvenir of the evening.'

She shook her head at her bulldog. 'Oh, Gladstone! Just as well you don't have pockets. Who knows what you'd steal!'

Wyatt laughed again. 'I sure hope you'll do me the honour of accepting that invitation I mentioned? Though, now I know to lock up the games room first. Until then, however, please excuse me. I make it a rule to retire early. After all, owls may be wise, but they aren't successful much at business.'

'Unlike your own commercial interests must be,' she said, thinking back to how many of the other men among the guest list she'd witnessed swarming around him.

'Only on account of my never deviating from my motto. Bid

dusk early goodnight so as to chide dawn for rising later than you.'

Eleanor watched him stroll away, smiling at the image of him chastising the sun from behind an enormous oak desk, polite and softly delivered though his reprimand would certainly be.

Like most social events she'd attended, the departure of the first guest set off a flurry of others. However, it seemed no one felt they could leave until enough effusive pleasantries had been exchanged in the hallway. To Gladstone, proceedings had dragged on far too long already. He sprawled his bulky form on to her satin evening shoes with a sharp huff.

'Oh, it's been so enchanting,' yet one more faceless woman said to Eleanor. 'New York's certainly had its eyes peeled wide open tonight by you, Lady Swift.'

The neatly trimmed whiskers of the man beside her nodded with an amused look.

'Oh, gracious, far from intentionally,' she said, while accepting her shawl from Clifford.

Mrs Vanderdale appeared, and the couple instantly stepped aside.

'Good night, Lady Swift.' Mrs Vanderdale hesitated. 'I shall decide when it will be best for you to visit the Ladies' Liberty Club and send you a note to that effect. To where shall I dispatch it?'

After her conversation with Mrs Dellaney, she wasn't sure now if she wanted to visit Mrs Vanderdale's elite club. But as she raised her hand to reply, she found to her bewilderment it contained a calling card. With her name and New York address on! Her gaze slid to Clifford, who merely stared back, his expression as inscrutable as ever.

'Oh, er, thank you. To here would be lovely.' She handed over the card. Mrs Vanderdale glanced at the address and grimaced. Eleanor turned away. 'Now,' she said, glancing across the sea of heads, 'I really must find Mr... oh, there you are.'

Dellaney had appeared in front of her, his eyes feeling a little too curious for her to be comfortable. 'Lady Swift. It has been a pleasure. However, too short a one. I insist you join another of my other gatherings in the near future. A far smaller, more intimate one.'

She was just about to thank him, but explain her remaining time in the city was already full to bursting, when he fixed her with a pointed look.

'Come to my *proper* home, Lady Swift. I'd love for you to see how Ogden P. Dellaney *really* lives. Only let me have your address this time. Tracking you through the *New York Times* is no way to continue our association.'

Mrs Vanderdale snorted and stalked off.

Eleanor watched her go out of the corner of her eye.

What's her problem, Ellie?

She shrugged. 'Er, thank you, Mr Dellaney. Your... *proper* home?' Her gaze roamed over the palatial hundred-foot hallway.

Dellaney nodded. 'You got it. It's in Bay Shore.'

Eleanor's eyes flicked to Clifford again, who gave an imperceptible nod. He handed Dellaney's beleaguered-looking valet another of the cards.

'Thank you, Mr Myers,' he murmured.

'Likewise, Mr Clifford.'

Eleanor tied her shawl loosely and looked around the hallway. 'Is Mrs Dellaney free? I'd like to say good night and—'

Dellaney waved a dismissive hand. 'She'll be somewhere. Don't stress yourself waiting on her account, though. Good evening. But not goodbye.' He brushed her fingers with his, making her shudder, and then marched away, leaving the last twenty or so guests staring after him, their own farewells dying on their lips.

Thinking that really had to be the end of the evening, Eleanor paused as she drew level with Myers. She'd made so many faux pas already, not to mention Gladstone's help in adding to them, she decided that thanking Dellaney's head of household couldn't do any more harm.

'Please do pass on my commendations to your team who looked after us all so well this evening, Myers.'

A wide-eyed gaze was her only reply.

'Seems you do have a lot to learn, Ellie,' she murmured, spinning around, expecting to be treated to Clifford's best admonishing look. But he was not behind her. He was, instead, nodding respectfully to a lady who was slipping him a card of her own.

She shook her head. *It seems, Ellie, your butler is in greater demand than you are!*

6

Outside, she stepped into the taxi with her butler's elbow for assistance so she could hold her gown tails aside.

'Ah, Iver, what a treat it's you again!'

'Yeah, yeah, lady,' her driver called gruffly, but he shot her a grin in his rear-view mirror.

'In you go, Master Gladstone.' Clifford hoisted the bulldog inside. 'Good evening, Iver. A long night for you, it appears.'

'Not as long as yours, Mr Clifford.'

Eleanor sat back as they pulled away and eyed Clifford thoughtfully.

He shifted in his seat. 'My lady?'

'Oh, just wondering how your evening at Dellaney's went?'

'As expected,' he replied enigmatically.

'Really? Well, on my part, I enjoyed myself but I'm not sure anyone said anything I could wholeheartedly believe they meant. And half the time I was entirely in the dark as to what they were even saying, what with their Americanisms and accent.'

'And yet, hearteningly, my lady, as you said, you were enjoying yourself. So much so, I suspect it was only the lure of your... ahem, pyjamas which finally led your feet to the front door on the heels of Mr Wyatt?'

'That and my stomach dancing the tarantella! Perhaps we might sit up just a while though with the pretence of playing chess?'

'The board is already set up.'

'Thank you. And rest assured, I shan't keep you up any longer than it takes.'

'Takes to what, my lady?'

'To drag out of you what on earth you were doing in the hallway being handed cards by strange women!' She waggled a finger at him. 'Yes, you were. Don't deny it. And if you say,' she deepened her voice in an imitation of his, '"alas, discretion forbids, my lady", I shall likely scream. Just so you know.'

'Ah!'

She noticed Iver was driving with his neck craned at an angle, evidently his left ear best for eavesdropping. She turned to him.

'So what's been happening in this exhilarating, never-seems-to-sleep city tonight, then?'

'Same ol' craziness,' he grunted back, stamping on the brakes so hard, she flew across the central gap into Clifford's lap. 'Just like these fellas here!'

'Ahem.' Her butler coughed. 'Iver, if we might—'

'Might what?' He indicated the road ahead.

She threw Clifford an apologetic look and scrambled up to lean over the back of the front seat. She peered through the windscreen at the shapes milling in front of the bonnet.

'Horses?' She fumbled for the door handle and stepped out.

Iver leaned the top half of his body out of his window. 'Say, fruitcake! You know the street's for driving down. Not staging a rodeo!'

'Real funny, buddy!' an incredibly thin man shouted while trying to grab the reins of one horse. 'You know, I'd laugh my pants off if they hadn't already gotten shredded when I tried to head them off. Darned barbed wire!'

Clifford, who had followed Eleanor out of the cab, hurriedly stood in front of her.

'My lady, "pants" refer to "trousers" on this side of the Atlantic.'

'Oh, for goodness' sake, Clifford.' She stepped around him. 'I've seen a man's ankles before!' But as she reached the front of the taxi, she stopped abruptly. 'Oh my!' The man's trousers were conspicuous only by their absence, save for a few tattered threads. She held her shawl out behind her. 'Clifford, please give the poor fellow this while we deal with these escape artists.'

He reluctantly did as she bid.

'Does the job, I suppose,' the man grumbled, wrapping it around his lower half. 'But hell, there ain't better be no one I know passin' this way!'

She tutted. 'If you tuck the ends you're holding into your waistband, you'll be fine and' – she waved a hand toward the six horses who were butting each other with long shrill whinnies – 'we can have this lot sorted in a moment.'

'Yeah, right. I like your optimism, ma'am. But I can't say I share it. I been trying to get the devils back in the lorry what broke down for the past half hour.'

'Then they must be tired by now. Ah! I know. Clifford, what have you got in your pocket in the way of boiled sweets?' She held her hand out as he passed her the striped blue and white paper bag he carried wherever he went.

'An excellent idea, my lady. Bravo.'

She nodded and looked into the bag. 'Perfect. Here, chaps.' She tipped a few mint humbugs into each of the other two men's palms, Iver having joined them. He eyed her ruefully and made a show of looking at his watch.

'Stop fussing. It'll only take a moment.' She walked slowly

up to the horse she'd singled out as the ringleader, clicking her
tongue softly and rustling the paper bag.

'Hello, friend. Who'd like a treat?'

The horse sniffed the air and then trotted over cautiously.
Nosing her palm, it accepted a sweet from her. As it sucked
noisily on it, she held up a halting hand to Iver and the stranger
who had crept forward. She stepped up and whispered in the
animal's ear, noting that instead of flinching or pulling away, he
breathed his warm, minty breath on her cheek. Slipping off her
satin heels, she hitched up her gown skirt and swung herself
onto the horse's back with ease, having learned to ride bareback
in Arabia from the Bedouin tribesmen. She gently urged it
forward, keeping the bag of sweets in front of its muzzle. The
other horses followed as she and the horse ambled over to a
fenced car parking compound she'd spotted.

A few minutes later, the horses, having all finished their
minty treats, were munching on the tufts of thick grass growing
along the edge of the car park. The stranger, meanwhile, had
gone off gratefully to repair his lorry.

Clambering back into the taxi, she smiled at the sight of her
bulldog's belly rising and falling as he snored, snuggled up
against the base of her seat. With a grunt, he jerked groggily
awake and shuffled up against her legs for an ear tickle.

'Not bad, lady,' Iver called as they set off again. He pointed
at the photograph on the dashboard. 'Not even my Sadie could
have managed gettin' those animals tamed like that.'

Iver was still chuckling over a titled English lady riding
horses bareback around New York when they reached their
apartment.

'Out you get, folks. And thanks for the entertainment.' He
waved Clifford's wallet away. 'Leave the fare with Marty tomorrow, and I'll grab it from him later. It don't do to carry much
dough around in the early hours.'

Eleanor paused mid yawn. 'Iver, surely you're off home

yourself now, aren't you? It must be gone one o'clock in the morning.'

'Ain't up to me, lady. It's up to New York. But after what you pulled off tonight, whatever this city's got up her sleeve is gonna feel pretty lame, I can tell ya!'

Having coaxed the sleepy Gladstone up the last of the steps to the front door Clifford held open for her, she waved over her shoulder as Iver's taxi drove away.

The sound of squealing tyres made her glance down the road. The roar of a far more powerful engine than Iver's filled her ears as the beam from the headlights of a speeding car cut through the gloom.

'NO!' she shrieked, a split second before the car hit the man in the road with a sickening thud.

7

In the stunned silence, Eleanor felt herself sway. It couldn't be! Her mind had to be playing the vilest of tricks. And yet there it was, the full, awful truth sprawled face down in the shadows of the middle of the road. Motionless.

'My lady, please!' she heard Clifford's urgent call as she sprinted down the first of the steps.

Heedlessly she ran to where a ring of people had already formed. As she pushed her way between two of the gawping onlookers, another man stood in front of her.

'You should back off, ma'am,' he said over the sound of more running footsteps. 'That's no picture any tootsie should see.'

'No more than all the horrors I saw as a nurse in the war. The man needs help!'

'Sorry, sweetheart.' He moved aside, calling, 'Let the lady, through. She's a nurse!'

The group fanned out sideways, revealing a sight that stopped her dead. Marty the doorman's crumpled form lay in a fast-growing pool of dark crimson. So much so, it was hard to believe there was any hope.

Nevertheless, she fell to her knees and reached out a hand,

hesitating at where to feel for a pulse. The only exposed wrist was a shape it should never have been and the neck so thick with blood pouring from the devastating head wound, her fingers kept slipping off. A faltering pulse finally tapped a failing rhythm against her fingertips.

He's alive, Ellie! But barely.

She bent down to his ear. 'Marty,' she said far more calmly than her racing heart could believe. 'Help will be here quickly.' In a city that never slept, she desperately hoped this included the ambulance crews. 'Just lie still and let me help you breathe.' Gently scooping the thick blood from his open mouth with one finger, she felt a faint breath. She leaned in closer to check she wasn't imagining it, only to realise Marty's lips were twitching as if trying to speak.

'It's best you save your energy. The ambulance will be here soon,' she said as confidently as she could.

But the faint voice came again. 'W... Why... why... m...'

She bent forward even closer, trying to catch his words.

'Mar...' The rest was lost to what she knew from her experience as a war nurse was the rattling breath of a dying man. Suddenly, his eyes flicked open. 'Why... Mary?' With one last spasm, his eyes closed again, and his head fell to the ground.

Sinking back on her heels, she clasped her hands together and sent a silent prayer heavenward for a tragically lost soul.

As she opened her eyes, she felt Clifford's comforting wool coat being draped around her shoulders. Numbly, she accepted his elbow to stand, feeling the world spin.

As they waited for an ambulance to arrive, a voice called out, 'Great, rubberneckers too! Like I need that, people. Get over there, all of ya. NOW!' A square-built policeman brandishing a baton marched up to the onlookers.

Eleanor watched as the crowd slouched reluctantly back on to the pavement. The policeman stared at her. 'Think you're special, lady? I said—'

'Ahem, Officer.' Clifford eyed him firmly. 'This is *Lady* Swift. Visiting from England.'

He looked over Clifford's impeccably attired form with a caustic eye. 'And that means what to me, Suitsville? She still gotta move when she's told.' He rocked back on his boot heels and slapped his baton against his palm.

'Officer. Sergeant. Whatever your rank is,' she said placatingly, aghast at his lack of compassion. 'Might you show a little more respect for the fact a poor fellow has died? And in terrible circumstances.'

He lifted his cap, looking her over as he scratched his head. 'Once you've seen one hit-and-run, lady, you've seen 'em all. He's just one more who'll sleep at the city morgue tonight.'

Before she could reply, a long black vehicle, chuffing sporadic plumes of smoke, drew up. Along its length, the words AMBULANCE. BELLEVUE HOSPITAL were picked out in white lettering.

The policeman shook his head. 'Should've called the meat wagon, not an ambulance.' He jerked a thumb at the crumpled remains of what had been a vigorous human being only twenty minutes earlier. 'Talk about wastin' the city's damn money.'

Eleanor's brow darkened. 'That, Officer, was a man. A good and decent person who deserves as much respect in death as he did in life.'

Clifford nodded. 'And unless you wish to be reported to your superiors, I'll thank you to moderate your language in front of her ladyship.'

The policeman rolled his eyes. 'Whatever you say, buddy.' He turned back to Eleanor. 'So you knew' – he pointed to Marty's lifeless form – 'that man?'

'We did,' she said through her chattering teeth. Despite Clifford's coat, she couldn't stop the shivers which had taken hold of her. 'But only a little. He was our... our...'

'The gentleman was our doorman, Officer,' Clifford said.

'Now, her ladyship needs to retire before shock and upset take any greater hold.'

The policeman raised his baton. 'Not so fast, chum. You'll both join the line with the others and I'll take your statements once I'm done here.' He strode over to the body, grumbling loudly to the ambulance driver.

'Come on, Clifford.' She cast a disgusted look over her shoulder at the policeman. 'The sooner we're done here, the better.'

As he accompanied her to stand near the others, she noticed that most of the onlookers had slunk off, leaving only a few remaining. She shook her head at Clifford's suggestion she might wish to shield her eyes from the view of the body being loaded into the ambulance.

'In a peculiar way, Clifford, it will be a snippet of comfort to see Marty driven away and not left lying abandoned in the road.'

He pressed a handkerchief into her hand. 'Hearteningly, my lady, the ambulance crew seem a far more humane pair than the callous representative of New York's police force we have had to deal with.'

Finally, the ambulance crew clambered back into their vehicle and set off, Eleanor thinking it resembled a hearse even more now she'd watched it being loaded with Marty's disfigured body.

'Goodbye, Marty. God bless,' she said sadly.

Her sharp hearing caught the muttered scoff of the policeman's voice. 'Like you knew him enough to care, lady!'

8

———————

To distract herself from her wrung-out emotions, Eleanor looked along the line of remaining witnesses still waiting for the policeman to make his way over. They included Iver, she realised as he tipped his cap to her, and a dark-haired chap, who stood slightly apart.

Clifford interrupted her thoughts. 'My lady, there was nothing anyone could have done. Not even if the ambulance crew had delivered poor Marty to the hospital while still alive. Regrettably, it was only a matter of time.'

She managed a wan half-smile. 'Thank you for reading my mind so well. At least on this occasion. But here we are again, talking of time.'

The policeman loomed into her view. 'Yeah. And that's enough talkin' about anythin' except answerin' what I ask ya.' He gave her a sharp look, then ran his eye along the rest of the group. That it now comprised only a few of the original onlookers didn't seem to worry him.

If he's even noticed, Ellie.

'Any others of you know that' – he caught Eleanor's eye – 'that guy that just got run down?'

Iver hesitated, looked along the line to the man standing apart from them, and then nodded. 'Sure. I saw Marty most days. I taxi this stretch and this building especially.'

'Then you stay right there. Anyone else know him?' the policeman asked, with little enthusiasm to Eleanor's ears.

Again, Iver's glance went to the chap on the fringe of their group, who took half a step forward with obvious reluctance.

'Yeah. I did. He was my brother.'

Eleanor's hands flew to her mouth.

'Oh gracious! I had no idea.' She went to console him, but he turned his back to her and stared at the policeman instead.

Clifford whispered to her, 'Grief takes many forms, my lady. Perhaps most notably with unexpected loss under such extreme circumstances.'

She nodded and tried to avoid staring at the man who had professed, or almost confessed, she thought with a frown, to being Marty's brother. But something inside her was desperate to find a resemblance. As if glimpsing even a glimmer of Marty in his brother might bring him back. But aside from similarly dark hair, which conversely held not a hint of Marty's effervescent waves, she could find nothing similar. Even his skin tone seemed darker, although she had to admit, the dim view offered by the street's gas lighting was shading everyone's faces.

The policeman pointed at the man with his baton. 'Right, you stay too. And you too, lady,' he added coolly to Eleanor.

'Swift. *Lady* Swift,' Clifford said pointedly.

He let out an exasperated sigh. 'And as her spokesman, you gonna insist on stayin' too, Suitsville, let me guess?'

Clifford's brows flinched. 'Categorically, yes.'

The remaining person, a wiry man with a pinched face, waved a calloused hand at the policeman. 'I didn't know him from Adam, but I was the last to speak to him. You want I should stay too?'

The policeman nodded. 'You might as well make up the numbers.'

'Officer!' she blurted out. 'What about the other witnesses who have slunk—'

'Now listen up and listen good,' the policeman said, frowning fiercely at her. 'What I say goes on account of this badge I'm wearin', see?' He indicated the silver-covered shield pinned to his jacket. 'And thank you for tellin' me the job I been doin' for seventeen years. So, you see the licence plate of the vehicle, did ya?'

'Sadly, no.' She looked hopefully at Iver, Marty's brother, and the pinched-faced man who had volunteered to stay. They all shook their heads.

The policeman grunted. 'Thought so. No one ever does. And if they do, they muddle up the numbers so much, it's just another waste of my time even writin' 'em down.'

That made her realise he hadn't produced a notebook of any sort. Clifford, however, was one step ahead of her. He waved his own slim pocketbook. 'Perhaps a few borrowed pages might be of assistance, Officer?'

'Smart alec, eh?' The policeman dredged up what Eleanor assumed was a police issue blue pad and a stump of a pencil from his trouser pocket. 'Right. The... deceased's brother first. Whaddya see? And keep it short.'

Eleanor's heart clenched for him. Despite his less than effusive approach to her, he'd just witnessed his own brother being fatally run over.

Marty's brother grunted. 'Yeah, I'll keep it short alright. But not because it suits you. I didn't see nothin' because I was in the lobby there.' He pointed over his shoulder at her apartment building. 'But I did hear some chump roaring his motor, then tyres shrieking on the road.' He looked down momentarily. 'And I think Marty called out. Then more tyres before the bang. When I got out the door, the car had already gone. I ran up to the crowd around...' He shrugged. 'Anyways, I sees her' – he nodded curtly at Eleanor – 'kneeling over Marty in the road.'

She shook her head sorrowfully. 'I just wish I could have done more.'

He flinched, then shoved his hands deep in his pockets. 'Yeah, well thanks for tryin', I guess.'

'Cabbie, next.' The policeman waved his pad at Iver.

'Ahem.' Clifford cleared his throat. 'Given the extreme distress so nobly endured, surely her ladyship might be next, Officer?'

'Surely she might not!' he said, imitating her butler's clipped English accent badly. 'Cabbie!'

Iver nodded. 'I'm pullin' off after droppin' the lady and Mr Clifford when I hear tyres shrillin' somewhere down behind me.' He stared upwards as if replaying the scenario on the dark swathe of sky visible between the buildings on either side of the road. 'So I looks in my rear-view mirror. Only that jerk what hit Marty had his lights up so blindin', all I sees is white. Bright, bright white. Like the pearly gates is openin' for me.' His world-weary face looked even more sombre. 'Only they was openin' for Marty.' He shook his head. 'Anyways, that jerk speeds off around the corner so I brake hard 'cos something doesn't smell right. Then, I stop and comes back to see what's what.'

'And what's what did you see?' the policeman barked impatiently.

'I sees a crowd. And when I gets through it, I sees that lady doin' her best for Marty. And doin' what no one else had the guts for. Not one of them lookin' on moved so much as a finger.' He hung his head. 'Me either. He was so broke up, I just stood and... gawped.'

Eleanor shivered again. 'Iver, none of us could have helped him any more after he had been... hit so hard.'

'Sure, but that ain't gonna help me sleep tonight any more than you.' He shrugged disconsolately.

The policeman rolled his eyes. 'If you don't all stop yakkin' so much, there's gonna be no night left for sleepin' in.' He pointed at the pinched-faced man. 'Short and sweet. S'all I want. Ya got that?'

The man nodded. 'Got it, Officer. Right. I'm not from around here. Passing thru, see. And man, was I lost. Only now, I wish I hadn't even come this way as it's my fault he's dead.'

The policeman leaned forward. 'You were drivin' the car that hit him?'

'Heck, no!' The man yelped in a panicky tone as he gestured down to his scruffy trousers and elbow-patched grey jumper. 'I'm booting it, like always. My kind can't afford no car.'

'Then why did you say it's your fault, muttonhead?'

'Because if you're lost, who's the one guy you gonna holler over to ask? The doorman, 'course. He knows every street in his neighbourhood.'

Iver threw him a look. 'So what? Us cabbies don't?'

'I wasn't starting it with you, so back off.'

The policeman scowled. 'Move it on. Like now! So you called the dead guy over on account of you bein' a tourist. And?'

'And he steps into the road to come over. Only just half the ways across, that car just up and out of nowhere smacked him so hard he flew over the bonnet.'

'That it?' At his nod, the policeman turned to Eleanor. 'You're up.'

She frowned. 'Up what?'

Clifford coughed. 'I believe it is finally your turn, my lady.'

The policeman pulled a face. 'We ain't playin' Parcheesi, chum.'

She turned to her butler for another explanation.

'Not a clue, my lady.'

She shrugged. 'Officer, I shall tell you everything I know. Or rather, what I saw, to be more precise. And then I trust you will answer my questions.'

'Trust all you like, lady,' he said without looking up from examining the blunt end of his pencil.

Dissatisfied but keen she might be able to offer something that would help catch the culprit, she shook away her irritation. 'Like the others have said, I heard tyres screeching on the road. Oh, actually only after I heard the engine rev very loudly. It was a long, dark-grey car, I think, although it's difficult to be certain of the colour under these lights. It had a mounted emblem of some sort of woman on the bonnet. It reminded me a little of the flying lady on the Rolls. Or the "Spirit of Ecstasy" as Clifford tells me is its correct name. Anyway, I did notice the number plate started with a five, I think?'

'Like a thousand do. That it? No make or model?'

'Officer, I have seen your American cars rarely.' She cast her eyes down, thinking hard. 'But I did see the driver. At least the little that was visible. They had a broad-brimmed hat pulled down low and a great thick wool scarf pulled up high over their mouth.' She looked up. 'Why would anyone be dressed like that in this heatwave?'

The policeman shrugged. 'How should I know, lady? This is New York. People dress any ways they feel. I stopped some lunatic from driving along the sidewalk last week and he was more naked than the day he was born! So what next?'

'And then I screamed out. For the driver to stop, that is, because I'd seen Marty step off the pavement. Only the driver didn't. They just... ploughed straight into him. Actually no, the car did swerve first.'

The policeman shoved his notebook and pencil back in his pocket. 'Simple hit-and-run. Driver lost control of the car, panicked when he saw bones flyin' over his windscreen. Shot off. Nothin' unusual. See it every day,' he muttered. As Eleanor went to protest, he raised his hand. 'Save it, lady. The witnesses have confirmed your guy practically stepped in front of the car. You'd a thought he'd know better, workin' in a street with these old gas lights. Can't see nothin' in between the parts they do illuminate. In fact, makes it worse.'

She gasped. 'Officer! Marty is dead by the hand, or wheels, of another. I won't accept you suggesting it was his own reckless fault.'

The policeman ignored her and waved his baton at the others. 'We're done here, people. Scram!' He turned to go.

'Names, Officer?' she called after him. 'Aside from mine, you haven't taken them from the other witnesses. How are you going to follow up with any of them?'

Begrudgingly, he stopped and pulled out his notebook and pencil again and wrote them down, adding their addresses at Eleanor's insistence. As the policeman strode off, she looked to Marty's brother, who stared back.

'If there's anything I can do, please—'

He raised a hand. 'Thanks, lady, but if you don't mind, I gotta go tell my ma her pride and joy is lying in the morgue!'

9

The following morning, having shared the last of her rather moreish breakfast with a still dozy Gladstone, Eleanor resolved not to put it off any longer. She hurried down the long parquet-floored hallway, past the curved glass wall which looked out onto the impressive balcony and on into the library. The shelves were crafted from some sort of rosewood, with an inlaid gold interlinked diamond pattern that coaxed one's gaze along the spines of the books. This intricate motif was also mirrored in the cobalt floor tiles and the vivid blue leather upholstery of the chair she dropped into at the imposing mahogany desk.

And then doubt elbowed her resolve aside.

'Gracious, Gladstone. However does one word a letter of condolence to someone one has never met? Especially when the loss was so unexpected and horrific?'

Full of sausages as he was, her bulldog seemed disinterested in her dilemma and more interested in making himself comfortable on the rug. She tapped her chin with the end of the fountain pen for so long she was sure it had left a mark. Finally, she shook her head. 'I'll only write all the wrong things now. Better to do it when I've thought more about what to say, don't you think, old friend? Do it at the right time, not in haste, yes?'

Her eyes fell on an open book on the desk, the page bearing just one line of boldly printed text: "The right time is any time that one is still so lucky as to have."

She nodded and flipped back to the cover. 'Thank you for the reminder, Mr Henry James. And you, Clifford!' Hunching over the notepaper, her pen flew across the sheet...

A while later, her butler stood by her side reading the result.

'Bravo, my lady. Not an easy missive to scribe.'

She shrugged. 'Somehow, it sort of wrote itself. Marty was such a fine chap. And thank you.' She gestured at the beautiful arrangement of white peace lilies he had ordered to accompany the card. She sighed. 'He was too fun and likeable to have departed the world so early. So please lead on, butler mine, whatever distraction you have come up with will be most welcome.'

'But not to Master Gladstone, it appears.'

She followed his gloved finger to where her bulldog had paused in his drowsy attempt to rouse himself sufficiently to greet Clifford. He yawned so widely, Eleanor feared he might dislocate his jaw.

'Want to stay here, Mr Lazybones?' His stump of a tail twitched hopefully. 'Off you go then.'

Gladstone collapsed back on the rug, his stiff little legs sticking out sideways. Clifford collected the floral arrangement and offered to take the envelope she still held.

'My lady, perhaps I can assist by delivering your condolences on your behalf? Enough courage mustered for one day, I feel.'

She nodded gratefully.

In the building's smart entrance lobby, however, Clifford's

comforting suggestion was thwarted by the sight of Marty's brother standing in as the temporary doorman.

'Morning, Earl,' she said tentatively. 'How are you holding up?'

'Up? Nothin'. I'm holdin' the door.' His expression darkened. 'Oh, I get it. Probably not as good as Marty though, you're thinkin'.'

'Not a bit. I meant that as you had the worst evening of your life last night, I imagine, I hope you and your mother are coping as well as can be expected.' She took her letter of condolence from Clifford and the lilies and held them out. 'Forgive me if it's not a convention here, but even though I'm a stranger to your family, I wanted to pass on my sympathies.'

From inside Earl's tiny office, a bell shrilled out.

'Mrs Melchum. Again!' he muttered irately.

'Keeping you busy, is she?' Eleanor said sympathetically.

'Only like her hand is stuck to her bell button. That's the fourth time already. And it's only ten in the mornin'! Too bad she don't get out more. For me,' he ended grouchily.

Thinking that Marty's way of grumbling about her cantankerous neighbour had been not only politer but also more sympathetic, she trod carefully. 'Perhaps whatever causes her to rely on a walking stick makes it hard for her to leave the building very often?'

'More like never leaves. But it ain't much at all to do with needin' the stick. She can get about fine enough.' He gritted his jaw as the bell started up again, more furiously this time. 'Man! She's lived here as good as twenty years and chose to lock herself up in that graveyard she calls her apartment from day one. Except for marchin' down here carpin' on when things ain't perfect. Which they never are for her!' He gestured towards the front door, indicating the conversation was over.

Halfway down the steps, her name being called out jerked her from her musing over why such a formidable woman as Mrs

Melchum would confine herself to her apartment. She spun around to see Earl shifting uncomfortably on the top step, still clutching the flowers.

'Er, thanks, I guess. For, you know, these. From my ma, at least.'

On the pavement, to her surprise, Clifford walked her away from the building before hailing a passing taxi. Once inside and on their way, he explained.

'Normally it would be... interesting, my lady, to listen to Iver's views on everything from the state of the economy to the state of his, ahem, personal health. However, I thought today you might prefer to feel free to unburden your thoughts at will as we journey? Without, as it were, concern for Iver's own upset over yester eve's tragedy.'

'Thank you. Although I'm still in the dark as to where we are journeying to?'

Ten minutes later, she found out as the taxi pulled up opposite a tall triangular building, embellished with four modest columns and a diminutive balcony.

'Delmonico's restaurant, my lady. Notable for pioneering the unorthodox practice of allowing ladies to eat at their own table unaccompanied by a gentleman.'

'Oh!' Her chin fell.

She looked up to see her butler shaking his head. 'Your reservation is for, ahem, two.'

'Clifford!' she gasped. 'You're actually going to break another of your rules and eat with me? In public? Oh, say you are!'

'Disgracefully, that is the intention, my lady. With your permission, of course? Purely in the name of any company being better than none for you today, I conjectured. Please forgive my overstepping—'

'Don't be daft. You're the best company. I've said so many

times. And together we can raise a toast to Marty. A non-alco-holic one, naturally.'

But as she went to step off the pavement to cross the road, a long, dark-grey car pulled up outside the restaurant. She froze. From the driver's seat, a solidly built man with a scarf covering the bottom half of his face eased himself out.

'Wait!' Eleanor cried, darting across.

'My lady, no!' Clifford's urgent cry sounded above the blare of the delivery truck's horn as the vehicle swept past, forcing her back onto the pavement.

'It's him!' she panted. 'The hit-and-run driver!'

Clifford stared at the man. 'My lady, a moment's logic would dictate—'

But she was already sprinting around the back of the delivery truck, which had juddered to a halt, the driver yelling furiously at another truck driver who had stopped, blocking his way. Both drivers aided the argument by leaning heavily on their horns.

By the time she had reached the other side of the road, the driver and his companion, who had got out of the car, were both being greeted by the restaurant's maître d'.

'You!' she cried, grabbing the man's elbow and spinning him around. 'Where were you last night? I—'

'He was with me,' his companion hissed, a tall woman, dressed in a fashionable fur-trimmed red jacket. 'In the hospital. Not that it's any of your business. Now nick off.'

Eleanor was flummoxed. 'Hospital? No, the ambulance came later. After it was too late. Too late because of you!'

She sensed Clifford behind her.

'You!' The man pointed a finger at her butler. 'Are you with this mentally aberrant female?'

'I am accompanying this lady, sir,' he said calmly. 'However, there is no mental aberration among our party, thank you.'

'Yeah! Then what's all her blather about some ambulance?'

Eleanor jumped in before he could answer. 'The one that took poor Marty away after you—'

'He what?' the woman snapped. She leaned into Eleanor's face. 'See this scarf he's wearing? That's hiding the scars that are still raw after they removed the bandages last night. So whatever you're babbling about, it doesn't concern my husband, right?'

'Oh, gracious!' Eleanor mumbled, abashed by the deep and angry red carvings now visible on both the man's cheeks and across the top of his lip. 'I'm so sorry. I thought—'

'You thought you'd just try and spoil his treat of being able to eat normally after two months!' the woman sneered, poking Eleanor in the arm. 'Take a hike, honey. And make it a long one.'

The couple walked into the restaurant accompanied by the maître d' and, confusingly, Clifford. She stood watching the traffic pass until he re-emerged, his expression as impassive as ever.

'If you will forgive yet another overstep on my part, I explained to the maître d' that I had been dispatched to cancel the reservation for Lady Swift. It is a small restaurant and perhaps the gentleman you accosted deserves to enjoy his first meal in months in peace?'

She groaned. 'Oh, Clifford, I'm so sorry for ruining our lunch. And for that poor man. Whatever must he think?'

'That he merely encountered yet another native of this ever-unpredictable city.' His brows flinched. 'However, if we might refrain from any further New York-inspired conduct?'

She nodded and slid contritely into the taxi he flagged down.

'The Grand Central Oyster Bar, please,' he called to the driver, before turning to her. 'An alternative luncheon venue, my lady. Hopefully, we can dine without a reservation.'

With a lurch, the taxi shot off.

Despite Eleanor's best efforts, however, she could not help jabbing at the side window as she pointed out cars that could have been responsible for Marty's tragic demise.

'What's the lady's deal with fancy cars, buddy?' the driver hollered back to Clifford.

'Just a touristic interest in the more luxurious models unseen in England,' he said nonchalantly.

'Ha! Then you wanna go where the bosses rule. They got heaps of 'em.' He turned to face them, ignoring that there was a long stream of cars crossing in front. 'You want I should go that way, lady?'

'Yes! Maybe. Hang on,' she added, having caught Clifford's cautionary look.

The taxi screeched to a stop. 'Well, which is it?'

She looked enquiringly at Clifford. 'What's the problem? We'll still end up at your delectable-sounding oyster bar.'

He lowered his voice. 'My lady, "bosses" are the leaders of criminal gangs here. We will likely end up at the bottom of the Hudson River! Especially if you spring out and accuse anyone of anything untoward as you, ahem, have done recently. With sincere apologies, but might it, perhaps on reflection, be better to return "home" as you referred to it so affectionately to eat? Along with a raft of your own cook's admirable fayre, one might choose early house pyjamas in the company of a snoozy bulldog?'

'And maybe a little time with my butler. If he's still speaking to me, that is?'

He pretended to consider the matter. 'I don't think it will be too protracted an affair to persuade him so.'

By the time she climbed into bed that evening, her thoughts were calmer and clearer.

Especially as a telegram had arrived from Hugh. She

pressed it to her chest, hearing his rich deep voice whisper the words to her:

> *Eleanor, my darling. Have stopped counting the days until you're home. Ticking off the hours and minutes until I can hold you in my arms. Have fun. Stay safe. Listen to Clifford, please! Hugh xx*

She dropped off to sleep almost immediately, dreaming of her handsome, dependable fiancé.

But less than an hour later, she jerked upright with a gasp, her forehead as soaked with sweat as her neck. The nightmare had seemed so real. And then it hit. It wasn't a nightmare. Marty's bloodied and broken form really had spoken to her just before he died.

'"Why Mary?"' she breathed aloud. 'Whatever did he mean?'

10

Despite the already stifling morning heat, Eleanor sprinted up the steps and into the police station, only to be met by greater chaos than in the clamorous streets she'd just left. A sea of men and women in various states of dishevelment shouted and gesticulated, while equally loud and animated uniformed officers manhandled them across the shabby, grey-walled reception area. Above the din, telephones rang shrilly. She wrinkled her nose at the stench of sweaty bodies hanging thickly in the oppressive air and shrugged at Clifford's arched brow.

'I can't see anyone free. Everyone seems occupied.' She looked around the bedlam. 'Doing whatever it is they are doing.'

He nodded and mimed her leaving and making a telephone call instead.

She shook her head. 'No. In person is the only way. And to our officer who came to the incident. Albeit begrudgingly. I need to tell him what Marty said before he died. Besides' – she waved at the unoccupied desks – 'there's no one answering the telephones, anyway!'

Before she could work out how to attract someone's attention, an authoritative voice blasted through the cacophony.

'ENOUGH!'

Amazingly, the raucous din stopped. Except the ringing phones. The man was fitter and more alert than any of the other policemen she'd yet seen, his more elaborate badge and demeanour suggesting he was the captain of this precinct. He jabbed a finger at the nearest policeman.

'Spread 'em out, will ya! Theft reporting, room one. Violent attacks, room two. Bodies found, room three. Anything else, come back later! Now, people!'

He spun on his heel and strode back down the corridor. The chaos erupted again, but this time it seemed more organised. Clifford respectfully waved Eleanor back against the wall as the policemen hustled two or three people each towards the doors indicated by their captain.

Finally, the hubbub diminished sufficiently for Eleanor to reach the reception counter and hit the top of the large, tarnished brass bell with her palm, instantly recoiling with a yelp.

'Ow!'

A crumpled midnight-blue jacket stood up stiffly from under the counter to reveal a greying moustache and weary eyes. 'Yeah, that happens a lot.'

She held out her palm, showing the deep red dent, and then pointed at the bell. 'It's lost its... thing on top that you hit.'

The desk officer leaned on both elbows. 'You think we ain't spotted that, lady?' His heavy brows met. 'Whatever you want, you gotta roll on off to rooms one to three or come back later. Captain said so. Okay?'

She smiled genially. 'Long night, Officer?'

'Will be. I just got on shift this morning.' He frowned. 'But say, what's that to you?'

'A great deal, actually.' She placed her handbag on the counter and clasped her hands together beside it. 'Now, I'm looking for a policeman.'

He rolled his eyes. 'Lucky shot then. The station's full of 'em.'

'How marvellous! But I need the right one, you see?'

He sighed. 'Lady, we're kinda stretched at the moment. All the time, actually.'

'I can appreciate that,' she said earnestly. 'So I won't take up more of your valuable time than I need to. Now, I'm trying to find a square-ish, I mean, sturdily built officer with mid-brown hair, grey-ish eyes and a rather, umm... domineering manner.'

He beckoned her forward. 'There are clubs here in New York for that kind of thing. This is a police station.'

Out of the corner of her eye, she caught Clifford's lips twitching.

She tutted. 'No. I mean, I'm looking for a specific policeman I met during a terrible incident.'

He rubbed his face with his hands. 'This cop got a name?'

'Undoubtedly. Doesn't everyone? But I don't know it.' She stretched up on tiptoe to wave at the officer's badge. Misjudging the distance, she poked him in the chest with the pin the badge was held on with, if his pained expression was anything to go by. 'Sorry. But he had a number on his badge like you do.'

'What's his number, then?'

She shrugged. 'Not a clue. I didn't think to take it during all the awfulness.'

The officer jerked his chin at Clifford. 'You with this lady?'

'For my sins,' she heard him mutter. He stepped up beside her. 'Yes, Officer. How can I be of assistance?'

'You understand much that comes out of her mouth?'

Clearly amused by the question, only Eleanor's eyes caught her butler struggling to maintain his impassive expression. 'On the rare occasion, Officer, yes. Perhaps, however, it might help if I just told you the policeman's number is 647?'

The officer grunted. 'Like yesterday, yeah.' He seized a

tattered clipboard and flipped up the top sheet. '647... he's on zero shift.'

Clifford nodded. 'Ah! Midnight start, correct?'

He nodded back.

Eleanor yanked her late uncle's watch from her pocket. 'It's almost eight a.m. now, so he should be here soon. Surely a shift isn't more than eight hours?'

The officer shook his head 'Nope. But only so as we can fit two in a day when we're short. Like always. But yeah, he'll get off at eight. For a bit, anyhow. You can wait right through that second door.'

The room was tiny, only the bare whitewashed walls free of clutter. Clifford quickly assembled a passable seat from a sturdy box, topped with a wooden tray and a thick sheaf of papers for a cushion.

She sat on it gingerly. 'As unorthodox as it is, it is surprisingly comfortable, thank you.'

He bowed and from a jacket pocket pulled out the reception bell and a domed nut from another. In a trice, he had it mended.

'I procured the nut from the noticeboard,' he said in reply to her silent question.

'And sleights of hand in a police station are a good idea, Clifford? Really?'

He dinged the bell in reply.

She did her best to tamp down her impatience. She took a deep breath and regretted it, as the air in the room was no fresher than it had been in the reception area.

A few moments later, the door swung back hard against the wall, the rear view of a uniform filling the opening.

'Real funny, Hank! You gonna wish you ain't never started.'

The policeman they'd been waiting for turned around and frowned at Eleanor, his weather-beaten face looking exhausted.

'So, you comfy enough? 'Cos we're here to protect civilians and serve the law, not pussytoe 'round settees and serve tea.'

She leaned forward conspiratorially. 'Don't let on but I'm more of a coffee girl, Officer...?'

'647. Like you don't know that, already.'

'Yes. And if you prefer to be addressed by your number, fine. It just seems rather unfriendly of me.'

'Don't fret none. Seein' as we ain't gonna be friends.'

Clifford cleared his throat. 'Officer, tiredness notwithstanding, a better-mannered approach to her ladyship would be appreciated?'

The policeman grunted. 'Save it, Suitsville. Tiredness nothin'! I'm bushed! Some drunk needed cuttin' down by his tie from tryin' to swing from the flagpole on ninth. Then two purse snatches, back-to-back, but a mile apart, of course. Then three smashed-in shop windows on twenty-eighth.' He threw his hands wide. 'Then I won the top prize. An arm! So cut me some slack.'

Eleanor shared a look of horror with Clifford. 'Someone found... *an arm*?'

'Yeah. In a cab. Now what's all this about? And make it real quick.'

Eleanor shook the image of a disembodied limb being driven around New York out of her head. 'I remembered something from the incident where poor Marty Morales, my doorman, was killed. You—' She broke off as he held up an imperious hand, which she noted had livid bruises down one side.

'Save your breath. It's already been signed off, see. Simple hit-and-run accident.'

She sighed in exasperation. 'Officer, it's really important—'

He yawned. 'Jeez! You don't think everyone thinks the same? Now, it's been a long night and I'm back on shift in—'

'Officer, it wasn't an accident!' she said louder than intended.

He stared at her for a moment, and then glanced at Clifford. 'You think this is for real, too?'

'If Lady Swift does, then most assuredly, Officer.'

The policeman stared at them for a moment, then threw his hands up. 'Alright. I get off shift in like fifteen minutes, once the reports are written up. I'll be in Frank's Lunch Car, behind the lot on Eighth and Forty-Third. I'll give you an ear, but nothing more.'

'Perfect. Thank you,' she said in relief.

'Perfect, my lady?' Clifford sniffed a quarter of an hour later at the door to the diner. 'Forgive my rendering an alternative opinion, but I fear even Gladstone would baulk at eating in such an establishment.'

She fixed him with a stern look. 'No, he wouldn't. You know he'll eat anything. Anyway, it smells of food and they've probably got some kind of sausage, so he'd be in there like a shot. And' – she stared at the ancient train carriage, abandoned it seemed on a patch of dirt – 'the inside has to be better than the outside, surely?'

In truth, she found the interior rather quaint, with its faded red booth-seating down one side. On the other, ten stools were set along the counter with a blackened grill behind.

As they entered, the four heads huddled over plates on the stools, and the three sets of uniformed policemen in the booth seats, turned and gawped at them.

'Yo!' A man in an apron behind the counter stopped flipping eggs and patties on the grill and looked them up and down in disbelief. 'You folk lost or actually want somethin' to eat?'

'Oh, the latter,' Eleanor said brightly. 'It smells wonderful.'

'No it don't,' a now familiar voice said behind her. She

turned to see Officer 647 standing in the doorway. 'Unless you're starved, that is.'

The man behind the counter pointed his spatula at him. 'Like you ain't in here any minute you ain't savin' the city, Balowski. So sit down, shut up and eat up.'

The policeman waved towards an empty booth and surprised her by waiting until she was seated to slide in opposite. He shot a look at Clifford, who was still standing.

'What? You can't sit with the lady?' Shaking his head, he shuffled along his bench seat to make room for her butler.

'Most kind,' Clifford said, perching on the edge.

They ordered, Clifford settling for a cup of coffee only, much to the policeman's disgust.

'Now,' she started in, 'I don't want to sour your breakfast, so before it arrives, I'll tell you why I'm sure Marty's death was no accident.'

Before she could, the food arrived. Two generously filled plates, followed by three mugs of what looked like lethally strong black coffee.

'Dive in.' He added several spoons of glutinous sauce to three large meat patties topped with fried eggs, two thick slices of bread and an enormous heap of fried onion.

Eleanor picked up her fork, a knife evidently not considered necessary. She tried a small mouthful of the patty first and found it delicious, if greasy. The policeman dunked his bread in his runny egg yolk, Clifford stiffening beside him. He then glugged a large mouthful of coffee and leaned back in his seat.

'When I took the witnesses' statements, no one else thought the hit-and-run deliberate.'

She bit back the reply that scribbling two lines of each person's account hardly constituted 'taking a statement'.

'No one mentioned it, I agree. But it all happened so fast. And I think I was in the best position to see. Which is why I was the only one who told you about the driver's strange attire and the fact that I'm now sure he swerved, both of which I find highly suspicious. There was nothing in the road to avoid, you see, except Marty and' – she swallowed – 'the driver did the exact opposite. He swerved *at* him, not *away* from him. I remembered it distinctly late last night.'

The policeman scooped more onion into his egg and shrugged noncommittally. 'That it?'

'No. The other thing that makes me sure this wasn't an accident is that just before he died, Marty came to and spoke to me.'

'Yeah?' His brows rose. 'Odd 'cos he was kind of broken up for sayin' much, I'd a' thought. So what'd he say?'

'"Why Mary."'

'Why Mary?'

She nodded, noting Clifford take a sip of his coffee and shudder.

The policeman chewed thoughtfully for a moment. 'You didn't say nothin' 'bout that in your statement.'

'I know.'

Clifford turned to him. 'Her ladyship was in a considerable state of shock.'

He grunted. 'And upset. Yeah, yeah, you said at the time.'

She grimaced. 'It wasn't just the shock, if I'm honest. I wasn't sure I'd heard him correctly and, ridiculously, at first, it didn't seem important. But now I'm certain that's what he said. Does "Why Mary" mean anything to you, Officer?'

He shook his head. 'No. And, lady, folk say crazy stuff all the time when they're breathing their last.' He mopped up the remains of the egg and onion juice with a stub of bread. 'I won't tell ya some of the things I've heard over the years. Make your wig spin if I did.' He pushed his plate away as if he was finished with not only his breakfast but also the conversation. As she went to speak, he raised his hand. 'I told you already, lady, the case is shut. Even if I thought there was something in what you just told me, we don't got enough men to waste on a lousy hit-and-run. I'd like to see the captain's face if I suggested it!'

Eleanor bristled. 'Well, thank you for your time, Officer... Balowski, I believe it is.' She rose and gestured to Clifford. 'Your breakfast is on me.'

The policeman stared at her. 'Huh? Don't see why?'

She pursed her lips. 'Because you at least listened. Good day.'

As she reached the door, the policeman called over. 'Forget the whole thing, lady. I know you don't like it, but in this city, no one cares about one more dead doorman.'

'You're wrong, actually,' she called back as she marched out. 'I do!'

11

Back at her apartment building, Eleanor hesitated in the hallway. At Clifford's enquiring look, she grimaced.

'It was such a shock, the police officer dismissing out of hand my suggestion that Marty's death was no accident. All I can think to do now is try to unearth some evidence he can't ignore by talking to the other witnesses. And that means talking to Marty's brother, Earl, as well, in the vague hope he'll be able to throw some light on why Marty might have been killed. But I don't think he's likely to be very cooperative.'

Clifford nodded. 'I fear you may be right. However, I also fear we have no choice.'

She sighed. 'I know, but he's not covering Marty's door duty today, it seems. That's a chap I haven't seen before.'

'I believe Mr Morales will therefore be found in the storeroom, my lady. I noticed what appeared to be a substantial delivery of essentials for the building being unloaded at the rear entrance earlier. However, it is hardly a fitting place for a titled lady—'

'Down those stairs over there, is it?' she called over her shoulder.

In the basement, the scrape of heavy boxes being dragged across a rough concrete floor suggested her butler had been correct.

'Morning? Is that you, Earl?' she called out as she rounded the bare brick wall into a room resembling a small warehouse-cum-ironmongers. Two tiny windows high up lit the space just enough for her to make out a rack of metal shelving filling one wall. A stack of ladders, a shop's worth of paint tins and a dozen or so empty tea chests filled half the floor. In the centre, a work-bench held groups of tools, trays of fixings, a lamp and a wooden box littered with a raft of tickets, the front marked MAINTE-NANCE REQUESTS – URGENT.

Clifford set down a wriggling Gladstone who she now realised he'd carried to save the bulldog's portly tummy catching on the hard-concrete edge of the basement steps.

A moment later, Earl appeared encumbered by an enormous crate. He stopped on seeing her.

'Whatever needs fixing, Lady Swift, you just gotta fill out a ticket on the desk upstairs like everyone else. Residents ain't supposed to be down here.'

'What a shame. It's admirably organised. No wonder this is such a wonderful building to stay in. But actually, it was you I came to see.'

Earl grunted appreciatively as Clifford took half the weight of the crate and helped heave it up onto the shelving. 'Me?' he said suspiciously. 'About what?'

'Breakfast.' At his puzzled frown, she held her hands up. 'I want to talk to you about Marty, if you can bear it. And I was hoping you might let me buy you a late breakfast so we can chat?'

He shook his head. 'I'm on duty for hours more before my break. And I gotta finish shifting the last of the delivery.'

'And you don't really want to talk to me, I know. It's alright.

But, Earl, I need to tell you something critical about... what happened to Marty. Please?'

After a beat, he shrugged. 'Five minutes. But I can't leave this building. It'll have to be at my place.'

He led them through the gloom of the storeroom's further recesses and up a ramp with a handrail either side to a tired-looking blue door. 'We gotta be quiet, though. My ma's asleep in the next room.' He winced as he reached for the handle. 'She's taken Marty being gone real bad.'

'Master Gladstone,' Clifford said sotto voce. 'Not a sound, sir.'

They all tiptoed into the cramped and near stifling room, which clearly served as the family's cooking, eating and living area. Eleanor was struck by how palatially appointed and enormous her rented apartment was in comparison. The only lavish item down here was the bunch of peace lilies she'd given to Earl with her condolences. That they had been placed in a nondescript glass jug didn't diminish the very evident care that had been taken over their arrangement. The simple framed photograph of Marty leaning against it made her heart clench for his tragic death. Never one to lord her privileges over others, she was anxious not to appear as though she was scrutinising Earl and his mother's vastly lesser circumstances, so settled into a hard wooden chair. Earl waved Clifford into the only other one, but her butler shook his head. Earl shrugged and took the seat himself. He nodded at her.

'What's eatin' ya about the accident, then?'

Time to bite the bullet, Ellie.

'I don't believe it was an accident, Earl.'

'Not an accident!' he hissed. 'Say, I don't mean to be rude, but that's a pretty wild statement to fling across our table.' He leaned forward. 'Do you know how much it would upset my ma to hear—'

'Hear what, Earl?' a woman's voice croaked from the doorway. South-east Asian was the closest Eleanor could place the accent.

'Ma!' Earl glared at Eleanor. 'See what you done now?'

'Oh, don't fuss.' His mother waved him off with a frown which deepened the lines in her soft, copper-skinned face. 'I'm wrung out from the upset, not an invalid, boy.' She pushed herself into the room in an aged wheelchair.

Eleanor rose. 'Mrs Morales, please forgive me if I woke you. And for intruding. Especially at this difficult time. I'm so sorry for your loss.'

Gladstone let out a soft whimper and trotted over to gently scrabble his top half up into the woman's lap. She ran a shaky hand over his ears and down the soft grooves of his jowls. 'Well, that's a nice hello, Mr Wrinkles.'

Earl waved at Eleanor, then at her butler. 'It's Lady Swift, Ma. And her help.'

'Whose name is Clifford,' Eleanor said, smiling.

'Mr Clifford, Lady Swift, welcome company can never intrude.' Mrs Morales smiled at each of them, which brought some life to her red-rimmed eyes. She rolled her wheelchair up beside Eleanor and tugged her back down into her seat, patting her hand. 'Thank you for the flowers. And for your words from the heart. Never expected the like from a lady such as yourself.'

'Marty brightened every day since I arrived, Mrs Morales.'

The woman sniffed back a tear. 'Earl, open the door to let this crazy heat out, there's a boy. Then tell me what you two were whispering about?'

'Nothin', Ma,' Earl said quickly, doing as he was asked, which brought only a waft of mustiness in from the basement. 'It was about nothin'.'

Her eyes narrowed. 'Earl Morales, you were a terrible liar as a kid and you ain't got better with age! So, don't play your mother for a fool!'

He shrugged. 'Okay. It was about Marty, Ma. But nothin'
you need to trouble yourself with.'

'I see.' She glanced at Eleanor. 'So this lady just happened
down to our home to talk nothin' with ya?' She turned to
Eleanor. 'You tell me so I don't gotta drag it out of Earl later.
'Cos I will and he knows it.'

Eleanor glanced at Earl, who nodded helplessly. 'Umm, if
you're sure, Mrs Morales. But it's not going to be an easy thing
for you to hear.'

The woman's face hardened. 'Can't be harder than hearin'
Marty's gone. The boy was only thirty-eight.'

Eleanor shook her head. 'He had such a... a cheery and
lively manner, I thought he was younger!' She took a deep
breath. 'Anyway, I asked Earl if he would give me a few minutes
because... well, to put it plainly I need his help in finding out
the truth about Marty's accident. Because I don't believe it was.'

At the woman's gasp, Eleanor took the handkerchief Clifford held out and pressed it into her hand.

'Thank you.' Mrs Morales wiped her eyes. 'You think
someone ran my Marty down on *purpose*? But why would they
do that? He was nothin' but a good heart who wouldn'a hurt
nobody.'

'I can't answer that yet,' Eleanor said. 'But the police have
closed the case. Which means that whoever was driving that car
will get off scot-free.'

'We know that.' Earl scowled, shoving his hands in his
workaday trouser pockets. 'That's on account of it bein' a hit-
and-run. An accident. That cop told us all at the time.'

She shook her head. 'And he didn't change his view at all
after I tracked him down to tell him what I remembered.'

Mrs Morales' dark eyes swam as she gawped at her. 'You
went downtown? To the police station? For my Marty?'

'Yes, of course.'

'Ma,' Earl interjected. 'Talkin' like this is only going to upset you more. Lady Swift, thanks and everythin', but we don't want—'

'Yes, we do,' his mother said firmly.

'Ma!'

'Ma, nothin'! Earl, if this English lady is kind enough to want to find out the truth about your brother's passin', you gonna do whatever she thinks might help.' She turned to Eleanor. 'Start by tellin' us what you told the cop, please.'

Eleanor recounted what she'd told Balowski, leaving out, however, the part about Marty's dying words. She wanted to tackle that with each of them separately. 'Which is why, when he refused to help, I came here hoping Earl could tell me something about Marty that could give me a lead on why someone would want him dead.'

'No can do,' he grunted. 'I've been outta the storeroom too long already. We need to wrap this up.'

'Yes.' His mother nodded. 'You need to get back. And then meet with Lady Swift later and tell her anything you know that might help.' She fixed him with a steely glare at his mutinous look. 'Yes. You. Will!'

Eleanor rose hastily. 'Thank you both. I'll leave you in peace now. We need to go and find Iver.'

Mrs Morales' eyes widened. 'Iver Driver, the cabbie?' She stared at her son. 'You never said he was there too, Earl?'

'Why would I, Ma? I was tryin' to stop you thinkin' the worst of it over and over.' His tone softened. 'You gonna cry all the colour outta yer eyes if you keep weepin' so hard.'

'Yeah, likely I will, but that won't stop me seein' justice done for my Marty, if Lady Swift is right. Which is why you gonna do as she says.'

'Okay, Ma,' he said grudgingly.

Mrs Morales turned to Eleanor, her eyes searching hers. 'That gonna be enough? You talkin' to Iver and Earl?'

She shrugged. 'Honestly, probably not, but it's a start. I also need to talk to another eyewitness who volunteered to stay, but I've no idea how to find him.'

Earl jumped in. 'He said he ain't from around here, so that's a non-starter.'

'Thank you,' she said, 'but there must be someone who can help.'

'I can.' A voice drawled from the open door.

12

Eleanor stared in amazement as Balowski stepped into the room.

What is he doing here, Ellie?

Before she could ask, Earl scraped back his chair and squared up to him. 'You got too much nerve comin' down here and listenin' in on matters that don't concern ya, cop. Now beat it!'

Behind him, Gladstone's hackles stood up as he growled.

'Matters that don't concern me, huh?' Balowski pointed at Eleanor. 'Then why did I get off the night shift to find her perched on a pile of broken junk at the station, waitin' for me on account of your brother?'

'Her!' Clifford tutted. '"To find *Lady Swift* waiting", I believe you meant.'

'Lighten up, Suitsville.' He looked at Mrs Morales and his tone softened. 'Sorry about your son, ma'am. And invading your place, but I was looking for her. *Lady* Swift.' He threw Clifford a pointed look. 'And since I was told upstairs she weren't home, I figured she'd be diggin' about down here 'cos her type never stop at no.'

Eleanor was flummoxed. 'But why were you looking for *me*?'

'Jeez! Force a guy to say it out loud, why don't ya.' He frowned. 'Alright, alright. Your story kinda got to me after breakfast. I can't pretend it changed my mind, but... well, it's been a long time since I met anyone on the streets who cared one iota for anyone. Especially a stranger.'

Earl jabbed a forefinger in the policeman's jacketed chest. 'Then you been on the wrong streets, double buttons. 'Cos we all look out for each other round here.'

'Sure you do,' the policeman said disparagingly. 'That's why she was the only one who went to help your brother when he was lying in the road out there?'

Mrs Morales reached for Eleanor's hand and squeezed it, her eyes filling. 'Earl never told me that.' She dabbed at her mouth with Clifford's handkerchief. 'I never saw the day comin' when I'd have an English lady, a cop, and my oldest son working together. But that's how it's gonna be. For Marty's sake.'

'No way, Ma!' Earl slapped the table. 'This cop don't know us and how we do things.'

'Then work with him, son, so he does!' She held up a stern finger. 'Enough carpin', now. I've spoken!'

Balowski grinned, then to Eleanor's surprise, pulled out his police notebook and stub of a pencil. 'How far you all get with what's what, then?'

Eleanor gave him a quick recap. 'So, I'm going to talk to Iver, then Earl, when he finishes work. And if you could—'

'Getta hold of the details for the scrawny fella who wasn't from around here. Shouldn't be too hard.'

He turned to go, only to jam shoulders in the doorway with Earl.

'Get yourself gone, cop,' he grumbled.

'Oh, go haul leather yourself.'

Their two sets of boots echoed off down the ramp.

Mrs Morales looked from Eleanor to Clifford. 'Now, what's my part in all this?'

She hesitated. 'You probably need to rest.'

Mrs Morales shook her head determinedly. 'No. I'll be fine stayin' up for whatever you're anglin' for, honey child.' Turning her wheelchair, she waved away Clifford's efforts to restrain Gladstone from eagerly accompanying her. 'Don't worry. Mr Wrinkles can help out. After all, we're going to need all the help we can get to find out what really happened to my son.'

Clifford caught Eleanor's eye. 'If you will excuse me, my lady, but I have some quite urgent household matters to attend to?'

She nodded back. 'Absolutely. Mrs Morales and I will be fine.'

Once alone with the emotionally exhausted but determined Mrs Morales, however, Eleanor wished Clifford had stayed. He possessed the conversational delicacy she lacked. Asking Earl if he would talk to her about Marty, his brother, had been hard enough. But she'd never needed to probe a grieving mother, especially one so recently bereft of her youngest son. Her 'pride and joy', as Earl had told her she referred to him.

'Steer me right, friend,' she whispered to the photograph of Marty beside the lilies on the table.

Joining Mrs Morales at the countertop, she held her hands up. 'I know you're perfectly capable, but I'm terrible at just sitting. May I help a little?' She shrugged. 'Although I should warn you, if Clifford were here, he'd mention my "helping" bears a striking similarity to "hindering".'

The older woman laughed wheezily. 'Now how's that for a proper lady! No good at lazing away the days and gets a real tickle outta being teased by her closest help. What is Mr Clifford, anyways?'

'My butler and, well, mostly everything besides. I'm eternally grateful to have inherited him, and Henley Hall, my house.' Her cheeks coloured as she cursed her runaway tongue at how that must have sounded.

But Mrs Morales shook her head and waved around the room. 'Oh, don't you go worryin' like that. Home's home, whatever it's missin' in fancy furniture and whether it's four rooms and a water closet or a draughty castle stuffed with paintings and a good-looking butler.'

Eleanor smiled in relief.

'How'd I know what you were thinkin', right?' The older woman slid Eleanor's letter of condolence out from down the left side of her wheelchair. 'The first time I read this, I knew anyone who can write that much heart into their words and not hide it was gonna have a face that was just as honest. Whether or not she wants it to be.' She pressed the notepaper to her chest. 'Honey, this letter has given me so much comfort, I can't tell ya.' She tucked it back carefully, looking Eleanor over with a playful expression. 'See, now I'm thinkin' maybe I oughtta call up to Mr Clifford to ask just how much mess his mistress is gonna make in my kitchen?'

Eleanor laughed. 'Lots, I assure you! But let me save you the trouble of asking how much and show you instead.'

Happy to be occupied while she worked out what she needed to ask, Eleanor donned the apron offered and set to on her task. Unexpectedly, this turned out to be washing a basket's worth of small orange and green fruits of varying shades in the tiny blue enamelled sink resting on four spindly legs.

'They're calamansi from the Philippines. Like me.' Mrs Morales arranged a line of different-sized glass bottles between them. 'They're a kind of cross between a lemon and an orange, I suppose. Now, split 'em. Hats off!'

Eleanor turned the first fruit in one hand and the unwieldy knife in the other, trying to decipher her task.

Mrs Morales tutted good-naturedly. 'Didn't your mama ever show you how?'

Eleanor shook her head sadly. 'She didn't have the chance. I grew up on a small sailboat. At least until I was nine. Then my parents disappeared one night and... and that was the last I saw of them.'

The older woman's face fell. 'Oh, dear Lord! I'm sorry. For a woman who can't move her own feet, I sure know how to go stompin' into someone else's troubles.'

'No need to apologise. It was a long time ago.'

'Don't feel like it though, child, I know.' Mrs Morales patted Eleanor's arm, her tone softer. 'Now.' She took the knife and waved at the fruit. 'Would your mama mind if I showed you how?'

'She'd love it,' Eleanor managed to say through the lump in her throat.

A few moments later, she was slicing away with her newly learned technique while the older woman pressed the results through a fine sieve. The glass bowl below gradually filled with buttery yellow liquid. Her teacher nodded approvingly.

'Then a scoop of sugar, a little honey for a treat and this handful of ginger for easin' the joints and we got the base of a juice fit for angels.'

Eleanor smiled as Mrs Morales steered her back to the tiny sink.

'You ain't done, titled lady. The seeds need separatin' and washin' next— Oh, but no they don't.' She clapped a hand over her mouth, tears spilling down her cheeks.

Eleanor bobbed down into the woman's eyeline. 'Gracious, what has upset you so much about that?'

Mrs Morales wiped her eyes. 'My Marty used to take them off and plant 'em quietly in any bit of ground he could find. Done it since he was a boy.' A sob of a laugh broke out of her. 'People walkin' through Central Park got no idea why there's so many trees sproutin' orange fruit in the season, he said.'

Eleanor swallowed hard. 'Maybe I could have some seeds to

take back to England and have Joseph, my gardener, plant them at Henley Hall? And, maybe, before I leave, you and I could go and visit Marty's trees? If, of course...' She tailed off.

The older woman nodded, a smile lightening her face despite her tears. 'I can't tell you how much that would mean to me. I got wheels. And you got arms to push.' Her eyes hardened. 'And let me tell you, Lady Swift. Between us all in this room, we gonna create a miracle in this town!'

13

The finished beverage was a delicious mix of sweet and tangy citrus flavours just bursting with sunshine. Eleanor savoured her first glass as they settled down together at the kitchen table. It was particularly refreshing with ice, given the heat, but her thoughts were getting more troubled with each sip.

Mrs Morales broke into her silent fretting. 'Earl swaps the empty delivery crates for things like ice when he can. It's a perk alright in the hot weather. Oh, he's a good boy underneath, though he ain't sunshine like you wrote about Marty bein'. And don't take any notice of Earl sayin' we don't want your help. We're used to keepin' to our own kind when trouble hits.'

'I understand. And I'll understand if you've changed your mind about talking to me now?'

'Nope!' Mrs Morales picked up Marty's photograph and kissed it. 'Truth is, when you was brave enough to tell me you didn't think it was no accident, it weren't such a surprise. My heart told me there was likely somethin' in that.'

Eleanor was staggered. 'It did? Can I ask why?'

'Honey, you can ask anythin'. I'll tell ya if it hurts too bad to answer.' She stared at the photograph. 'Oh, I ain't said nothin' to Earl, but Marty was off somehow for a while.'

'"Off?" As in not himself?'

'That's it. And now I think of it, it started before he lost his last job a few months back.'

'With Mr Dellaney?'

This time it was Mrs Morales' turn to be surprised. 'He told you he got fired from there?'

'Not exactly. Marty said he used to work for him. Then he clammed up and left me with a warning not to take any wooden—'

'Nickels. Well, that says a lot. Marty loved his job there at first. He was the chauffeur to Mr Dellaney himself.'

Eleanor raised a hand. 'Please, can we go back a step? I didn't understand what Marty meant about nickels?'

'He meant don't get cheated or go in blind with his old boss. You see, that Mr Dellaney, he got the whole world lickin' his feet. They probably made of gold too, just like the rest of him. But he did my Marty down. My boy came home one day lookin' real cut up, sayin' that Mr Dellaney had thrown him out. And with the promise he'd never work as a chauffeur in this city again.' She frowned as she clucked her tongue. 'Mr Dellaney was as good as his word, too. Marty couldn't get a job drivin' so much as a horse cart after that. He bucked up a little after a few months when the doorman job came up here and Earl helped him get it, but it weren't the same.'

'What was Marty like outside of work?'

'Exact same as the kid my husband and me nursed all the miles from the Philippines to here when he was two and Earl was almost four. Marty was... not secretive.' She thought for a moment. 'More kinda private, I guess. He was happy on his own. He liked doin' his thing. But in between, he was the most attentive son any mother could ever wish for. Only, he never said much 'bout anythin' that was goin' on with him.'

'What about his passion? He was such a spirited chap, I can't imagine he didn't have one.'

'Sure did. Cars. Oh, he loved cars right from when they started appearin' and takin' over from the horses that used to be king in this city. Got a job washin' 'em at a showroom and was as happy as a bird. Then he moved up and worked for a monied modern family who had their own car.'

'So how did he end up working for Mr Dellaney?'

'Do you know, I can't honestly tell ya. There was a spot of girl trouble, I think, but course he wouldn't say enough that made any sense. Then he ended up switchin' chauffeur jobs a few times before landin' the big deal with Dellaney. Then that went sour and Marty never said why either.'

Eleanor's ears had pricked up. 'What did you know about his girl problem?'

'Nothin', honey. If he ever even had a girl at all, I'd 'a been the last to hear, though we was real close in other ways. Like I said, he just kept his business to himself. I only think it was girl trouble that made him move jobs because a mother has a feel for things like that.' She took Eleanor's left hand and smiled at her engagement ring. 'See, I knew you had to be spoken for. What's he like?'

'Oh goodness. How to describe Hugh?' Eleanor's shoulders rose with happiness at the thought of her far too handsome fiancé.

'Tell me his last name so I can get a picture of him.'

'Seldon. Detective Chief Inspector Hugh Seldon.'

Her eyes widened. 'A policeman! Girl, don't you do anythin' you're supposed to! Ain't he supposed to be a banker or a lawyer or just too rich to have to do anythin' at all?'

'Probably, if society had its way. But my beloved uncle Byron, who so kindly left me his estate and the title that came with it, would definitely have approved of Hugh. I'm sure he would, because Clifford does.' She sighed. 'Sadly, I didn't know my uncle very well. He took me in when my parents disappeared but was always travelling.'

Mrs Morales winced. 'Boarding school?'

'Yes. And then back to Uncle's for the holidays, where poor Clifford had to wrangle with my having no concept that his precious house rules weren't there to be broken.'

The older woman chuckled. 'And both of you been squabblin' since the day you came back on account of inheritin' the house?'

'Much to his secret delight. And Hugh's, actually. The two of them together are incorrigible. In fact, before I knew Hugh properly at all, he colluded with Clifford on my birthday. With his help, he kept it a surprise and drove all the way down to where I was holidaying on the south coast of England to take me dancing.'

Mrs Morales clapped her hands. 'Girl, he is a keeper!'

'Even though he's a policeman?' she said tentatively.

The older woman shrugged. 'Unlike most around here, I ain't got no truck with the police. The straight ones, that is. Underneath that uniform, they're just regular folk, like you and me.'

'Including Officer Balowski?'

'He came lookin' to help you 'bout Marty, didn't he?'

They sipped their juice in companionable silence for a minute.

Mrs Morales paused in stroking Gladstone's ears and sighed. 'I ain't told you nothin' of help 'bout Marty, have I? Is there somethin' else I can do?'

Eleanor bit her bottom lip. 'Yes. But it's a big ask.'

The older woman stared at her, eyes brimming with tears. Her voice came in barely more than a whisper. 'You wanna look inside my baby boy's room, don't ya?'

· · ·

Outside the narrow wood door, which looked as if it might have been seconded from an old wardrobe, Eleanor stepped aside for Mrs Morales to enter first.

She stopped her wheelchair dead. 'Oh no. He was so private 'bout his affairs, he didn't like no one in his room. Not even a pretty girl once in a while. More's the pity. And not his mama, neither.'

Eleanor held up her hands. 'Then I shouldn't—'

The older woman fixed her with a firm look. 'You should do whatever you think will help us find out the truth. I trust you, honey.' With a few well-practised manoeuvres in the restricted passageway, she wheeled herself back to the kitchen.

Eleanor took a deep breath, opened the door, and stepped into the tiny room. A single iron bed, dressed with clean but faded blue sheets occupied one end, while a washstand fashioned from a tea chest inset with a shallow bowl occupied another. In between, a small brown rug covered some of the bare wood floor, while hooks nailed to a curtain pole served as hanging space.

It was the far wall which caught her attention, however. A collection of tin toy cars sat on a set of shelves. Obviously cherished, despite the dents and scraped paint, each had a hand-written card listing the make, model and year of manufacture.

As she turned to examine the room again, her skirt swished some loose papers off the bottom shelf. She bent down to retrieve them and noticed a battered wicker laundry basket under the bed. A quick foray through the pockets of a pair of trousers waiting for wash day made her cheeks burn with shame. However, they yielded nothing. She returned them to the basket and straightened up, muttering, 'This is hopeless. Marty, help me, please! For your mother's sake.'

But no answer came. Resignedly, she knelt down to return the wash basket to where she had found it. Giving it a gentle shove, she frowned. Something was stopping it. She knelt down again and peered under the bed. Nothing. Her fingers crawled forward until she had to lie on the floor.

Her stomach did a somersault. Two of the nails that held the floorboards in place were slightly proud.

Why, Ellie? Unless...

She winkled the board free with a knife she found on the bottom shelf and, cursing her lack of foresight in bringing a torch, reached down tentatively into the hole.

Metal, Ellie!

She pulled the item out and stared at it. It was a toy tin delivery van, larger than the other models. She pondered the toy for a moment, turning it slowly in her hands. Why wasn't it on the shelves with the others? Had Marty hidden it because it was valuable? A collector's antique, perhaps? Her nose wrinkled. Unlikely, as it was in particularly poor condition, missing most of its paint, but also one of its tin wheels. The moulded rear section stamped with the word "GASOLINE" also felt loose. And then it fell off.

Speechless, she sat staring at her lap. Or rather, at the five rolls of banknotes the truck had deposited there.

14

'Here we go! Lecture time!' she whispered to Gladstone, who was sprawled across her lap, with his tongue flapping in the welcome breeze floating in through the drawing-room windows. For, rather than diminishing, the unseasonably early heatwave had increased.

Clifford pursed his lips. 'My lady, yet not one hour ago you were evidently spreadeagled under a dead man's bed, rooting under his floorboards. Alone!'

'And in his laundry basket.' She hid a smile at Clifford's horrified look. 'But I did discover those rolls of banknotes.' She grimaced. 'The only thing is, I don't know how to bring them up with Mrs Morales. I mean...' She looked at Clifford, a pained expression on her face. He nodded.

'I agree, my lady. It is hard to believe a mere chauffeur, and then doorman, could possibly have come by such a large amount of money in any legal manner.'

'Exactly! And how is that going to go down with his grieving mother?'

'I can only think extremely badly. Perhaps we should keep your discovery between ourselves until we have had time to at least consider an alternative explanation?' He pulled out his pocket watch. 'Which unfortunately cannot be now, as Mr Morales is due in a moment.'

'Bother!'

She hurried to the staff eating area just off the kitchen.

'Hello, ladies.' Her staff jumped up from the table and shuffled into a line. After they'd curtseyed and disentangled an exuberant Gladstone from their legs, she sat down and waved them back into their seats.

Mrs Trotman tugged Polly down beside her. 'Park your skirts and start in on your tea, my girl. He'll be here any minute.'

It had been Clifford's idea for Eleanor to be taking tea with her staff when Earl arrived in the hope it would put him at ease. In England, she often did, preferring it to eating alone in the vast dining room. The table she now sat at was occupied mostly by a large oval plate filled with a selection of simple but delectable-looking pastries and scones, both of the savoury and sweet varieties. As Mrs Butters poured Eleanor a steaming cup, all eyes swivelled to her.

'Oh, right. Er...'

'I believe "dig in" would be appropriate, my lady,' Clifford said as he arrived. 'Followed immediately thereafter by,' he cleared his throat, '"and get a wiggle on already".'

The ladies broke into giggles. Despite her unease at her upcoming meeting with Earl, Eleanor laughed as well.

With Gladstone chewing on a baked bone, they all tucked in, the ladies launching into tales of their jaunts outside the apartment building. Even somewhat abridged as Eleanor was sure they had to be, given that Clifford was present, their retelling of their amusing experiences soothed her nerves.

'And then the man had the cheek to say, "This ain't no playground, it's a museum!"' Mrs Trotman chuckled. 'Then he shooed us out with a broom.'

Mrs Butters nodded. 'It was a quality one, mind. Plenty of

strong bristles and the sort of handle you can keep a good grip on. So I stopped him huffing long enough to ask where I could get one.'

Eleanor laughed out loud. Even Clifford's lips quirked.

The doorbell rang. Clifford disappeared to answer it. A moment later, his voice came from the hall.

'We are through here. Do join us. Yes, naturally, her ladyship too.'

He stepped around into the alcove, followed by a bewildered-looking Earl.

'Ah, hello, Earl,' Eleanor said genially.

Clifford waved him towards the empty chair between Mrs Trotman and Mrs Butters, the former of the two patting the seat encouragingly.

'We don't bite, Mr Morales. Not hard, anyhow.'

Mrs Butters poured him a tea.

'Pastries are going fast, mind, especially in the seats occupied by these two young 'uns.' She indicated Polly and Lizzie. 'So, best not dally, if I were you.'

Earl stared around the table, his eyes coming to rest on Eleanor. 'I thought you wouldn't, you know...'

'Relax with my staff?' She shrugged. 'They're more like family, you know, Earl.' She smiled affectionately at them all. *It's true, Ellie, we've been through a lot together since I inherited Henley Hall. Good times and bad.*

As Earl drank his tea and ate a selection of the pastries and scones, the ladies and Clifford kept him engaged in easy chatter. Eleanor chipped in occasionally, but mostly held her tongue, trying to sum him up by discreetly watching and listening.

'See, I'd say the south streets are gonna be more fun for you, ladies,' he said less gruffly than Eleanor had heard him speak before. 'You should try the market down that way, too. It's way cheaper and better than the one nearest here.'

'Right.' Mrs Butters slid a hand around Polly's arm and

dragged her up. 'Come on, my girl, let's go look at Mr Clifford's map and start planning our next little trip out.'

Earl nodded as they disappeared. Without any coercion, he reached for another pastry.

After a discussion about the merits of the boiler system with Clifford, and the vagaries of the lift, Mrs Trotman rose. 'You've given me an idea there,' she said to Earl, without adding what exactly it was.

'I'll watch so as to know for next time,' Lizzie said, following her out.

Earl shook his head to himself, looking around the empty seats.

He's either relaxed enough to be helpful now, Ellie, or he never will.

She put down her cup. 'I hope you don't mind me saying that the time I spent with your mother earlier was really heart-warming. She's a wonderful lady.'

He shrugged. 'Ma's the best. Just don't upset her if you ever want to hear the end of it.'

She smiled. 'Oh, I think that's supposed to be a mother's job. But maybe you got a raft of tellings-off over squabbling with Marty when you were growing up?'

'Maybe,' he said non-committally.

Fearing he was clamming up, she caught Clifford's eye.

'Mr Morales,' he said. 'The rental of this apartment has proven most successful due to the exemplary team of staff here. However, your brother hadn't been employed here as long as yourself, I believe?'

Earl rolled his eyes. 'No, I got him the job about three months ago. Left out all the other stuff and just buffed up how great a doorman he'd make to the building owner.'

'Which he did,' Eleanor said genuinely. 'So you were right. The... other stuff obviously didn't affect his work.' She took a sip of tea. 'Whatever it was?'

Earl swallowed his mouthful of pastry. 'Marty had a real short fuse for bad luck or bad times. If things were good, Marty was good. But if not, well, you get the picture.'

'Like before he... you got him the job here?' She held her hands up. 'Mind you, being sacked is no fun for anyone.'

Clifford raised a finger. 'That is sacked as in "fired", Mr Morales.'

Earl stopped frowning. 'Right. Maybe, but Marty was sore long before he got the boot.'

'An unhappy employment from the outset then, perhaps?'

Earl grunted. 'He liked it fine at the start. That Dellaney has a fleet of cars you wouldn't believe. Marty drooled over 'em. Seemed to sour quick though. He'd only been employed for a few months. So, when he was fired, you'd have thought he'd be happy it was over. But nope!'

Eleanor's brow furrowed. 'Did he say why he was fired?'

Earl laughed without humour. 'Marty never said nothin'. Probably just missed drivin' his precious cars. Always wanted to be a chauffeur. Used to make pretend, by sittin' in boxes when he was a kid.' He shook his head disparagingly. 'Chauffeurin's just bein' someone else's drivin' monkey. Only perk is bein' seen out in a fancy car wearin' a fancy uniform, far as I can make out. But Marty lived for it.'

Eleanor's thoughts flew back to the banknotes she'd found under Marty's bed. 'Well, it was a well-paying job. I mean, by the sound of it. Surely he would have missed that?'

Earl looked at her as if she'd fallen from the moon. 'Thought you of all people would understand that?'

She didn't.

Earl shrugged. 'It weren't no high payin' gig. Men like Dellaney make money to keep it, not to give it to the likes of his staff.'

'Ah! I see. And Mr Morales, your brother really didn't give you any clue as to why he lost his position?'

Earl shook his head and swigged the last of his tea. 'Only thing I remember now was he blamed the bucket lickspittle.' At their confused looks, he translated. 'The guy who cleaned Dellaney's cars. Temples, I think. Anyway, Marty said the guy ratted him out to Dellaney, then slid right on into Marty's place in the drivin' seat. Course Marty said everythin' he told Dellaney was lousy lies, but who knows, right?' He pushed his chair back and stood. 'That's it. The Marty show's over. I gotta get to work.'

'Yes, of course.' Eleanor rose with him. 'One last question. Did Marty ever mention a girl called Mary?'

Earl's lip curled. 'You got a funny idea about Marty. He wouldn'a said nothin' if he had every doll in New York called Mary that he was makin''—'

'Up to,' Clifford said quickly.

'That what you call it in England? Don't try using that on a doll here, Mr Clifford. You won't get so much as a flash of a lacy underlayer.' He turned to Eleanor. 'I came here 'cos Ma ain't one you can say no to and the day still be worth gettin' up for. But I've said all there is 'bout Marty. Thanks for the pies. And if you want to know more about how Marty lost his job, why don't you ask Dellaney himself? Or Temples, the guy who stepped into his shoes?' At the door he swung around. 'Marty and me might not have been like best buddies, but we were still brothers. And I'm not just gonna stand around and do nothin'. Whoever did this to my brother is gonna pay!'

15

The taunting sounds of the lift descending and rising to every floor but Eleanor's wasn't the source of her agitation this time.

'You're sure an evening gown is the only correct option, Clifford?' She ran her hands uncomfortably over her bare arms. Looking down at her embroidered gown's pretty scalloped neckline, it suddenly felt far too revealing. 'Dellaney said it would be an "intimate" affair. I cared for neither his word choice, nor tone of voice.'

'The *married* Mr Dellaney?' Clifford's brows flinched. He slipped Gladstone's lead into her hand. 'One moment please, my lady.'

He swiftly reappeared with her beaded lace overwrap in complementary seafoam and emerald-green with floaty butterfly sleeves which swung in perfect folds against her forearms. She gratefully slid into it and then fastened all the pearl buttons which ran up to a high satin collar. 'Much better, thank you.'

'Don't see how,' a cantankerous voice called out.

'Mrs Melchum!' Eleanor whispered.

'And the cherished Catamina,' Clifford whispered back.

'Tail already twitching. Lift wars, ahoy!'

'Good evening, Mrs Melchum,' Eleanor said, ignoring Catamina's long and spiteful hiss at Gladstone.

'Is it?' the older woman snipped. She looked Eleanor over with a critical eye. 'Going out?'

Remembering Earl's grumble that her neighbour's irritability was probably due to her rarely leaving the building, she tempered her reply. 'Just popping to a quick little thing. Uptown, I believe you describe it as.'

'This is New York, Lady Swift,' she said drily. 'Nothing is little. Nor quick. Neither can one simply "pop" anywhere. This city will see to that. And that outfit looks like it took a half day to decide on.' Catamina gave a haughty yawn and turned her back to Eleanor.

'Thank you for your compliment,' Eleanor said, struggling to restrain a clearly feline- frustrated Gladstone.

The lift having arrived, Clifford opened the door.

Mrs Melchum's curiosity seemed far from sated as she stepped in after the Siamese. 'Dinner, is it? Theatre?' She flicked her eyes disdainfully to Eleanor's butler. 'And with your help, I see.'

'Actually, Clifford is just accompanying me to Mr Dellaney's house so I don't have to travel alone.'

'*Ogden* Dellaney?' Mrs Melchum's voice held a peculiar tone Eleanor couldn't place. Before Eleanor could reply, Mrs Melchum gestured impatiently for Clifford to close the lift door on her and her cat. With a clunk and a whirr, the lift descended. The woman's words floated up the shaft to Eleanor's ears. 'A word of advice, Lady Swift. Make sure you leave with what you came with!'

Eleanor shot Clifford a confused look but received only a raised brow in return.

Having waited impatiently for the lift's return, Eleanor jumped in and then out in the foyer, before hurrying to the basement stairs. At the top of Mrs Morales' wheelchair ramp, Gladstone let out a woof and nosed the tired blue front door open. She followed the excited bulldog into the tiny kitchen.

'Oh my! Oh my!' Mrs Morales said in awe, one hand cupping Gladstone's wobbling jowls in her lap, the other holding Eleanor's arm out to one side. 'Just look at you. Honey, I didn't think you could be more beautiful, but you're fit to join the angels up with my Marty.'

'Thank you.' Eleanor swished her sleeves out like wings. 'I wish I could fly up and see him.'

'And maybe Mr Clifford would have the heart to push me in my chair across the skies to come with ya.'

'Willingly, madam,' he said, bringing a smile to the woman's exhausted face.

'Forgive us descending on you unannounced.' Eleanor perched on the edge of the nearest of the two chairs. 'But we both wanted to check you're as well as can be?'

Mrs Morales smiled wanly. 'Oh, with the way I'm bein' fussed and spoiled, I'm doin' fine enough.'

'That's good to hear. Earl is looking after you, then?'

'In his own way.' She flapped a hand. 'I ain't grumblin'. He's doin' his best. But sure was a treat to have your ladies call. Oh, they are such a welcome wash of sunny mischief, 'specially the two young'uns. Have they told ya the best of their tales since they been here, Mr Clifford?'

'Thankfully not, madam,' he said earnestly.

She chuckled and squeezed Eleanor's hand. 'Now, get your beautiful dress and face gone from my kitchen. You got far better things to do with your time. This is New York City, case you hadn't noticed.'

'I have.' Eleanor shook her head. 'And she's proving just as unexpected as everyone keeps warning me she is. But actually, tonight I'm going...' She caught Clifford's quiet cautionary cough. 'Umm... uptown.'

'Then let's hope uptown is ready for a visit from Lady Swift. Thank you for comin', honey, Mr Clifford, and darlin' Mr Wrinkles too.' She gave Gladstone's ears one last loving ruffle. 'Don't be shy comin' again any time you three have a minute with nothin' to do.'

Out front, Earl hailed a taxi for them.

'Well, if it ain't Lady Luck,' called the gravelly voice from the driver's seat.

'Iver! Good evening.' She leaned in the front passenger window. 'It's lovely to see you, too.'

Especially as you need to grill him on the hit-and-run, Ellie.

Iver rolled his eyes. 'Oh yeah, says the dame who's been avoidin' me.' He raised his heavy greying brows. 'Ain't that the truth?'

'Perhaps a little.' She shrugged sheepishly. 'Please don't take it personally. It was only—'

'On account of Marty? Figured so.' His already disconsolate tone softened. 'Poor kid. That was no way for anyone to go. 'Specially a good one like him. Ain't nothin' we can do for him now.'

Except get justice for him and his family, Ellie.

Iver pulled his cap down harder, then jerked a thumb at the back of his taxi.

Once she, Clifford, and the wriggling bulldog were inside, she leaned forward. 'Actually, Iver, I believe, there might be a lot we can do for Marty. If you're willing, of course?'

Iver graunched the taxi out of gear and turned slowly to stare at her. 'Help Marty? Lady, he's gone, he's... *dead.*' Beckoning to her butler with a gnarled finger, he lowered his voice. 'Mr Clifford, I gotta tell ya we got clinics for the hysteria here in New York. Really hope it ain't already too late, s'all I'm sayin'.'

'Most kind, Iver,' he said in his ever-measured tone over

Eleanor's gasp. 'But I can assure you there is no mental... irregularity manifesting in her ladyship.' He peered sideways at her. 'And yet this is the second time such an accusation has been levelled at her ladyship in less than twenty-four hours...'

She hid a smile. 'I'll deal with you later!' She turned back to Iver. 'I didn't mean we could bring poor Marty back. I meant that we might be able to get justice for him.'

'Justice?' Iver let out a long whistle. 'Lady, you think that car slammed Marty on purpose?'

'I do.'

For a moment, he was silent. Then he glanced at Clifford and back at her. 'Mr Clifford, too?'

'Yes. Which is why we need your help.'

He stared forward and hunched his shoulders. 'Me! I'm just Iver Driver. Ask anyone. What can I do? Drive, that's it. Period.'

Eleanor shook her head. 'Not the case, Iver. Please, for Marty. Can we just sit here a moment and talk?'

Clifford held his wallet up so Iver could see it. 'Naturally, your time sitting here will be compensated, not only the miles travelled.'

'Like that's what I'm concerned about right now.' He pulled his cap further down and stepped out.

Eleanor groaned. 'Oh, no! Where's he go—'

She broke off as he opened the rear door and slid inside. He sat in the spare seat, facing them. Gladstone decided the moment needed enlivening with an enthusiastic bulldog charge, licky welcome at the ready.

'Yuck!' As Clifford coaxed Gladstone back and pinned him gently against his suited legs, Iver held his hands out. 'So, here I am, Lady Swift.'

'Thank you,' she said with relief. 'All we need you to do is recount everything you remember from dropping Clifford and me at the apartment building's steps onwards, the night Marty died.'

Iver's mouth turned down. 'Don't see as it's gonna help. You were standin' right there when I told that cop the whole story the other day.' At her pleading look, he held up his hands. 'Okay, okay!' He gathered his thoughts. 'Let's see. So, from the beginnin' then.'

Only a few sentences into the taxi driver's recollections, she stopped him.

'One moment, Iver. You remember the pinched-faced fellow? The witness to the hit-and-run the officer questioned? Said he wasn't from around here?'

He nodded.

'Well, did you notice him before you pulled away after dropping us off?'

He thought about this for a second. 'I think so. In fact, yeah, I sees him waitin' on the sidewalk, alright.' He held his hands up. 'Can't mean anythin', though.'

'Maybe. Maybe not.' She frowned. 'You said "waiting" not "standing"?'

Iver nodded. 'Yeah. He looked like he was waitin' for a bus, but ain't no buses come down this road.' He slapped the seat, making Gladstone jump. 'But he was waitin' for Marty to cross so as he could ask him directions, course, that's why.'

Something was still bothering her, but she couldn't pinpoint what. Clifford glanced at her and then at Iver. 'Had the gentleman called out to Marty at this point, do you know?'

'Don't think so. And he weren't no gentleman.'

Eleanor frowned in confusion. 'Why not?'

He snorted. ''Cause soon as the cop turns his back, he don't scram like the others. He stays to hear all the worst of it. Like it's not enough he sees Marty fly over that car and smack onto the road.'

'You don't think he was just trying to be helpful, then?'

He shook his head. 'Lady, don't you get it? Folks are too busy fighting with this city and each other. They ain't got time for bein' helpful, 'cept that real odd outta towner I've been drivin' around.'

She leaned forward. 'Who's that?'

Clifford pointed a respectful finger at her. 'Ahem, yourself, I believe, my lady.'

Iver nodded.

She laughed, but the niggle was still there. 'You really think that man stayed just out of some kind of macabre interest, Iver?'

'Sure do. New York's a spectacle, alright. But Marty goin' so… so broke up like that. That was somethin' else.'

His already downcast expression took an even more doleful turn.

'Last question,' she said quickly. 'Was there anything else that struck you as odd at the time of the accident?'

He shrugged, then his face creased. 'There was somethin'.' She and Clifford leaned forward. 'That guy you were just askin' about. The rubbernecker. He told the cop he hollered for Marty 'cos he was lost and wanted directions. But when I pulled up to drop you off, he was just waitin' like I said. And while you was gettin' out, no one called out to Marty. I'd a' heard.'

'You're sure?'

He nodded. 'And then, as I'm pullin' away' – he lifted his hand and adjusted an imaginary rear-view mirror – 'all I sees is the back of his head like he's now lookin' down the street, not at Marty who was still on the other side of the road to the guy. It must have been after that he called out.'

Clifford shared a look with Eleanor.

'So he wasn't looking at Marty,' she said slowly, 'which he would have been doing if he was trying to attract his attention.'

Clifford nodded thoughtfully. 'Indeed, my lady. Instead, it seems he was looking—'

'In the direction the car that killed Marty came from!'

16

'Stop!'

Eleanor spun around and stood, waiting.

Outside her apartment block, Clifford walked down the road towards her with a measured stride. Twice he glanced behind him, but each time shook his head and continued. Finally, he stopped, five or six shop fronts from her. Glancing at the apartment block once again, he called, 'This is the nearest I believe it could have been, my lady.'

'Excellent!'

Iver scratched his head as they cast their eyes around the kerb and road where they were standing. He looked from one to the other.

'Okay, what's this all about? You makin' me wait, I get that. Everyone makes the cabbie wait. He don't count for nothin'. But keepin' a swell like Dellaney waitin'? That's another matter!'

Clifford glanced at his watch. 'We'll only be a few minutes more and you'll still have time to drop Lady Swift at Mr Dellaney's residence no more than her usual twenty minutes late.'

Eleanor resisted rising to the bait. 'We worked out, Iver, that the driver who ran Marty down must have been waiting somewhere down the road.'

'But not so far down that they couldn't see our pinched-faced fellow giving the signal that he was about to get Mr Morales to step into the road.'

Iver gasped. 'You think that's what he did, Mr Clifford!'

He nodded. 'We do, Iver. And as it was evening, as it is now, with the gaslight illuminating only some areas and throwing shadows over the others, we estimate the car must have been parked waiting with its engine running somewhere between where her ladyship and I are standing.'

Iver's brows knitted. 'Okay, I can buy that. But what you hopin' to find?'

'We've no idea,' Eleanor called as she walked slowly towards Clifford, who was now walking towards her, eyes on the ground. 'But when we find it, we'll let you know.'

Clifford raised a hand, and they both stopped. 'I think, my lady, given that the other two vehicles parked here,' he indicated a beaten-up lorry and an even more beaten-up sedan car, 'have not been moved in some time, I conjecture, the driver must have been parked opposite one of these three shop fronts. In fact' – he pointed to the nearest two – 'one of these, otherwise the driver's view would have been obscured by the lorry itself.'

Eleanor nodded as they both scanned the area he had indicated. A moment later she waved Clifford over. He and Iver joined her, both dropping to their haunches. 'What do you think?'

Clifford bent down and picked up a cigarette end. Iver frowned.

'It's just some butt-end some guy passing flicked in the road!'

Clifford shook his head. 'The weather has been dry since yesterday evening, and this "butt" is not old. Rather I would say it has been dropped fairly recently. Certainly in the last few days. Secondly, as you suggested, most people,' he said with a sniff, '"flick" their ends into the road. This is far too close to the kerb.'

Eleanor nodded. 'More like someone waiting in a car dropped it out of the window.'

Iver shrugged. 'Which means it could be anyone who parked there in the last twenty-four hours.'

Clifford straightened up. 'Indeed, it could. It is, however, a fairly unusual cigarette. A French Gitanes. No filter and made from a mixture of black tobacco and therefore more pungent.'

Eleanor grimaced. 'I remember them. On the French Riviera everyone was smoking Gauloises or Gitanes cigarettes. The rich set mostly Gitanes.' She shrugged. 'However, Iver is right. It could have been dropped by anyone. But let's both keep our eyes open as we go and see if we spot someone we figure might be a suspect smoking that particular brand. It's a long shot, and even if they do, it doesn't mean they dropped this one.' She caught Clifford pulling his pocket watch out. 'Okay, come on, Iver. I can't put it off any longer. Let's get to Dellaney's. But if he gets too familiar, or handsy, I might just forget I'm a titled English lady!'

As they headed back to the taxi, Clifford shook his head. 'That is unlikely to happen, I'm sure.'

She frowned. 'Why?'

'Because, my lady' – he glanced away, a twinkle in his eye – 'you would have to remember you are one in the first place.'

17

'Expectations exist only so one can exceed them.' Ogden P. Dellaney smiled smugly. Too smugly, and too close to Eleanor's ear for comfort. 'Just as I imagine yours were, Lady Swift, on seeing Glory Gates for the first time.'

Eleanor willed her best guest smile not to falter. Dellaney's words had been delivered, not as a question, but as a statement. And being told her own mind always rankled, particularly when it was wrong. Dellaney's second mansion, his 'proper' home, as he called it, was indeed breathtaking. But she had seen and stayed in Ottoman and Indian palaces on her travels, and they made Glory Gates seem... somehow vulgar.

She turned her hard-won alcohol-free cocktail in her hand. 'Honestly, Mr Dellaney, I came with no expectations. An open mind sees so much more, especially when travelling, I find. After all, what a shame it would be to miss the world's wonders because one packed the blinkers of home in one's case.' She broadened her smile. 'Don't you agree?'

The clench of his jaw suggested he didn't. Any man who had a replica French Renaissance chateau built only an hour and a half from his already enormous town mansion would surely expect to be considered right on everything? However, his thirty-four bedrooms, forty-three bathrooms, two ballrooms, recital suites, portrait galleries and endless reception rooms suddenly seemed to displease him. His dark eyes almost vanished in his deep frown. Evidently even the palatial four-storeyed glass atrium housing a veritable jungle of tropical trees and exotic birds they were standing in had lost its lustre at her refusal to be told what to think. She reminded herself why she was there; to ask about the night of Marty's death and find out if Dellaney had an alibi. Not wanting to appear any ruder, she swallowed her irritation.

'This is, without doubt, however, a beautiful and extraordinary home.'

Her host's humour seemed restored, his ego soothed, as his frown turned back to a smug smile. 'Yes. The most extraordinary, actually.' He stepped even closer. 'I must show you every inch... of her.'

Her skin crawled. *I don't think so, Ellie!*

'I imagine I'm far from your only guest tonight, Mr Dellaney?' she said hastily, fearful the answer might be yes.

He smiled slyly. 'Now that would hardly be the thing, Lady Swift. You and me all alone in Glory Gates? The others are gathered in my observatory. And as I've told you before, do call me Ogden.' He pulled out a gold cigarette case and offered her one. Her heart quickened. Someone who had a replica French chateau as a home might also smoke French cigarettes! She hid her disappointment. American Cravens!

After coaxing Gladstone to join them in ascending to the top floor in the grandiose glass and gold lift, she followed Dellaney out as he gestured to a spiral staircase.

'I'm afraid it's on foot from here.'

She quickly scooped Gladstone's portly frame up with a grunt. 'No, after you.' She had no desire to have this over-familiar man so close behind her on a confined staircase. At the top, the room they emerged into was just one more ocean of the finest leather upholstery, marquetry inlaid wall panels, priceless-looking objets d'art and gold light fittings. On every side, however, a set of arched open French doors led out onto a wraparound balcony, allowing uninterrupted views of the vast landscaped gardens. And, this evening, allowing guests to cool down in the continuing heatwave.

Her host left her in the company of Mrs Vanderdale, who had just come in from the balcony and disappeared back down the staircase.

'Ah, Mrs Vanderdale, good evening. What a remarkable house.' Eleanor waved her butterfly sleeves to get the most of the welcome breeze.

'Can't say I notice any more.' Mrs Vanderdale's mahogany curls bounced against her flawless cheeks as she gave a cursory glance around.

Eleanor shrugged. 'Well, I think Glory Gates is delightfully... theatrical somehow.'

Mrs Vanderdale snorted. 'Of course it is. This is Ogden's slice of living like the theatre stars he secretly idolises. Sometimes, I wonder if it's the only reason he funds those Broadway shows.'

'Theatre?' Eleanor failed to hide her surprise. 'For some reason, I imagined Mr D— Ogden, would only be interested in far more serious business pursuits.'

Mrs Vanderdale shook her head. 'He is. He invests in Broadway mostly so he can hobnob with those same movie stars.'

Wyatt appeared from the other side of the balcony. 'Good evening, Lady Swift. Howdy, Gladstone.' He ruffled the euphoric bulldog's ears. 'I was beginning to think you weren't coming.'

'Me or Gladstone?'

He laughed. 'The both of you.'

At that moment, their host reappeared. 'What's the conversation, people?'

Mrs Vanderdale smiled sweetly. 'Lady Swift was most intrigued to learn about your Broadway connection, Ogden.'

'Eminent connection, Lavinia.' He turned to Eleanor. 'You're a devotee of the stage, then?'

She held her hands up. 'Actually, I can't honestly say I've had the chance. I only returned to England a short while ago in real terms and, in truth, I've been rather too caught up with things to go to any productions. I did join our village's local amateur dramatic society, though, which was fun.'

Dellaney and Mrs Vanderdale shared a disbelieving look.

Wyatt nodded encouragingly. 'Like community theatre, as we call it in America?'

'If that's a group of locals who have no training and are happy to make a fool of themselves having a go at acting anyway, then, yes.'

'And you joined that!' Mrs Vanderdale's tone said it all.

Dellaney was regarding Eleanor with intense curiosity. 'So, what is it that keeps a titled English lady too caught up to go and enjoy the best that culture can offer?'

Her brain froze. She could hardly explain it had been investigating a raft of murders she'd been unwittingly embroiled in.

Unexpectedly, Mrs Vanderdale came to her rescue. 'Ogden, how many times do I have to tell you that we ladies lead a life you have no business knowing about?'

'Too many to care for,' he said tartly.

Eleanor stepped in. 'You seem to be forever entertaining, Ogden. How do you find enough time to see the plays yourself?'

'Oh, it's not so much seeing them, though they are spectacular, obviously. It's more being immersed in the life of theatre. The scripts, the actors, the stage sets.'

'And the door takings,' Mrs Vanderdale sniped.

Wanting to be anywhere but amongst their seemingly

constant digs at each other, Eleanor reminded herself why she was there.

'I know Atticus likes to retire early, do you do the same, Ogden?' She laughed. 'Of course, you can't have done the evening I first came around to your Manhattan residence, although you could have retired when the last of the guests left, whatever time that was?'

He looked at her oddly. 'Actually, I was grateful you started the stampede with Atticus here. Everyone followed almost immediately.'

'Oh, shame. Did the evening not go as you planned then?'

'On the contrary. As it happens I... had a migraine and needed to retire once everyone had left.'

With only his staff to verify that, Ellie. She frowned. *I wonder how Clifford is getting on discreetly interrogating them?*

Mrs Vanderdale looped her arm over Wyatt's. 'The strain of being King of New York starting to show, Ogden?' She looked Eleanor over. 'What about you then, Lady Swift? A young woman on her first trip to the Big Apple as it seems to have been named now. I don't believe you went home and straight to bed like a good girl?'

Eleanor ran her hands down her arms. 'Actually, I witnessed an... accident and tried to save a man's life.'

Wyatt shook his arm free of Mrs Vanderdale's grip. 'Very noble, Eleanor. Can I say without offending you that you're every inch what I could never have expected?'

'Yes.' She smiled, but it faded at the memory of Marty's fatal injuries. 'But I only did what any of you would do, I'm sure.' She chose her words carefully, noting only Wyatt had nodded. 'The poor fellow was hit badly by a car outside my apartment building.'

'These things happen,' Dellaney said offhandedly. 'If one is incautious.'

'Was it someone you knew?' Wyatt said.

'Actually, it was someone I, and Ogden, knew. The doorman at my apartment building.'

Mrs Vanderdale tapped a nail against her glass of evidently medicinal champagne and looked with amusement at Dellaney. 'Why would Ogden know your doorman!'

'His name was Marty,' Eleanor said. An emotion passed over Dellaney's face, too fleetingly for her to place it. She kept her tone light and her eyes on his. 'I believe he used to be your chauffeur before you sacked, sorry, I mean fired him?'

Anger flashed across his face this time. 'Staff come and go like the seasons, Lady Swift. This... Marty may have been one of them at one stage, I really can't recall.'

At the head of the stairs, Eleanor spotted Mrs Dellaney. Dellaney glanced over and scowled. 'Now, please excuse me. Do enjoy the rest of the evening.' He stalked off, brushing past his wife without a word.

With a careless toss of her blonde coiffure, Mrs Dellaney tottered over on even higher heels than Eleanor had seen her in last time. Wyatt offered her a gentlemanly nod. Mrs Vanderdale, however, seemed to be looking the woman up and down disdainfully without disguising the fact.

'Good evening, Mrs Dellaney,' Eleanor said brightly.

'Evening, Lady English.' Mrs Dellaney shook her head. 'No, Lady...'

'Swift. But don't worry. I can't imagine how you keep up with the names of all the guests you must have in a week. Particularly with the theatre connection. Ogden was just telling us about his interests in Broadway.'

Mrs Dellaney rolled her eyes. 'Don't you mean boring you with? But maybe he found enough manners not to detail how he only devotes his time to the long-legged investments he can get his claws into.'

Uncomfortable with Mrs Dellaney's rather disparaging tone, Eleanor looked to Wyatt for help. 'Might that be similar to a "long-term investment", as I remember overhearing my late uncle mention years back?'

His eyes flicked to Mrs Dellaney, then out into the throng of guests. He waved a hand at no one in particular. 'No, Lady Swift, it very much wouldn't. Ladies, would you excuse me, please.'

'Oh dear.' Eleanor turned back from watching him walk away, noting Mrs Vanderdale's half-hidden smirk.

'Oh nothing!' Mrs Dellaney said. 'But I see I wasn't clear at all. I was trying to warn you, Lady Swift, since you're just the sort of long-legged investment Ogden *can't* resist. And as you don't know him at all,' her tone darkened, 'I'd suggest unless you want a ton of trouble, you stay away from him.' She turned and tottered away, calling over her shoulder, 'And I don't mean from me!'

18

Mrs Dellaney's revelations had left Eleanor with a sour taste in her mouth. She vowed to keep as far from Dellaney as her investigation would allow, something that might prove difficult as he had abruptly sacked Marty and she needed to find out why. In the end, it probably had nothing to do with Marty's death. But then again, it might have.

Wyatt appeared again out of the throng and offered her his elbow. 'I overheard the last of that. I've got the feeling you've had enough of Manhattan high society for one night, and would prefer to retire to your pyjamas, as you enlightened me last time. Let me walk you to the door.'

How Clifford had arranged for Iver and his taxi to be waiting at just the moment she needed them, she had no idea. But she was grateful for both familiar faces and wasted no time imparting what she'd learned.

'Dellaney insisted he had a migraine and went straight to bed after we left the night Marty died,' she said quietly to Clifford as she climbed in the back seat and they set off.

He looked unconvinced. 'Remarkably well covered up, if I

may say so. Poor Lizzie is prostrate in the dark when one afflicts her.'

She nodded. 'I thought the same.' She lowered her voice further. 'The only other useful piece of information I gleaned was from Dellaney's wife.' She recounted what the tipsy woman had revealed. 'Not much help. What about you? How did you get on with the staff? Apart from Mrs Dellaney, if you could ever find her sober enough to ask, they seem to be the only ones who could back up Dellaney's alibi.'

He pursed his lips. 'From what I observed, none would dare contradict anything Mr Dellaney said. Indeed, I feel they would say nothing unless instructed to do so by Mr Dellaney himself. And would then only repeat verbatim what they had been told to say.'

'But, Clifford, you always manage to wheedle some revelation out of the staff.' She hid a smile. 'After all, staff do like to gossip about their employers, don't they?'

He eyed her aloofly. 'I shall ignore that jibe, my lady.'

She laughed. 'It was a joke and you know it. Although, it's often been true, and helpful, when we've needed it.' She clicked her fingers. 'What about Myers, the butler? You always get on with your counterparts.'

'Tighter lipped than a clam, my lady. No matter how artfully I trod.'

She lapsed into thoughtful silence as they crossed the river back into Manhattan itself.

'How was the party?' Iver interrupted from the front.

'Oh, you know me and formal occasions by now,' she said airily, not wanting to get distracted from her conversation with Clifford. However, as she half-turned back to him, she gasped.

'Iver! Stop!'

The taxi lurched to a halt, flipping Gladstone onto his back.

'My lady?' Clifford helped the bulldog back onto his tummy.

'Sorry, Gladstone. But there. Look!'

She pointed through the window at a smart-fronted workshop on the other side of the road.

He followed her finger and raised an eyebrow. 'I fail to see—'

'The car!'

On the far right of the forecourt, under a streetlight, a long, dark-grey saloon was parked.

Iver stared at it. 'That sedan? What's the deal?'

Her butler shook his head. 'My lady, I rather hoped we'd conceded you had accosted sufficient innocent drivers across the city already?'

'Innocent ones, yes. But that.' She leaned further out of the window and stared harder at it, looking for the emblem she'd seen before. The number plate read 534-577.

The number plate of the car that hit Marty started with a five! But then again, Ellie, thousands do as Balowski pointed out.

She pulled her body back in, opened the door and scrambled out of the car, Clifford's imploring words falling on deaf ears. With a weary headshake, he joined her on the pavement. The workshop appeared closed up for the evening, unsurprisingly, as it was now nearing ten o'clock.

'I know you think I'm getting hysterical about finding the car that hit Marty, but this time I'm right. Come on. Stealthy does it.'

She walked further along the street until she was past the garage, and then quickly crossed the road and doubled back, Clifford following. Using the wall which formed the end of the forecourt as cover, she crept on until she was tucked halfway along the car. Closer beside her than he would normally countenance, Clifford held up a questioning gloved hand.

'What now?' she whispered. 'Yes, good question. However, as you have clearly worked out, I haven't got a plan. Other than to look for damage or any other clue that this was the last thing poor Marty saw before his world went forever dark.'

Her breath caught as she stole up to the bonnet. Up close the emblem looked like the one she'd seen. A naked lady in silver, rather like some sort of nymph. And the chromed bar between the headlights was stove back into the engine grille and the windscreen cracked.

'Clifford, this has to be it!'

'Er, folks,' a voice called from the shadows. 'There's nothin' to see here. Shop's closed.'

She spun around. A man in a dark overcoat with his hands behind his back stepped into a shaft of light from a street lamp.

She frowned. 'I know you.'

'Don't see that you can, ma'am,' he replied nervously. 'We ain't met.'

'No, we haven't formally.' She stepped forward, grateful that Clifford was beside her. 'But you're... Oh dash it, my memory for names.' She jabbed at her forehead. 'Mr Dellaney's chauffeur!'

'Mr Temples,' Clifford said, *sotto voce.*

'Yes, Temples, I remember now.' She waved a hand behind her at the battered car. 'What a mess. Mr Dellaney wasn't hurt, was he?'

He looked at her askance. 'You're Lady Swift. I thought you were at Glory Gates tonight with Mr Dellaney?'

'Oh, I was. And he seemed fine. But I've learned you boys wouldn't say if you were injured. Even if your leg was hanging off. Clifford is the worst for that.'

Temples turned his chauffeur's hat in his hands, speaking hesitantly. 'Mr Dellaney weren't drivin' the caddy. Nor in the car when this' – he nodded to the damaged car – 'happened.'

So it's a Cadillac, Ellie. 'Then who was?'

'I've no idea.' He looked over both shoulders. 'It was missin' from Mr Dellaney's garages the night it happened. I tried to tell him but he was throwin' another party and sent me off in a temper. That Mr Dellaney's got a real bad temper. Not speakin' out of turn, Lady Swift,' he added hurriedly. 'Anyway, followin' mornin' I found it back where it should a' been all along, lookin' like that, so I brought it here for repairs. This garage fixes all Mr Dellaney's cars. I just leave them here and collect it when they're done.'

And all evidence of the hit-and-run gone, Ellie.

She shared a look with Clifford. She'd seen and heard the chauffeur trying to tell Dellaney, so that part of his story, at least, was true.

'Stolen and then returned, Mr Temples?' Clifford's tone was dubious.

'No. Darn well borrowed. Without permission. Again! This is the staff car, see. It's only used by them to run errands. And only a few can drive her. And it's only for bona fide trips on Mr Dellaney's account. But nobody so much as asked me that night. Ain't the first time, neither.'

'How long have you been Mr Dellaney's chauffeur, Temples?' she said casually.

He hesitated. 'Couple of months or so, maybe. Ain't really been countin', Lady Swift.'

'What happened to the previous chauffeur?'

'I... I don't know. Mr Dellaney just up and blew worse than a hurricane on fire at him like he does sometimes. Ripped this coat and cap off of him. Then threw him out the door.'

The image of the rolls of banknotes she'd discovered under Marty's floor jumped into her mind. 'It's a good job though, I imagine?'

'Real great. Er, thanks for askin'.' He rubbed the back of his neck. 'Say, don't mean to be rude, but why the—'

'Especially with the... bonuses?'

His mouth fell open. For a moment he said nothing, then shook his head. 'You don't wanna be talkin' like that around here. A high-ridin' dude like Mr Dellaney's got ears, and eyes, on the streets. You talk like that and Mr Dellaney gets to hear it…' He turned even paler. 'I gotta be back at Mr Dellaney's place. He don't like it when I'm late.'

He hurried over to the road and hailed a taxi.

She watched him go, then walked back to her own taxi with Clifford. As they climbed in, Iver looked at her in the rear-view mirror.

'So, any more interruptions you want I should know about before I drive you home?' he said sarcastically. 'Or maybe now you want I drive you someplace else?'

She nodded. 'Actually, Iver, yes.' She turned to Clifford. 'Dellaney threw Marty out, and according to Temples, in a violent temper. And the car that ran down Marty came from Dellaney's garages. I'm not saying Dellaney's responsible for Marty's death, but I am saying it's time he got a visit from the New York Police!'

19

'But when will Officer Balowski finish his shift?' Eleanor tried again. 'I'm a... friend.'

The desk officer shook his head. 'No, you're not. I seen you before. And Balowski will get off shift when the city's done with him and spits him back in here.'

At the policeman's raised voice, Gladstone let out a flurry of barks. The desk officer leaned over and pointed a finger at him.

'Can it, mutt!' He peered harder at the bulldog. 'If that's what you are.' He jabbed his finger at her and Clifford. 'Now, if you got somethin' to report, get reportin', I'm busy.'

Eleanor was close to the last of her patience. 'Alright, Officer, then I need you to write down everything I'm going to tell you.'

'Sure.' He slammed the records book in front of him shut and folded his arms against the large damp patches of his blue shirt.

She gritted her teeth. 'Officer! I believe I have got evidence in a murder case. Although at the moment you've labelled it a hit-and-run and closed it.'

The desk officer yawned. 'Keep goin', lady. You're hilarious.'

Eleanor ground through the remains of her teeth enamel. 'I need someone to understand that a man named Mr Dellaney needs investigating. Him, or one of his staff—'

'Whoa!' The policeman's face paled as he lowered his voice. '*The* Dellaney? Mr Gold Towers? Mr "I own this city" Dellaney?'

She nodded. With a jerk, the officer whipped around from behind the counter faster than a greyhound after a rabbit and shoved her towards a door in the corner.

'Wait in there, lady. And keep quiet, will ya!'

A minute later, Balowski's curt voice came from the doorway. 'What is it with you?' He bowled in and pointed at Clifford, who was trying to restrain Gladstone's ever eager welcome. 'And save it, Suitsville. You should a' stopped her.'

'He tried,' she said, jumping to her butler's defence.

'Then you should a' listened. Jeez! Lady Swift, you get dropped on the head real hard as a kid or somethin'?' Before she could reply, he waved an imperious hand. 'Walk. No talk.' He glared at her. 'Until I say you can.'

The 'walk' was more of a silent frogmarch, leaving her with the feeling a grim-faced judge wielding a gavel could well be waiting at the end of it. Or a cell. But to Clifford's evident horror, and Gladstone's panting delight, they were herded to the rear entrance of Frank's Lunch Car. The side which housed the rubbish bins. And the host of stray cats busy strewing the contents out onto the dirt.

Inside, the diner seemed to be occupied entirely by police uniforms.

'Just can't stay away, eh, Balowski?' the beefy aproned owner called over the squeal of the meat chunks he was pressing onto the grill.

Balowski scowled. 'Leave it, Frank. I ain't in the mood. Make it three and sharp.'

Clifford's attempt to protest was wasted, as Balowski had already stalked to the furthest booth, waving an irritated hand for the two of them to follow. The lone policeman occupying it looked up with questioning blue eyes as Balowski rapped the table with his baton.

'Got worse than barrel dregs this time.'

'Oh, I don't know.' The other officer grinned at Eleanor. 'I'd say you're punchin' way above your weight there.'

'Yeah.' Frank appeared, thumbs tucked in his apron straps. 'But no makin' out in the booths.'

'Only on the counter!' the policeman chuckled.

Clifford closed his eyes in despair while the policeman rose and slid out. Grabbing his half-finished plate of what seemed to be a grilled meat sandwich, oozing with thick yellow sauce, he waved Eleanor into his place. Bending down, he whispered loudly, 'Play gentle with Balowski. He don't get out much.'

'Beat it!' his colleague grunted, stepping awkwardly over Gladstone.

'Actually,' she said genuinely as Balowski slid in opposite her, 'I would imagine you get out *too* much. Always patrolling the streets, I mean. But home, I imagine you see far too little of that.'

Like Hugh, Ellie.

She wondered where Balowski lived. And if there could be anyone understanding enough waiting when he finally did make it home? But scanning his exasperated expression told her he was not in the mood for chit-chat.

Frank slid three mugs of steaming black liquid and three empty plates onto the table. He added a deep metal dish bearing a mound of golden-brown parcels which smelled so good, Eleanor's stomach let out a loud unladylike gurgle. He laughed.

'Holler if that don't show your belly who's boss, lady.'

Dropping a ripped-off section of cardboard scattered with overcooked meat scraps in front of a delighted Gladstone, he went off.

Passing Eleanor a pristine handkerchief, Clifford swallowed hard as he served her with a mug and plate. He looked searchingly around at the counter, but Balowski tugged him down onto the booth seat beside him.

'No, there ain't no fancy linen, nor silver spoons for the lady. She got fingers that can lift a Johnny cake, ain't she? It's only fried cornmeal balls filled with syrup. Besides, we ain't here to eat.'

Although that didn't stop him from tucking in, Eleanor noticed as she joined him. After he'd finished his first of the mysteriously named treats and swigged it down with what she was delighted to find was surprisingly good coffee, he sat back and stared at her.

'You know, you got a lot to learn about New York.'

'I'm trying.'

'Try harder! And fast.' Scooping up another of the moreish bun affairs, he waved it at her, lowering his voice. 'You can't just bowl up, accusin' a cheese as big as... *him* of anythin'. Not him. Not no one on his staff, neither. Nor no one he does business with. Get it?'

She shrugged. 'I hear what you're saying.'

'That ain't enough. Not even a start.' Balowski rose and peered cautiously over the top of the booth. Satisfied they weren't being overheard, he slumped back down, his voice so quiet she had to lean in to hear him. 'Dellaney, he's so powerful, he's got friends at City Hall and' – he nodded towards the other tables – 'on the force.'

She didn't miss that Clifford stiffened at this last revelation.

'But I never said that. Got it?' Balowski watched them

nodding in unison before continuing. 'Dellaney's got interests on Broadway, too, see.'

'Oh, he was talking to me about those yesterday evening.'

Balowski's eyes turned to saucers. 'Now, explain to me, Lady Swift, if you thought he was a dirty cat, why the heck were you with him last night?'

'To check if I was right, of course. I went to his house at Bay Shore to discreetly interview him.'

'Discreet! You?' Balowski scoffed. 'See, now that must mean something different in England.' He turned to Clifford. 'Am I right?'

Her butler's lips twitched as he took a suspicious sniff over the rim of his coffee mug. 'I fear I might incriminate myself if I were to answer that, Officer Balowski.'

This seemed to amuse them both. Eleanor gave a mock huff. 'What's the importance of Dellaney's links to Broadway, though? I would have thought his most powerful connections would be with politicians or financiers, for example? Not actors.'

Balowski nodded. 'Like I said, he's got them all in his pocket. But Broadway, well, it ain't just a lot of fancy theatres and huffy darlin's who like dressin' up and struttin' about on the stage.'

'Then what else is it?'

Again, Balowski rose to peer around the diner. Satisfied, he sat down. 'All I'm sayin' is whatever you want that ain't legal, you'll get it there. And easy.'

'Like alcohol?' she whispered.

Clifford caught her eye. 'Like any and every vice, I believe Officer Balowski is saying, my lady. And likely, also where justice of questionable morals is dispensed readily.'

'You got it, Suitsville. In Broadway, see, the high and mighty what serves justice in the courts rub shoulders and drinks with them that dispense it with blackjacks and guns. And I ain't gettin' involved with that mob for nobody and no one.'

Eleanor's head fell to her chest. She took a deep breath. 'But, Officer, that means we need your help all the more! I don't know enough about New York. Anything much, actually, it is quickly becoming obvious. But you saw what someone did to poor Marty.'

'So? You think this badge was easy to get? You think it's easy to get another job that pays even squat in this city?' He shook his head. 'And ain't no job gonna do you any good with a smokin' hole burnin' in your chest.' He took a swig of coffee. 'You should leave it now a dude like Dellaney's involved, Lady Swift.'

'But I can't.'

He held her gaze. 'Why?'

'Because everyone else is.'

Aware that Balowski was watching her intently, she returned to her coffee and took the next bun in the seriously dwindled pile that Clifford had repeatedly declined to try. She crossed one set of fingers under the table.

'Darn dames!' Balowski muttered into his cup. There was silence for a minute. Then he rubbed his face with his hands. 'Alright, alright! I must have lost my mind, but I'm still in. Though, you got to promise me one thing before we're done here?'

She sighed with relief. 'Fire away.'

'Now, first off, no more ragin' into the station shoutin' wild accusations about the suited money in this city. In fact, no comin' to the station at all. Not for nothin'. Not even if your precious help here gets stolen. Deal?'

'Deal.' She smiled at her butler. 'I'll come and rescue you myself.'

'If you absolutely must, my lady.'

Balowski shoved himself off the end of the booth seat and strode to one of the other tables.

'Hey?' she groaned. 'But we haven't agreed—'

'Patience, my lady.'

Balowski reappeared with the blue-eyed officer. 'He works traffic. And he's straight. He'll sniff around quietly and see if there's anythin' on the car.'

'Dellan—' She jumped as the second officer raised his hand as if to clamp it over her mouth. 'Ain't none of us gonna say that name, are we, lady?'

She nodded contritely. 'Got it. Really.'

The traffic policeman smiled at Gladstone, who was still busy licking his cardboard plate for any remaining morsels. Balowski ran a hand down his buttoned jacket.

'Meanwhile, no guarantees, but I can try and find out certain people's whereabouts at the time of the hit-and-run. Which, you don't need to keep sayin' it ain't. But I can't ask nothin' direct about our main man, remember?'

She nodded. 'Asking about that person too obviously might get you into trouble.'

'Ain't no "might" about it. Captain would have me in on the spot so he could rip my head offa my neck and then shove my baton way up inside to work me like a puppet. All the top cats protect each other and who knows who all of 'em are, right?'

'Gracious! I really appreciate you sticking with this. All the more with what is at stake for you.'

'Yeah, whatever. Anyways, I got the address that scrawny witness guy gave, like you asked.'

'So why are we still here?' She jumped up.

''Cos it's too late to go callin' until tomorrow,' Balowski grunted, rising himself. 'And, besides, there's one final condition.' He picked his cap up off the table. 'If word gets out 'bout what we doin'...' he held her gaze, 'you'll pay for my funeral.'

20

The following morning in the taxi, the neighbourhoods they were zigzagging through were descending from the less wealthy to the positively impoverished. Opposite her, Clifford's gaze became increasingly concerned.

After weaving down the same street a second time, Balowski shoved the driver's shoulder.

'Cabbie! What kinda game you playin'?'

'No game, Officer,' came the reply from a gap-toothed grin. 'Figured you fancied a ride around with the pretty lady, seein' as that address you gave me don't exist.'

'What?' Eleanor cried, staring at the policeman.

'Just let us out!' Balowski barked at the driver.

With Gladstone pausing at every broken gatepost and fire hydrant, they checked with the few people they met who would talk to them. But it seemed the taxi driver had been correct. There was no such number. And no such road.

'We're done here,' Balowski said firmly.

Eleanor nodded resignedly.

'That it?' He frowned. 'No insistin' we ain't done until our boots got no soles? You never take "no" for an answer.'

Out of the corner of her eye, she caught Clifford nodding to himself.

'Maybe. But don't you see? I don't have any idea at the moment as to how we'll manage to track him down, but the fact that the witness gave a false address is beyond suspicious. He must be involv—'

'Lady.' Balowski's tone was incredulous. 'It would only a' been suspicious if he *hadn't* given a false address. I bet the name he gave is just as phoney too. Jeez! I told you. No one in this city wants to get involved in anyone else's troubles.'

Clifford nodded. 'The only suspicious element, if I might be so bold as to suggest, is that he stepped forward to give a statement at all.'

Balowski jabbed him good-humouredly with his baton. 'You got your eye on my badge, Suitsville? 'Cos you're right on the money 'bout that.'

She shot Clifford a puzzled look.

'Then why have we traipsed all the way out here to the Lower East Side, I think you said, and trudged around these streets looking for what you already had a suspicion didn't exist?'

Balowski grunted. 'To check if I was right, of course.'

She felt abashed. 'Apologies. And thank you for being so conscientious.' She looked between them hopefully. 'So, we need to plan our next step. And it has been a while since we ate. Officer, can I buy you lunch?'

'From anywhere except Frank's,' Clifford added quickly, with a shudder. 'For the love of gastronomy, anywhere else!'

With Balowski reluctantly agreeing to eat somewhere other than his favourite diner, a taxi deposited them a few doors down from her apartment building.

'Oh, you gotta be kiddin' me!'

Eleanor cocked her head. 'Problem, Officer?'

'Yeah, problem!' Balowski waved his baton. 'The tables have got cloths on 'em for a start.'

Clifford nodded. 'Yes. "Tablecloths."'

Balowski scowled. 'And it says something about "speciality seafood"! This ain't no joint for beat cops.'

'Precisely,' Clifford said firmly. 'It is "a joint" which is almost acceptable for a titled lady to be seen, and dine, in.'

Balowski folded his arms. 'No way am I goin' in there.'

'Then forgive my error in assuming your word was your bond when you agreed to assist her ladyship with the investigation.'

Eleanor watched their silent stand-off with fascination, for once unsure if Clifford's ability to keep his impassive demeanour would beat a manner as belligerent as Balowski's.

She shouldn't have doubted him.

'What kind of butler are you anyway?' Balowski scowled and shoved Clifford ahead of him up the steps.

'Score one to you,' Eleanor whispered as her butler drew level.

'Naturally,' he whispered back.

Inside, the place was empty except for a middle-aged couple drinking coffee and poring over what looked like newspaper reviews of Broadway productions.

'Lunch platter for three to share, is it?' the pretty young waitress asked once they were seated.

Clifford nodded. 'That will be perfect, thank you.'

Balowski stopped suspiciously eyeing the glass of mint-infused cordial they'd each been served on arrival to slap Clifford's suit-jacketed shoulder. 'So, finally you gonna eat somethin'.'

Eleanor shook her head. 'No, Officer, there'll just be all the more for us two.'

A few minutes later, she took a sip of the delectable

smelling oyster chowder. The soup was accompanied by individual lobster-shaped baskets filled with miniature herby bread rolls. In the centre of the table, the waitress had also set down a long, green boat dish. The dish was laden with baked clams, shrimps, fish-shaped pots filled with pâtés and mousses, and shell-shaped pots filled with clear jellies peppered with more seafood. Balowski eyed it all dubiously. But once he'd started in, he ate with gusto. As they ate, they discussed their next move.

'Well, we can't just scour every street and building in New York for our missing witness,' Eleanor said. 'What ideas have you got?'

Balowski added a generous slathering of mousse to a prawn and swallowed it. 'Ideas ain't my strong point. That's why I'm a beat cop.'

'But you know this city inside out?'

He nodded.

Clifford arched a brow. 'No disrespect, Officer, but if that were the case, would not the false address the witness gave struck you as such?'

Balowski ignored the remark and crammed more aspic-suspended seafood into his mouth and grimaced. 'People pay good money for this?'

'Well, someone knows who our witness is, and where he is,' Eleanor said determinedly. 'So we'll just have to start asking. And without delay.'

'Brilliant plan, Lady Swift,' Balowski said sarcastically, waving a bread roll. ''Cos the city's only home to, er...'

'In excess of five million people according to last year's census.' With a pained expression, Clifford flicked Balowski's breadcrumbs from his jacket sleeve.

'Jeez! That your idea of rousin' night-time readin'? Sure, ain't mine. That'd be—'

'No doubt something one would not mention in the presence of her ladyship,' Clifford said firmly.

'Boys!' She gave them both a stern look. 'There's a time for squabbling, and it isn't now. We have to find someone who might know the witness.'

Balowski grinned. 'Say!' He pointed at the waitress who had served them. 'This skirt might know him. Hey, doll!' He let out a piercing whistle, causing Clifford to wince.

The young woman hurried over, looking surprised at how she'd been hailed. 'Is there somethin' wrong?'

'Yeah.' Balowski smiled sweetly. 'We need to know the name and address of a guy we don't got no picture to show ya. A guy who would never step into a joint like this, and who don't live in anywhere even a tenth as fancy an area as this. But he does like hangin' around neighbourhoods like this and rubber-neckin' at accidents.'

The waitress' hands flew to her face. 'Oh, like the one in the street here late the other night?'

Eleanor jerked up straighter. Then her shoulders slumped. The restaurant would have been closed. The waitress couldn't actually have seen anything. 'You probably read about it in the newspaper, did you?'

'No, miss, I saw it.'

Eleanor gasped. 'You witnessed the accident?'

'No, but I saw all the commotion after.' She looked at Eleanor in awe. 'And I saw you, miss, runnin' over so brave to try and help.'

Eleanor's brows shot up. 'This restaurant is open that late?'

The waitress shook her head. 'Oh, no. We closed two hours before, miss. Same as always. But the kitchen girl's sick and well, I needed the extra money with my husband all laid up, so I stayed on, helpin' chef clean up. Then layin' the tables for the mornin'.'

Clifford gave her an encouraging smile. 'And after the ambulance left, and the commotion died down, did you keep watching through the front window?'

She stared down at the floor. 'Maybe, sir.'

'Right up to when this officer' – Eleanor indicated Balowski hopefully – 'was questioning me and a few others?'

The waitress shook her head again. 'No, miss, I never saw that. I got four little ones at home. Had to finish up quick after the ambulance left.'

'Oh.' Eleanor failed to hide her disappointment.

'Sorry, miss.' The waitress smiled apologetically. 'But I'd already lost a bit of time dealin' with that needleneck chicken grinder as hammered on the door 'bout twenty minutes before it all happened.'

Eleanor shrugged. 'I had this down as being only a fish restaurant.' Ground chicken didn't fit at all with the mostly seafood menu, nor the quality of the food they'd sampled.

Balowski, however, seemed animated. 'Real needleneck chicken? Workpants with too many bags?'

'That's the guy,' the waitress said excitedly. 'He came knockin', hissin' for an under-counter beer, so I sent him off. We're abidin' by prohibition in here. Honest, Officer. But he didn't like that and stomped off to wait on the kerb, right along there. Least, that was the last I saw of him and good riddance. Next time I see him when I'm on the rides, I'll make sure I don't give him the time of day.'

Eleanor's stomach skipped. 'So you recognised him?'

'Only from the Nickel Empire, miss.'

Balowski stood and took a bow. 'And thank you, Officer Balowski!'

Clifford coughed pointedly. 'For following her ladyship's insistent suggestion to start asking around. Well done indeed!'

21

Another taxi ride led them to Stillwell Avenue, a hectic subway station where none of them could hear each other, no matter how loud they hollered in each other's ears. Clifford bent awkwardly with Gladstone in his arms and tapped Eleanor's wrist before pointing to her handbag with a cautionary gesture. However, they were soon crammed so tightly in the stiflingly packed carriage that there was no chance of anyone picking anyone's pocket. Her butler's discomfort, however, didn't diminish as it also forced him into being sandwiched up against her in public. Eleanor, on the other hand, was too distracted to notice as she peered out of the window.

'Clifford, look!' She pointed out of the grimy window as their train rattled over Brooklyn Bridge, grumbling along one of the central tracks beside cars, vans and horses fighting for space on the adjacent roadway.

'A far too oversubscribed, if admirable, piece of engineering, my lady.'

Balowski rolled his eyes.

As the train clattered on, Eleanor tuned in to the fact that everyone around them seemed to be holidaymakers. This was

further confirmed by the occasional flash of swimwear underneath clothing and the plethora of picnic baskets shoved into
her shins.

The train finally pulled into a station, Gladstone letting out
a flurry of woofs as the doors opened. It was obviously a
terminus as a sea of passengers swept out, carrying Eleanor,
Clifford and Balowski with them. A short while later, they were
disgorged, along with the tidal wave of humanity, into the
open air.

'Oh my!' she said as she stared up at the gold-topped
columns supporting the letters 'LUNA' in metalwork.

'Luna Park, Lady Swift. We're at Coney Island,' Balowski
said in response to her questioning look.

'How marvellous! But what on earth did the waitress say to
lead you here?'

The officer tapped his nose and gestured onwards.

'Coney Island is also known more locally as "Nickel
Empire", my lady,' Clifford explained as they dodged the crowd
to keep up with the striding Balowski. 'The train fare was
dropped from ten to five cents, or a "nickel" in local parlance.
Now even those of modest means can afford to travel and this
has turned Coney Island into the largest resort in all of New
York, if not America.'

She gawped as rides of every conceivable nature roared and
twisted past in all directions, including dizzyingly tall helter-
skelters which wound through fake mountains and a remarkably lifelike Great Wall of China. The three of them, and Gladstone, struggled through the packed pedestrian walkways,
passing shooting galleries, ornate shopfronts, circus tops, casi-
nos, theatres, hotels, and music halls. And even though she'd
recently eaten, her stomach rumbled as she passed stands, cafés
and restaurants offering food from every nation on earth.

With an effort Eleanor finally drew level with Balowski,
trying to remember what he and the waitress had said.

A needleneck chicken grinder with workpants with too many bags, or something like that, Ellie.

She raised her voice over the bedlam. 'So, our witness works on a... chicken stand of some sort?'

Balowski shook his head. 'What a New York greenhorn! Nope. "Needleneck chicken" means "scrawny".'

'Ah! And "grinder"?'

'It's his job. He turns over the motor and keeps the carousel spinnin'.'

'So "workpant bags"?'

'Pockets to you. He's got 'em running down each leg. Now we know for quick reachin' of his tools.' He pointed ahead. 'The carousel is just up there by Shoot the Chutes.'

'Of course it is.' She shared a mystified look with Clifford.

The carousel turned out to be spinning rows of brightly painted horses, dragons and, bizarrely, ostriches, their necks clutched by whooping children. Standing against the central pole, hands in his pockets, was the very man they'd come to question. Unfortunately, he spotted them at the same time they spotted him.

'Dash it!' Eleanor yelled, sprinting around the still spinning carousel after his fleeing form. 'Don't let him get away.'

'Like that was my plan!' Balowski hollered back as he shot off around the other side of the ride. Behind the carousel, a long run of tall, tented stalls, all perfect for ducking through and hiding in, stretched ahead. She looked around for their man, but he'd vanished. Clifford was also nowhere in view. Then a series of uncharacteristically ferocious barks cut through the cacophony from somewhere five or six stalls along. Balowski appeared beside her, panting heavily.

'Great! We've lost the witness and Suitsville.'

'Actually' – she cocked her ear, straining to locate the barking more accurately – 'I think you'll find they are in the very same spot!'

They set off toward the sound of the commotion and soon spotted Gladstone scrabbling up the legs of their witness, growling ferociously, while Clifford wielded the giant mallet from a nearby ring-the-bell stall. She joined her butler and bulldog.

'Good work, chaps.'

'Thank you, my lady, but Master Gladstone deserves the bulk of the credit for running him to ground with an uncharacteristic turn of speed.'

Balowski jabbed his baton under the man's chin. 'Why'd'ya run, grinder?' he growled.

'Why'd'ya chase me?' the man shot back.

Eleanor smiled at him. 'Because we need to ask you a few questions, that's all.'

He jutted his chin out defiantly. 'Lady, you and I don't got no business together. And there's nothin' I got to say to him.' He jerked his chin at the officer.

'Strange,' she said evenly. 'You were very keen to talk to him last time.'

He stared at the three of them. 'This 'bout that hit-and-run?'

'If that is what you are determined to keep calling it, yes.'

'But I told him what I saw that night.' He tried to squirm out of Balowski's grip, but that only made him move closer to the still fiercely growling Gladstone. 'And this the thanks I get for tryin' to be helpful!'

'Over-helpful, one would definitely say,' Clifford said. 'But evidently it is. Perhaps if you were to tell us why you were really there, and what really happened, you might elicit a more favourable response from Master Gladstone and ourselves.'

But despite all their threats and entreaties, the man insisted he'd been passing and every word of the statement he'd given that night was true.

'Last chance.' Using both hands, Balowski grabbed the

man's collar and lifted him onto his toes. 'You gonna tell us the truth now or not?'

The man's face turned from defiant to terrified. 'Listen,' he pleaded. 'I've family. Don't you understand?' He turned to Balowski. 'You understand, Officer, don't you?'

Balowski dropped the man and spat on the ground. 'Yeah, I understand. Now, scram!'

Eleanor watched in dismay as their one possible source of information sprinted away through the tent flaps. She tried to restrain her irritation at Balowski for letting him go.

'All that tracking him down and we learned nothing from him.'

'Uncharacteristically defeatist, one might conjecture, my lady.' Clifford tipped his head at Balowski.

'Learned nothin'!' Balowski smirked. 'If that's nothin', I'd like to know what is! Besides, he wasn't goin' to tell us anythin' more, no matter how much we put the fear into him.'

Eleanor looked from Balowski to Clifford and back. 'Why not?'

''Cos he was already terrified. He didn't have room for any more.'

She nodded. 'I can see that. But what did you – *we* – learn?'

'I'd say given what you told me earlier, he was paid to distract your Marty guy so the driver of the car could line him up and—'

'Yes, thank you, Officer,' Clifford said quickly. 'Her lady-ship doesn't need any more of an image. I also suggest that our supposed witness was coerced into delivering a false statement after the incident?'

Balowski nodded. 'Yeah. And if didn't, he'd wind up wearin' a pair of concrete boots at the bottom of the Hudson. And any family he got, right alongside him!'

22

Eleanor tumbled out of the taxi and back into the madness of Downtown Manhattan. His customary two respectful steps behind, Clifford followed with the scampering Gladstone, who was fixated on the endless whiff of food that tickled his shiny wet nose. Despite her companions, however, she felt alone amidst the multitude of people surging around her. Invisible even. Just one among five million. No wonder life didn't stop here. Not for anything. Not for anyone. No one stood out. Nothing was odd or extraordinary. Anything and everything went.

Even murder, Ellie!

The thought jerked her back to the present. She hurried to follow Balowski, who was already climbing the police station's crowded steps. Behind her, Clifford called out.

'My lady! Remember—'

What he was going to remind her about was interrupted by Balowski.

'So, what happened to our deal? You were gonna stay the heck outta here?'

Ah! That was what you were supposed to remember, Ellie.

'Sorry, yes. I was miles away. I'll—'

'YO! BALOWSKI!' a voice shouted. She caught the sight of a paper being waved in the air.

'Over there,' she said helpfully.

'I've got ears! And eyes!' Balowski growled.

At the top of the steps, the blue-eyed traffic policeman from the diner beckoned them. After a quick glance over his shoulder, he thrust the paper into Balowski's hand. 'Accident reported on Lower East Side. That's the address and—'

'Lower East Side!' Balowski scowled. 'So, I give a darned bean because?'

The policeman rolled his eyes at Eleanor. 'You see, lady, that's why I'm head of traffic and he walks the beat.' He tapped the paper. 'Read the licence plate, bozo.'

'Captain's comin' in his blackest temper!' a panic-stricken younger officer hissed as he shot past.

The blue-eyed policeman caught Balowski's arm. 'Just step careful in takin' the lady, yeah?'

Balowski nodded as he hurriedly shoved the paper into his pocket. 'Sure. I'll be real careful.'

'Lower East Side?' Clifford's brow was etched with concern as they hailed a taxi.

She threw her hands out. 'It's the same number plate as the car that hit Marty! We have to go.'

He looked to Balowski for support.

He shrugged. 'Hey, don't ask me to try and stop that wild cat from doin' nothin'. You're her keeper!'

She climbed into the taxi. 'Dash it, chaps, I'm not a zoo exhibit!'

Twenty minutes later, however, she felt exactly that as they wove down the inappropriately named Orchard Street, composed as it was of six-storeyed monoliths of forlorn tenement blocks. Hundreds of hungry eyes stared back at her from every precariously hanging balcony and fire escape, the many babies and children making her heart ache for the fragility of their uncertain future. Tattered and patched awnings hung out over many of the ground-floor doorways, doing a poor job of shielding the inhabitants from the already fierce sun. Broken carts and ragged stalls of make-and-mend goods choked the pavements.

She shifted uncomfortably in her seat, feeling wretched for having so much when these people had only a dilapidated roof above their overpopulated heads. But equally guilty for not having considered her own ever-thoughtful butler. This had to be an unwelcome reminder of too many of his childhood years, one of the few snippets of his life he had uncharacteristically shared with her one difficult evening. Orphaned and then left unprovided for on the sudden death of his guardian, he'd found himself alone in the world on the eve of his twelfth birthday. The streets had been his only home from then on.

She caught him watching her. 'I'm so sorry, Clifford,' she mouthed.

The taxi veered into a narrow street devoid of life save for a lone policeman on the corner, scratching his head, staring blankly at his notebook. Balowski leaped out before the vehicle had finished lurching to a halt. Clifford waved his wallet at the driver.

'Kindly do not leave on any account. And if you will watch the lady's precious bulldog, a double fee will unquestionably be yours.'

The driver nodded enthusiastically. 'You got it, pal! I'll wait and keep him company, alright.'

They joined Balowski on the pavement to the unsettling sound of the taxi's door being locked behind them.

Still, Gladstone's safe, Ellie.

She turned to the policeman, whose haggard expression

made her wince. He greeted her with a tip of his cap before eyeing Balowski circumspectly.

'She with you?'

'Only 'cos I ain't shaken her off yet.'

Balowski looked amused by his own joke until the policeman pointed at Clifford. 'Suits your kind of thing as well as pretty ladies, eh? Weird.'

Balowski slapped the other's notebook. 'Cut the clownin', will ya? Anyway, what you doin'? Writin' down the number of cracks in the sidewalk?'

'Funny! No, I got sent down 'cos we got a call at the station 'bout an accident.'

Eleanor caught Balowski's covert hand gesture to tread carefully.

'Did you?' she said innocently, looking around. 'It's all been cleared up very quickly.'

The policeman stared at her wearily. 'No, lady. The vehicle is in the next street.'

He led the way. Eleanor stopped, her eyes widening.

'Oh gracious!'

The car was slewed diagonally across the pavement, its bonnet wrapped around a lamp post bent at near right angles, windscreen shattered, driver's door hanging open.

The policeman studied the wrecked car unemotionally. 'Dumb fool lost control and whacked into the only street lamp left in the whole crummy street.'

Eleanor's brow creased. 'Why would there be only one street light left?'

He stared at her as if she were from the moon. 'On account of all the others bein' hacked down by the residents with heck knows what and sold for scrap, obviously.'

'Oh goodness.' She glanced around. 'Where is everyone?'

'Waitin' till we've gone, lady.' The policeman looked from

her to Clifford with a puzzled frown. 'First time in New York, then?'

'Indeed, Officer.'

'Ah! That'd explain it. How's she treatin' ya'll?'

As Clifford replied, Eleanor slid away to examine the car.

'This is definitely the same one,' she whispered to Balowski as he appeared at her elbow. 'The number plate's the same: 534-577.'

'Licence plates ain't hard to switch from one vehicle to another.'

'True. But it's a Cadillac and the bonnet emblem is the same, a winged nymph. And you can still just about see the damage at the front from the first hit-and-run, even though it's been repaired.'

Balowski grunted. 'Alright. Maybe it is.'

She frowned. 'But there's more damage on the driver's door and the side of the bonnet.' She crunched over the broken glass to peer inside. 'Odd. That part can't have hit the lamp post.'

As Balowski returned to the policeman, Eleanor went to follow, but something caught her eye. Instinctively, she bent down and picked it up. It was a scrap of paper. She debated whether to drop it again, but there were no waste bins in the street.

Not that one more bit of paper will matter, Ellie. The street is hardly clean.

Nevertheless, she had a pathological hatred of littering and slipped it into her pocket.

Balowski turned and waited for her to catch him up. Not surprisingly, she conceded. He'd probably broken some fearful police rule in going out of his precinct. And by obtaining information from a colleague. And getting mixed up in matters that shouldn't concern him. She remembered his words in the diner. *Dellaney, he's so powerful, he's got friends at City Hall and on the force.*

She shivered, wondering if the policeman her butler was talking to right now was one of them.

Perhaps that's why Balowski's shadowing you, Ellie?

She spotted Clifford had his eye on her as well.

'How fortunate that someone reported this, Officer,' she said nonchalantly.

The policeman scowled. 'You think so? I was doin' just fine at the precinct. Didn't need to get poked down here.'

'I'm sure. But you probably had a few witnesses offering a statement?'

He shook his head. 'Lady, there weren't no witnesses. Least none who'd come forward. These folk go to ground like roaches the second a blue uniform appears.' He closed his notebook and shoved it in his trouser pocket.

She sighed. 'And let me guess. You won't be knocking on doors to solicit any eye-witness accounts?'

'Ain't no point. No one in this neighbourhood would so much as open the door. This is the kinda place where everybody minds their own business... for health reasons.'

'How tragically ironic. It seems such a sad and unhealthy area.' She looked to Balowski to check he wasn't about to clamp her mouth shut. He nodded imperceptibly. She took that as she was okay to continue. 'So I was wrong a minute ago. What I should have said is how unusual then that the accident *was* reported?'

The policeman shrugged. 'Probably 'cos stiffs pull flies fast in this heat and the body was inconveniencing someone.'

The indifference in his tone made her stomach clench. She recalled the extra damage to the car. 'Did the driver hit something before crashing?'

'Not *something*. *Someone!* Made a pretty mess of him, too. His—'

'Officer!' Clifford said sharply. 'I'll thank you to consider the lady's sensibilities.'

Looking aggrieved, the policeman scuffed a boot heel across the pavement. 'What's she come to an accident for if she's the squeamish type?'

Eleanor shuddered. That explained the extra damage to the car. 'So, who was the injured person?'

The policeman rolled his eyes. 'Like, how should I know? Nothin' in his pockets except half his insides—' Clifford shot him an admonishing look. The policeman held his hands up. 'Look, he didn't have no identification. But who's gonna carry anythin', even a nickel, through here? Only a madman waitin' to get hustled.'

'I see. Well, where has the ambulance taken the person?'

'Ain't no ambulance arrived. And ain't one comin' neither. Only needs the—'

'Meat wagon?' she said with sickening dread.

'That's it.'

Balowski shrugged. 'Morgue likely ain't gonna identify him neither. Bodies with no identification usually get an unmarked coffin right off the slab.'

Ever able to read her mind, Clifford stepped around to face her. 'My lady, please.'

'We promised,' she hissed. 'For Marty.' At his reluctant nod, she addressed the local officer. 'So where is the body?'

'Under that ripped tarpaulin. Got slammed clear off the pavement and onto the road.'

With Clifford striding by her side, she hurried off to where he'd pointed.

'Say, who is this lady?' she heard the policeman mutter.

'Oh, jeez, just one of those dames with a thing about stiffs,' Balowski's words followed her, sounding so convincing, she winced.

But as they reached the crumpled heap sprawled face down on the pavement, Clifford tried again. 'My lady, we should leave identifying the body to the authorities.'

She hesitated, then slowed down, allowing the policeman and Balowski to catch her and Clifford up.

'Please check once more, would you, Officer? And...' She glanced beseechingly at Balowski.

The policeman knelt down and pulled aside the shroud. Eleanor instinctively looked away.

'Nope. Like I said, means nothing to me but I don't know no one from this neighbourhood.' He rose and dusted down his trousers.

Balowski nodded. 'No one I know, either. Though...' He scratched his head. 'Now I think of it, he does look familiar.'

She steeled herself and turned around.

'Oh, my!'

23

The increasing heatwave was surely enough to wilt even the oysters in the shallows of Hudson Bay. It certainly wasn't conducive to seating five in any semblance of comfort in the cramped and airless Morales' basement kitchen. Gladstone, however, was faring a little better than most. Spreadeagled with his belly pressed onto the cool hearthstone in front of the cooker, his ham-like tongue flicked repeatedly into the bowl of water Clifford had set down for him. Rather irritatingly, Clifford seemed the exception to the general heat malaise, appearing as composed as ever.

Eleanor fanned her face with her notebook and looked around the group, searching for a positive that might rally them all. Before this blow to their investigation, she'd already been struggling to unite the motley crew which made up their so-called team. After this latest setback, the next half hour was critical. She and an out-of-uniform Balowski sat, squeezed shoulder to shoulder, in the family's only two chairs. Balowski's grey shirtsleeves were rolled up past his elbows, damp patches already under his arms.

Mrs Morales clucked her tongue at Eleanor's butler as he

topped up everyone's glasses with iced calamansi juice. 'Mr Clifford, this cop's off duty. Earl too. Can't you take the weight of those long suit pants of yours just this once?'

Before he'd managed more than three respectful words of dissent, she slapped the top of the empty tea chest beside her. 'Fella, if you in my kitchen, you gonna sit! And no polite "madam" backchat gonna change how it is. I got a broom in easy reach that says so. And Earl'll tell ya how that goes.'

Despite the situation, Eleanor hid her smile at her butler being chastised like a stubborn child.

'Comfy, Clifford?' she said impishly as he perched on the edge of his makeshift seat, minutely adjusting the crease of his suit trousers. His hand strayed to his tie.

'Incontrovertibly so, my lady.'

'Fibber!' she mouthed.

Mrs Morales banged her glass on the table, calling the meeting to order. 'So what's brought us all together right now?'

Bite the bullet, Ellie.

'Mrs Morales, so far we've identified two possible suspects who might have been driving the car that... that knocked Marty down. Dellaney, as it was his car and he had a row with Marty and sacked him out of the blue, so there seemed to have been some bad blood there.' She shrugged. 'Not a lot, I know. Our other possible suspect is Temples, Dellaney's current chauffeur, who was responsible for getting Marty sacked, it seems, and took over his job. Apparently, they also had a feud, according to Earl there, and Temples obviously had access to the car used in the hit-and-run as well. We are investigating other avenues, but that's where we were up to.' She grimaced. 'However, I'm sorry to have to tell you this but another person was hit, fatally, by the same car which struck Marty.'

Earl's boot heel scraped across the wooden floorboards. 'Oh yeah? When'd that happen?'

'Street in Lower East Side,' Balowski said, watching Earl closely.

'I said, "when", not "where", custard ears.'

'I heard ya,' the officer grunted.

'Well—'

'It was this afternoon, Earl,' Eleanor said quickly. 'Officer Balowski, Clifford and I went straight there.'

'Honey!' Mrs Morales reached for Eleanor's hand. 'A beautiful butterfly like you don't need to go seein' more horrors.'

'Quite,' Clifford said pointedly. 'Thank you, madam.'

Eleanor patted the woman's hand in return. 'I'm glad I did... in a way, because it meant I could identify the body.'

Balowski looked peeved. 'Yeah, well, I told you why I couldn't recognise the body at the time. I'd never met the dude and photos in the dog wrappers ain't never that clear.'

Eleanor and Clifford both glanced at Gladstone. Mrs Morales chuckled wheezily. 'Not somethin' for wrappin' Mr Wrinkles in. He means pictures in the newspapers.'

Eleanor's frown remained. 'So why are they called "dog wrappers?".'

''Cos you wrap your hot dog in 'em to keep the sauce from drippin' onta ya clothes.'

Clifford shuddered. 'Thank you for clarifying the matter, madam.'

Mrs Morales turned to Eleanor. 'So, who got taken from his family this time?'

She hesitated. 'Dellaney.' Out of the corner of her eye, she tried to gauge Earl's reaction, but he showed no emotion she could spot.

'Marty's old boss!' his mother said breathlessly.

'Exactly. And probably the leading suspect for Marty's death up until now, as I said. Which means our investigation has lurched right back to the start line!'

Mrs Morales seemed to be taking the news well.

She hasn't realised the implications yet, Ellie.

Mrs Morales shrugged. 'If he was the sinner behind our Marty bein' gone, then justice has been done. Amen.'

'Actually,' Eleanor said tentatively, 'it's not as simple as that. What's worrying me is that *if* Dellaney was responsible for Marty's death and then someone else killed Dellaney...'

Mrs Morales shook her head. 'You think there may be *two* killers?'

Balowski tapped the tabletop with a finger. 'Possibly. But if it *is* two different murderers, it's almost certain Dellaney was killed in that copycat hit-and-run for one reason only.' His gaze shot across the table.

Earl leapt up, knocking over the tea chest. 'Revenge, right, cop? Which you're suggestin' could only be somethin' Ma or me would a' done, since Marty didn't have no one else close to him. My ma's in a wheelchair so she ain't been drivin' no car. So what you really sayin'? It was me what killed Dellaney? 'Cos if so, you gonna arrest me now?'

Balowski regarded him coolly. 'Relax. No one's accusin' you of nothin'. Why don't you tell me where you were this afternoon, right around the time of the second hit-and-run?'

'None of ya business! And, besides, cop, I ain't that dumb. You ain't said when it was, so how should I know?'

'CHILDREN!' Mrs Morales barked. She broke into a fit of wheezy coughs. After passing her a glass of water, Clifford turned to Balowski.

'The likelihood of Mr Morales being able to access Mr Dellaney's staff car is remote, although not impossible. I would have thought it a more likely scenario, however, that a member of Mr Dellaney's own staff is responsible.'

'Like the chauffeur, Temples?' Mrs Morales said.

Clifford nodded. 'Yes. He may have made a show of trying to tell Mr Dellaney the car was missing the night of the first attack purely to deflect suspicion from himself. But, on reflection, it would seem unwise to use one of Mr Dellaney's own cars.'

Balowski gave him a slow handclap. 'Well done.' At his confused look, he laughed. 'Let me explain. I got news none of ya know yet, see. Happened as I came off shift. That Temples guy has been arrested for the hit-and-run on Dellaney. As the chauffeur, he obviously had access to the car seein' as he's in charge of the whole of Dellaney's fleet. Just so happens, I agree that you'd think he'd use an unknown car to run his boss down. One that couldn't be linked to him so easily. But then again, people are dumb sometimes. I come across it every day.'

Mrs Morales pointed at Balowski. 'Officer, that all you got on this Temples chauffeur?'

'No, ma'am. The boys also got evidence he's been stealin' off Dellaney. Simple deduction then. Dellaney gets wind and threatens to turn Temples over to us boys in blue.'

'So Temples kills Dellaney before he could?' Eleanor's expression gave away how unconvinced she felt. 'Listen, I know Temples is... *was* number two on our suspect list, but doesn't it all strike you as—?'

'Suspiciously convenient?' Clifford said. Balowski nodded in agreement. Clifford arched a brow. 'Yet you said the police have "evidence" that Temples was stealing from Mr Dellaney?'

Balowski nodded. 'You don't miss a thing, do ya, Suitsville? Yeah, I did. But who knows, right?'

Eleanor frowned. 'Let's focus on the biggest question, please. What on earth was Dellaney doing in such a rundown neighbourhood when he was killed, anyway?'

Balowski shrugged again.

'Beats me,' Earl said. 'He was dirt, but didn't like gettin' dirty. His type never do. And Lower East Side ain't exactly sanitary.'

Mrs Morales nodded slowly. 'So, just goes to show, money

ain't no salvation from gettin' what's comin' to ya.' She swung around to Balowski. 'So how'd it happen?'

'Well, local beat cop reckons driver lost control of the vehicle and then whacked into Dellaney. That's what the anonymous caller reported, anyway. Only—'

'It's too convenient again,' Eleanor said thoughtfully.

'So if it ain't the chauffeur, it must be me!' Earl snapped. 'Right, cop? That's what you swingin' back round to again!'

Eleanor jumped in to keep the two men from getting into another spat. 'None of us have any theories on who else could have been driving, Earl.' She hesitated. 'We do have another possible suspect. For Dellaney's death, anyway. Mrs Dellaney. I know her marriage wasn't a happy one. But unless there are two killers, we haven't got any motive for her killing Marty, but we're still digging.'

Once outside, Eleanor turned to Balowski. 'Do you really think Temples is our killer?'

He scratched his head. 'Honestly, I don't know. But what I weren't gonna say in there' – he nodded back towards the Morales' basement flat – 'is, the cops that arrested Temples, ain't ya know... good cops.'

'Oh my! You think the arresting officers might have planted the evidence?'

'Maybe. Wouldn't be the first time. And my gut is tellin' me somethin' ain't right. But if it ain't the chauffeur, then who? Mrs Dellaney or...' His gaze strayed back to the Morales' basement again.

She followed his gaze. 'Do you really believe Earl might have done it?'

He shrugged. 'I ain't sayin' he's helpin' me think otherwise. Wouldn't say where he was at the time Dellaney got hit. He also got cause.'

'Revenge for his brother's death,' she said quietly.

'Sucks, but yeah. Tell ya one thing, Lady Swift, that area it happened in this afternoon is known for being controlled by...' He looked around.

'Gangsters?' Eleanor whispered.

'Right again,' Balowski said. 'And those underground cats can magic any car outta any garage or repair shop and get it back without no one and nobody seein' a thing 'cos everybody looks away.'

'The banknotes,' Clifford muttered.

'Of course!'

Balowski frowned. 'What banknotes? We workin' together or not, Lady Swift?'

'Yes. I just haven't had a chance to tell you.' In truth, she wasn't sure what had made her hold back on telling Balowski about her find under Marty's floorboards. Whatever it was, she couldn't delay any longer, so she brought him up to speed. 'Which means,' she finished, 'maybe Marty got caught up with these gangsters while working for Dellaney?'

'Or,' Clifford said, 'Mr Dellaney *was* the gangster.'

'And those bankrolls are the bonuses Marty got for deliverin' illegal goods under the pretence of chauffeurin'?' Balowski said thoughtfully.

'Or perhaps for simply turning a blind eye?' Clifford said. 'And perhaps he was sacked, or fired, because he finally refused to continue playing any part in whatever illegal activities Mr Dellaney had involved him in?'

Eleanor nodded. 'Which would explain why Dellaney made sure he never worked as a chauffeur again. But then why not kill Marty at the time? Why wait until now? And why was Dellaney then killed?' She scratched her cheek. 'We need to find out more about any shady dealings Dellaney was involved in.'

Clifford coughed. 'Perhaps, my lady, given our uncertainty

as to whether Mr Morales is implicated in the second hit-and-run...'

She and Balowski nodded. 'I agree. Best to leave Earl out of any further investigations for the moment.'

'I'll find out what I can,' Balowski said with a grunt. 'Quietly!'

She ignored the dig. 'And I'll take up some of those invitations from Dellaney's crowd. Minimum, I need to speak to Atticus Wyatt and Mrs Vanderdale, they seem to have been closest to him. And Mrs Dellaney, of course.'

As they walked around to the front of the building, she sighed. 'Have we actually got anywhere today?'

'Our chief suspect has been eliminated from our suspect list,' Clifford said. 'If only by dint of him being literally eliminated. That is progress. Of sorts.'

She groaned. 'And we have three suspects for Dellaney's murder already. Temples, Mrs Dellaney and... Earl. Which means we might only be able to gain justice for Marty and his mother by proving that her only surviving son needs to be sent to the gallows.'

'Electric chair,' Balowski said matter-of-factly.

'Electric... oh, my!'

24

Eleanor smiled as her hostess appeared. 'Mrs Vanderdale, good afternoon. I must congratulate you on your remarkable club. It has left me feeling quite inspired.'

And she meant it. The interior of the imperious four-storeyed building which spanned an entire corner of two roads, was markedly different from the stiff gentlemen's clubs she knew back in England. The normally masculine dark-wood panelling, heavy leather seating and libraries filled with earnest tomes had been replaced with rich-textured upholstery, bright airy vestibules and a myriad of elegant-legged bureaus.

Mrs Vanderdale's personal secretary had led her into the crisply modern reception room, which was softened by ivory and sky-blue latticework panels adorning the walls between the sections of silk chinoiserie print wallpaper. A tall vanilla carousel held a selection of local, national and international newspapers and a raft of political pamphlets. Carved into rose marble spanning one wall was evidently the club's motto: *Grace in Strength*. Below, an arresting lifesize portrait of the founder, Mrs Lavinia Vanderdale, occupied pride of place.

Standing underneath it in a saffron tailored suit, the lady

was even more striking in real life. Mrs Vanderdale's cupid bow lips curled into a knowing smile.

'You might feel inspired now, Lady Swift. But wait until you have seen the campaign suite, the library, discussion chambers, research rooms, auditorium, dining facilities, and health spa. To name just a few.'

'Gracious. How industrious you all are.'

Mrs Vanderdale turned and beckoned for Eleanor to follow, her diamond bracelet-clad wrist catching the light. 'Lady Swift, here in New York, and America as a whole, we women are in our ascendency.'

Eleanor drew level. 'Womankind has come a long way in society's eyes, I'm delighted to say. But we are still far from being considered on an equal footing to our male counterparts.'

'Not "womankind",' Mrs Vanderdale said with a condescending flick of her mahogany curls. '"We women" of the Ladies' Liberty Club. The elite of emotional intelligence, intuition, determination and wealth.' She waved Eleanor in through a pair of double doors. 'And the minimal criteria for an invitation to join my association. Of which this, my office, is the nerve centre, since it is where I think best. Sit.'

Eleanor stepped across the cream and silver flecked marble floor to the matching plushly upholstered settee.

As Mrs Vanderdale paused to seize a note from her vast desk, Eleanor glanced around. In each of the six deep alcoves, an exquisite floor lamp modelled on a lavish arrangement of ostrich plumes threw a spotlight up onto the intricate ceiling mouldings. The silk damask wallpapered walls were adorned with a continuous run of framed photographs. All of which had Mrs Vanderdale front and centre.

The efficient clip of heels heralded the private secretary bearing a tray of drinks.

Mrs Vanderdale gestured for her to place it on the equally oversized coffee table.

'You'll take iced coffee, Lady Swift, I'm sure?'

'Sounds intriguing. Thank you.'

It tasted as delicious as it was refreshing. She sipped it slowly, floundering for a topic that might draw this woman out. 'Perhaps you have time to tell me what prompted you to start the Liberty Club?'

Mrs Vanderdale raised her eyebrows. 'I should have thought it obvious. However, I shall indulge your curiosity.' She folded her neat curves into the deep-buttoned seat opposite. 'The coming together of influence.' She paused, seemingly to study Eleanor's reaction. 'That has rested entirely in the male domain since before time was first recorded. But the legacies of women of influence have gone largely unnoticed. And, therefore, unrecognised. Why? Because, unlike the men, they did not pool their influence! My club is correcting that costly error.'

'A worthwhile endeavour, indeed,' Eleanor said.

'Lady Swift. The members of my club have the combined standing, reputation and funds to effect change, improvement and reform no man would dare dream about in this city. Or beyond.'

'Perhaps also the ears of those in power in areas where women have not yet made sufficient inroads?'

'You mean their husbands? Don't be coy, Lady Swift. In New York we say what we mean. But, yes, I won't deny that influence can be applied in all spheres where necessary. However, a vast proportion of the wealth and power in New York, and beyond, is already held in the hands of wealthy widows. Like myself.'

While admiring the women's ethos, Eleanor wasn't warming to her boastful manner. 'Well, you certainly have an eye for finding the right building. This one seems to have worked out just so for all the club's many activities.'

Mrs Vanderdale sniffed. 'Just so? I do not accept such mediocrity! Which is why I personally had this designed and built by the city's most notable architect. At my own expense.'

'Built to order?' Eleanor couldn't help marvelling.

'Naturally. Never underestimate a determined woman, Lady Swift. This building is a symbol for what the Ladies' Liberty Club stands for. In short, we define society. We are not defined by it!' Her hostess studied Eleanor's face intently. 'Now, it's your turn. The society wedding of the year to be held in London soon, then?'

'There is? Whose?'

Mrs Vanderdale's flawless brow furrowed fleetingly. 'Why, yours, obviously. You are engaged. We touched on that at our first meeting.'

'Oh, yes. The wedding.' Eleanor gulped. 'That won't be a huge affair. Neither of us are keen on pomp or ceremony.'

'But it's your wedding day! Surely, your betrothed will insist on nothing less than nuptials fit for a' – she cast a withering look over Eleanor – 'princess?' She shook her head. 'However do you manage in English society, Lady Swift?'

Eleanor smiled sweetly. 'By relying on my wits and committing a spectacular number of faux pas.' She took a measured sip of her coffee. *Come on, Ellie. You're not here to bicker. You're here to find out who murdered Dellaney. And Marty!* 'Mrs Vanderdale?' Her hostess looked up. 'I'm sorry, but I assume you've heard about... Ogden?'

'That he is dead? Yes.'

'My sincere condolences. It's a great tragedy. Perhaps it was insensitive of me to call on you today?'

'No. Life is fragile, Lady Swift. As a widow, I have learned that mourning another cannot, and must not, end one's own life in reclusiveness and tears. It's so unproductive. And tiring.'

'It's a fine-sounding philosophy and obviously brings you a lot of comfort. I'm sorry I didn't get to know him better, however. What was he really like? Ogden, I mean.'

Mrs Vanderdale shrugged one shoulder. 'Nothing more than you witnessed yourself. Driven, temperamental, loyal only as he saw fit. With, like most men, an ego as fragile and petty as a stubborn child.'

'Poor Mrs Dellaney. She must be distraught.'

Or not, Ellie, if she was the one behind the wheel of the car that killed him!

'Distraught, nothing. Flora stayed with her husband, like many of us women do, for one thing. His money.' At Eleanor's look, she laughed curtly. 'And why not? Again, like many of us women, she'd tired of his affairs long ago. As I believe she told you, more or less.'

'His business affairs kept him away from home a lot, then?'

Mrs Vanderdale leaned forward and stared at her. 'I cannot understand how you English get by with all that reserved politeness. No, not business affairs, Lady Swift, *extramarital* ones.'

So that confirms Mrs Dellaney had a motive for killing Dellaney as you knew, Ellie. But still not for Marty.

'Ah. Yes, Mrs Dellaney did hint at that when I spoke with her briefly.'

'But not as much as Ogden himself did by pursuing you.'

'Me! Oh goodness, no. He was just a little... more familiar than our over-polite English way dictates.'

'Nonsense! If only to his mind, you were obviously the most attractive of all his guests.'

Eleanor shook her head. 'I don't believe that to be the case at all. Especially at his first party. There were scores of beautiful women. I imagine I might have been something of a novelty, that's all.'

'I said "all his guests". Ogden was equally drawn to both sexes outside of his marriage.'

'I see.' Unsure why her hostess had decided to reveal this unexpected side to Dellaney's life, she nevertheless needed to capitalise on it. 'Well, I hope his... predilections didn't gain him any enemies? Male, or female?'

Mrs Vanderdale looked at her oddly. 'The only people who don't have enemies in this town are nobodies. Anybody who is anybody has enemies. But in a city as hypocritical as New York, the difficulty can be being certain who they are unless one is shrewd enough.' She gestured over Eleanor's face. 'I don't suggest you try moving here, Lady Swift. Just friendly advice.'

Eleanor bit back a withering retort. 'Oh, I have no intention of doing so. Much as I am delighting in most of what the city has shown me so far.' She took another sip of her coffee. 'I imagine at least that you and Atticus will be a comfort to each other after Ogden's passing? The three of you seemed good friends.'

Mrs Vanderdale snorted. 'If Ogden and Atticus were friends, then I've flown to the moon. On a cow. They made a show of being so for business reasons, that's all. Everything in this city is for show.'

Which rather goes against her earlier remark, Ellie, that in New York you say what you mean. Obviously, not to the person's face, however. Only behind their back.

'It was a very convincing show,' Eleanor said genuinely.

Mrs Vanderdale laughed. 'It's all about as real as the stage sets of Ogden's precious Broadway shows. Behind the scenes, Ogden and Atticus were at each other's throats.'

Perhaps you've found someone else who would have been glad to see Dellaney out of the way, Ellie?

'Gracious! But what were they fighting about?'

'Ogden was an arrogant fool. He thought he could get away with... certain things right under Atticus' nose. But Atticus is much smarter than that. And much smarter than Ogden ever was.'

Eleanor's thoughts were racing. 'Get away with what?'

Mrs Vanderdale leaned back in her chair. 'Now that would

be telling. You seem particularly interested in their relationship though, Lady Swift?'

'Oh, just trying to get the measure of the people I keep meeting at various functions. I don't want to make one of my usual conversational blunders, especially where Atticus is concerned. Friend or no friend of Ogden's, he's still bound to be affected by the other's passing.' She finished the last of her iced coffee. 'I'm seeing Atticus tonight. He invited—'

'I know.' Eleanor frowned. Mrs Vanderdale rose. 'I'm afraid I must be getting back to work. You'll take lunch here, I'm sure.'

Eleanor rose too. 'Actually, that is a very kind offer, but one I must decline.'

Her hostess raised a surprised brow. 'I can't imagine what you find more inviting than lunching at the Ladies' Liberty Club? We have one of the best French chefs in Manhattan. However, it is your business.'

In the oval reception area, Eleanor paused by the gold-lettered roll call of members inscribed in a magnificent slice of rose marble. 'How fortunate you ladies all manage to get along so well. No feuding like the gentlemen.'

Mrs Vanderdale's eyes narrowed. 'Our members do not feud. They understand the power of cooperation. However, outside of the club, it's a dog-eat-dog world, Lady Swift. It is what makes New York such a fun city to do business in.'

25

Eleanor was grateful it was Iver at the wheel of the taxi. In Clifford's absence, Iver's familiar world-weary face and mono- logue of never-ending opinions on every subject felt comfort- ingly grounding in this alien city. And, she had to admit, much as she wanted a companion to discuss what she'd learned about Wyatt, Gladstone was a lousy listener. Unless, that was, the conversation revolved around sausages.

'Where on earth are we now?' she called over the raucous din of blaring horns and yelling voices. She peered through the windscreen. 'Oh, my! There's more commotion in this one place than the rest of New York put together!'

'Ha!' Iver called over his shoulder. 'Thought you ain't been to Times Square yet, lady. So I brought ya this way round. No extra charge.'

'I would never have suspected you of trying to overcharge, Iver,' she said with a poker face that would have done Clifford proud. She stuck her head out of her window to take in the incred- ible spectacle. Far from being an actual square as she'd imagined, it struck her as the busiest and most disorganised intersection of roads she'd ever seen. Hordes of people shuffled between a sea of trolley buses, vans, cars, carts and horses in an area designed for not even half the number. From every inch of pavement, monolithic buildings towered up to the sky, many thirty or forty storeys. That many sported advertising boards at least four floors high she found staggering. Life in New York had done the impossible. Suddenly, it had become even busier, noisier and bigger!

Feeling her neck crick, she dragged her head back in. 'Oh gracious, Iver! Just look how packed even the road itself is with pedestrians.'

She pointed at the jostling sea of men sporting pale-grey fedoras with wide, almost uniformly black bands. In contrast, the women wore a rainbow assortment of hats but were equally treating the road as if it were the pavement. Much to the irritation of the fist-waving drivers of the many taxis, horse-drawn wagons and overloaded open-topped double-decker buses all caught up in the jam.

'Everyone's headin' for Broadway, 'course,' Iver said. 'Don't you realise you're almost in the heart of theatreland?'

She sat back. 'Please take your time, Iver. I'm not due at Mr Wyatt's place for a while yet and I'd like to do a little sightseeing as we drive.'

'Like I got any say in that!' He leaned out of his window and hollered pointlessly at the seething crowd, 'Sidewalks are on the sides of the street and are for walking on! Clue's in the name!'

Eleanor, however, was delighted their progress had been reduced to a crawl. Save for the choking vehicle fumes, that was. The extra time gave her the perfect chance to drink in every inch of Broadway, the very area which seemed to have become central to the investigation. Although how it might relate to Marty's murder, she was at a loss.

Her hungry gaze was drawn to the seemingly only stationary person on a street corner. In rolled-up shirtsleeves and red braces, he grimly hung onto the post of the placard he was holding aloft. She could see he was yelling something, but had no hope of catching his words. Nor of reading his sign from her angle of view.

'Look at that fellow, Iver. The "broadside" I think you called the protesters we encountered before. He's got no chance of an audience. The crowds are fixated on their evening's entertainment to the point they've entirely lost any sense of self-preservation!'

He rolled his eyes. 'He ain't no broadside, lady. He's advertisin'.'

'Advertising what?' She stared again as the man turned to face the taxi. She read his sign aloud. '"The Lyceum Theatre. See the play everybody's talking about!!!"'

Iver nodded. 'Yeah, all the theatres advertise like that. The Lyceum is one of the best around. We gonna pass it in a minute if these numbskulls'd only move.'

'There she is,' he called a few minutes later. 'The Lyceum. Prettiest of the lot. Almost as good-lookin' as my Sadie, but don't go tellin' her I said that.'

Eleanor studied the imposing Beaux Arts building. Above the impressive wavelike stone canopy spanning its width, six Corinthian columns towered up to the second floor, flanking the three deeply inset arched windows. Above that, a balustraded balcony ran the full span of the building. But the most eye-catching feature was the five-feet-high flames burning fiercely from the giant torches above the columns.

'So what's the play everyone is apparently talking about?' she mused as they drew level. A cold frisson shot down her spine as she read the name emblazoned on the theatre's enormous billboard. *Why Marry?* Her beau's all too recent proposal still rang in her ears. And she'd said yes. Eagerly. So why, then, had the play's title made her shiver?

Iver waved a newspaper over his shoulder at her. 'Reviews

are good, but it's supposed to be a comedy! How can it be when it's all about divorce?'

Maybe that's why you went cold, Ellie! You're not even married yet!

'Divorce?' she said breathlessly.

He nodded. 'Yeah. That's why it's called *Why Marry?*, see? Why marry, if it ain't gonna last?'

Her eyes widened. With his strong New York drawl, he had strung out the word 'Marry' to sound like 'Mary'! Just as Marty used to do back at her apartments with the word 'carry'. 'You want I should *carry* your bags, Lady Swift?'

She gasped. *Perhaps Marty's dying words were 'Why Marry?', not 'Why, Mary?', Ellie.*

If so, what did it mean?

'Iver, please stop. I need to go and talk to the theatre manager.'

He pulled over and chuckled. 'And you only havin' got as far as that engagement ring I seen on ya finger. Yet you still gonna give that fella a piece a ya mind about there bein' nothin' funny about divorce. Good girl!' He jerked his thumb at the legions of excited theatregoers swarming in through the Lyceum's doors. 'Betta elbow ya way in through the stage door if ya want to find him before the show's over, though.'

She climbed out and came around to his side of the cab. 'Good advice. Please wait for me here. I won't be long.'

She failed to hear Iver's reply, because coming out of a department store across the road, dressed in blue silk, was someone she badly wanted to speak to. Hurrying across the road, she just caught her prey before she got into the waiting limousine.

'Please forgive me for stopping you in the street like this, Mrs Dellaney, but I didn't know if you would be up to receiving visitors?'

The chauffeur, who was holding the door open, took a step

forward. He looked more like a bodyguard, well over six feet and as muscle bound as an ox. Mrs Dellaney waved him back and stared at her indifferently. 'Lady Swift, isn't it?'

Eleanor nodded. 'Yes. My heartfelt condolences. I'm so sorry.'

'Heartfelt condolences? Oh, I see. Because of Ogden's accident,' she said rather casually.

And rather soberly, Ellie?

'Well, thank you, I guess.' She seemed to catch on to Eleanor's surprise. 'Lady Swift, Ogden and I were not happily married as I'm sure you worked out the moment he started chasing you around our home at that first dreadful party you came to.'

'Goodness no, it wasn't like that!'

'Please! Don't bother to deny it. The very moment I saw your photograph in the *New York Times*, I said to myself, "Flora, she'll be at Ogden's very next evening affair. And then straight into an actual affair with him, if he gets his way."'

Eleanor gasped. 'I would never!'

Mrs Dellaney shrugged. 'It wouldn't have mattered one iota if you had. Not to me. Ogden was committed to one thing only. His libido.'

'Then I'm doubly sorry for you. But it was still a terrible accident to have happened.'

'Maybe it was. Maybe it wasn't.' Mrs Dellaney spread her hands. 'An accident, I mean. Plenty of people would have been happy to have seen him dead.' She smiled cruelly. 'Me included.'

Eleanor shivered. 'Do you have any idea, apart from yourself, who—'

'Might have wanted him dead?' She laughed curtly. 'Take your pick. Ogden wasn't a popular man among his friends or enemies, if you know what I mean.' Her expression hardened.

'But if you're fishing for tidbits, I'll tell you something you can gossip about.'

'I wasn't going to pry any further,' Eleanor said.

Mrs Dellaney's grim smile made Eleanor's skin creep. 'Well, I'll tell you something for nothing anyway, Lady Swift. At the time of his death I was out getting my revenge on my so-called husband. But not by running him down.' She smirked. 'Although if I'd thought of it, it might have been even more satisfying. Good day!'

She passed the chauffeur her purchases who opened the boot, or 'trunk' as Iver had informed her was the 'correct' term and placed them inside. Eleanor started.

Is that a large-brimmed hat and scarf thrown in the far corner of that vast luggage space, Ellie?

Before she could think of a way to get another look, the chauffeur closed the boot and a moment later the limousine merged into the sea of traffic. Deep in thought, Eleanor carefully made her way back across the road to the Lyceum.

At the theatre, she didn't have to wait long to get someone's attention.

'Don't you see you got Gloria Swanson waitin' out in the street like she's a nobody, Johnny!' a voice called. 'Let her in, you dunce. The redhead!' The doorman spun around with a horrified look. Catching Eleanor's eye, he strode forward, parting the crowd.

'So sorry, Miss Swanson. Right this way.'

Rather ashamed this was far from the first time she'd taken advantage of her similarity to the famous American actress, she simply smiled and let him lead her inside. The doorman yanked the door shut, leaving them in a dim corridor which led to a narrow staircase at one end and a chaotic overflowing costume area at the other. Trying to cover up that the musty air infused with the heady mix of grease paint and liquid paraffin was threatening to make her nose wrinkle, she beckoned him closer.

'The stage manager, please, dear boy. It's urgent.'

A minute later, a harassed-looking man in his early forties dressed in a vibrantly chequered waistcoat with a purple bow tie appeared. He was clutching a thick sheaf of scripts with both arms and dragging on a huge cigar. 'Miss Swanson?'

'Oh, where?' she replied innocently, peering over his shoulder.

'Wretched idiot, Johnny! It's not her!' he bawled at the startled doorman before glaring back at her. 'So if you're not Miss Swanson, whaddya want?'

She thought fast. 'Well, I'm reporting for—'

'Oh, I get it.' He slapped his forehead with the scripts. 'You one of them modern dolls that work on the newspapers? And you want an insider take on the play and cast? Horse's mouth quote to get you a leg up with the newspaper boss? Well' – he scanned her face – 'I'd say you got another way you could do that. But what the heck, you're too pretty to say no to. You got one minute. So ask. And ask fast.'

'Er, thank you. This play. *Why Marry?*'

'What about it?'

She realised she wasn't really sure what it was about it she wanted to know. 'Has... has it been playing long?'

The manager looked at her as if she were simple. 'Where you been, lady? It's a smash hit! We only put on the best shows here at the Lyceum. That's why a dude like Mr Dellaney bought it as his flagship theatre.'

She started. 'Was Mr Dellaney backing the play?'

'Sure. He owned the theatre, so he naturally backed the play.'

'Owned? As in past tense?'

He nodded.

'So, who owns it now?'

He shrugged. 'An anonymous buyer. Bought the rights to the play as well. A smart operator, for sure. Seems like this nameless dude has bought up a lot more theatres and plays too. He'll be rollin' in dough with the investments he's pulled off. Everyone's talking about it in the business. Word is, he was taking Mr Dellaney to the cleaners before Mr Dellaney got hit by that car.' He frowned at the sound of shrill ringing. 'Say, that's the five-minute bell. Now, scoot. And don't write nothin' derogatory in that rag of yours or I'll know about it!'

Back out in the street, she looked up and down the square. But no matter how hard she stared at the parked vehicles on both sides, she couldn't see Iver and his taxi. Standing on tiptoe didn't help, so she swung herself up onto an ornate street lamp to peer over the crowd. But still, she couldn't spot her transport home.

'Dash it!' she grumbled, squinting through the chaos of vehicles and people. 'He must have been forced to wait further down.'

'No, sweetheart. That ain't the reason.'

Staring up at her was an athletic-looking man in a smartly tailored suit. His neat moustache, however, failed to hide the long scar running up from his top lip. Without warning, she felt her fingers being prised from the post and then she was tottering on both feet on the pavement.

'We sent him off,' his equally slick-haired and sharp-dressed companion grunted.

'I was quite capable of getting myself down, thank you,' she said firmly. 'And why on earth did you dispatch my taxi off to goodness knows where?'

'Because you don't got no need of it.'

The man with the scar leaned in so close she shuddered at the feel of his breath on her cheek. 'Feisty ain't a good plan right now, sweetheart. You're going to come with us for a little chat. And any messing about, and your evening out in Broadway is gonna end badly. Real badly.'

26

Eleanor was led along the street, pinned by the arm each man had slung tightly around her shoulders. Had anyone in Times Square so much as glanced their way, they would have seen only three good friends entering a diner, bent on a long-missed catch-up.

'No fuss and you might just walk outta here,' the scar-faced man hissed as they slid into the furthest seating from the door.

Play it cool, Ellie. No one knows you're here. You need to get yourself out of this. If they'd meant to do you any harm, they'd have done so out in the anonymity of a crowded street.

'Coffee, darlin'?' the scar-faced man said as a waitress appeared. Before she could reply, he put his arm around her again and cupped her chin as if being affectionate. 'Yeah, she'll take a shot. Make it three.'

Alone with the two of them, she gathered her wits and glanced around, assessing her chances. Since they'd sat down in the booth, the ones on either side had mysteriously emptied.

Maybe not the time to try a little Bartitsu self-defence, Ellie. Who knows what they're carrying under those jackets?

She smiled at her two abductors. 'Do you know, gentlemen,

I couldn't in all honesty recommend you travel to England in the hope of picking up nice girls. I think you'll find they'll consider your strong-arm wooing tactics rather gauche and oafish.'

'What?' They stared at each other.

'We ain't tryin' to pick you up!' the scar-faced man snarled.

She let out a long breath. 'Now that is a tremendous relief because neither of you is really my type.' She adjusted the sleeves of her dress and then moved onto the pleats of her skirt. 'I assume then you just fancied swinging me down from my perfectly positioned perch where I was searching for the taxi you decided I didn't need any more. In which case, lesson number two, chaps; don't make decisions for a girl without even consulting her.'

'Okay, you wanna be consulted. We can do that. No problem,' the first man said in a menacing tone which sent a shiver down her spine, given that he'd managed it while smiling genially. 'See, we was being helpful. Came to give a warning on account of thinking you'd wanna stay alive. But maybe we was wrong? Maybe you've always wanted to see the bottom of the Hudson River? In concrete boots?'

'No,' she said falteringly. 'Because, well, they don't sound very flattering at all.'

The second man leaned across to her. 'Nor very easy to keep breathing in.'

They broke apart as the coffee arrived but she grimaced as the scar-faced man yanked her wrist sharply up behind her back with a warning glance. Judging by the way the other diners around her had quietly crept away without a word being spoken, she doubted if the waitress would, or could, help her anyway.

He looked her over. 'You got balls, sweetheart, I'll give you that. But cut it out. Right?'

'Cut what out?' she said indignantly. 'Sightseeing in Broadway? Asking taxis to wait and expecting them to be there when I come out? Really, chaps, you need to be clearer.'

'Then let me spell it out for you.' The first man, whom she realised was the real spokesman of the pair, slowly thumbed open his jacket. Her eyes widened as he tapped the long-bladed knife nestled against the silk lining in a purpose-made and expertly crafted leather clasp. 'Stop sticking your nose into matters that don't concern you. Or you might find—'

'Find what, gentlemen?' Clifford's ever-measured tone interjected. Her butler stood in a commanding stance blocking both men's exits, one hand filled with string-wrapped parcels, the other pulling open his jacket to reveal a ready-cocked pistol.

Oh, thank goodness, Ellie! You were doing fine on your own, but a little extra assistance, especially of the armed variety, wouldn't go amiss.

'That was a question,' Clifford said calmly. 'Do I need to repeat it, gentlemen?'

'Nope.' The man re-buttoned his jacket even more slowly than he'd undone it. 'But I hope that white steed you charged in on can gallop faster 'n a super-tuned motor. Because if your friend here don't stop what's she's doin', we're gonna come back. For both of you. And we ain't gonna be so friendly.' He stood with that flawless smile again. 'Excuse us now, won't you?'

'Oh, Clifford, thank you.' She flapped him into the opposite seat as the men left the diner.

His brow flinched. 'My lady, if we might adjourn from the site of such a discomforting meeting? To somewhere... let me think, oh, I know, *safe*.'

'It's safe here for a minute. They've gone and they know you're armed. The coffee smells divine-ish and besides,' she smiled sheepishly as she whispered, 'I confess, for the first time, my knees are feeling a tad wobbly. That was all so unexpected.'

'And perilous to life.'

'They weren't going to kill me in a diner. It's full of customers. Witnesses.'

'All of whom would have turned a blind eye, I very much fear.' His expression fell grave as he lowered his voice so she had to crane across the table to hear him. 'My lady, remember the words of our officer regarding the, ahem... other activities which are more than commonplace in Broadway?'

'Ah! I do. Then you're right, we should probably go.' They stood to make their way out of the booth, but she paused before they headed to the door. 'But wait a second, Clifford. How on earth did you find me?'

'We are both indebted to Iver, my lady. He parked around the corner and watched the two men march you into the diner. He then ran to the renowned Candy Emporium across the street as he remembered I had told you I would be shopping for souvenir tins of tootsie roll sweets for each of the ladies and informed me of your predicament.'

'Oh, Clifford, I am sorry. I may be a trifle impetuous on occasions.'

'But very impressive nonetheless,' a nasal voice said. From the booth next to them, a man in a trenchcoat with a wide-brimmed fedora slid sideways into view along the back of the seat.

'Were you talking to us?' She noted the man seemed to have one blue and one green eye.

'Why, yes, ma'am.' He jerked his chin out at the street where the two men had been swallowed up by the crowds. 'Very impressive, I said. In that you've managed to attract some heavy attention in a very short time.' He waved at the empty seat opposite. 'Please. Sit a moment.'

'No, thank you,' Clifford said firmly.

The man shrugged. 'The lady might want to hear this. It's to her advantage.'

Intrigued, she nodded to Clifford and slid into the opposite seat.

The man chuckled. 'I like your style, lady, so I'm going to cut you a break here. My client, whose identity must remain confidential, you understand, has an interest in a related matter to yours.'

Dash it, Ellie, how come even complete strangers seem to know what you're up to?

It seemed her face had given her away. The man nodded. 'That's right. Your secret isn't so secret, ma'am. Now, don't that strike you as a little... worrying? So many people know what you're looking into. And where, so as they can pick you off a single lamp post in all of New York?'

Clifford gave her a long-suffering look. 'A lamp post, my lady? Please tell me otherwise.'

She shrugged. 'I was looking for Iver.' She turned back to their mystery companion. 'What else have you got, because that's old news.'

He nodded. 'Maybe. And maybe it's old news that the people you're attracting the attention of own this city. From the bottom, right to the top, and back down again.'

'It is. And so far I haven't learned anything to my advantage I didn't already know, Mr...?'

'"Mr" is just fine.' He rose and brushed past the end of the table, knocking Clifford's parcels to the floor.

'Oh, most kind,' her butler said as the man helped him retrieve them. The man then nodded to each of them and walked to the door. 'My point, ma'am,' he called over his shoulder as he left, 'is you want to be careful whose company you're keeping! It could be deadly!'

27

Eleanor stared up at the ocean of yellow stone. It reminded her of a sandcastle village of endless towers topped with sculpted turrets she'd built with her father one glorious day on the remotest of island beaches. She took a deep breath. After the events in the diner only an hour ago or so, she was still a little shaky. But after Mrs Vanderdale's revelation that Dellaney and Wyatt had been at each other's throats, she'd persuaded Clifford that she should keep her appointment, however late. She looked down as the door opened to find Wyatt, cigarette in hand, smiling back at her.

'Oh gracious, it's you!'

He laughed. 'Yes. I live here, remember?'

'No, I meant I expected your butler or valet to greet me.'

'Well, Eleanor, I sure hope I haven't offended you by welcoming you to my home myself?'

'Not at all,' she said, delighting once again in his relaxing Southern drawl. 'I confess, I'm always happy to escape a little formality.'

'Me too. The Texan desert hasn't any regard for social airs and graces.'

She laughed. 'Well, that's just as well given how disgracefully late I am. I apologise again.'

'No problem. You rang in time for me to reschedule dinner, so all is well.'

He offered a courteous elbow and led her across the vast two-storeyed circular entrance hall past the most exquisitely carved staircase she'd ever seen. And then on past a twenty-foot mural dominated by the incredibly long horns of a massive, dappled brown and white cow.

She ran her finger in the air along the length of its curved horns, which would have embarrassed the tusks of even the most giant of African elephants. 'Is this to scale?'

'Why sure. Some are up to eight feet. He was one of the cattle on my ranch.'

He steered her towards the palatial marbled and glassed-over walkway she could see through the horseshoe arch. 'Where's Mr Gladstone tonight? I thought he always accompanied you?'

'I feared if I brought him along, neither your billiard balls nor leather slippers would be safe.'

He laughed easily, which she'd found so charming each time they'd met.

'A drink, Eleanor? You'll forgive my adhering to prohibition, I hope?'

'Categorically. I have been too. By the way, what brand of cigarette is that?'

He looked at her oddly. 'Black Cat. Nothing special. Why?'

Blast, Ellie! It didn't smell like a Gitanes, but best to check.

She shrugged. 'Oh, I just wondered. I thought recently of taking smoking up, but I don't really like the taste.'

He nodded. 'I smoke several different brands, depending on my mood.'

'Really? Any... foreign brands?'

He shook his head. 'No. I'm quite patriotic that way.'

She was soon settled into a sumptuous seat at the rear terrace's beautifully dressed dining table which looked out onto the Hudson River, her nose tingling with the delectable spring scents of roses, hyacinths and columbine. The wide river was peppered with red-funnelled ferries, flotillas of Lilliputian tugboats, smart port patrol boats and a handful of determined fishermen rowing their tiny open craft out from the shallows. The scene couldn't have been more of a contrast to the congested chaos of the city's roads.

In her hand was a flute of ice-cold mint and lime delicious-ness and before her a plate of delectable crab and shrimp canapés. And kissing her face, the most welcome breeze. It was all too relaxing for words, and yet she needed to ruin it all by probing for information on the ghastly topic of murder. She rallied herself.

'What a wonderful haven of tranquillity you've created, Atticus.'

He nodded. 'I need a slice of peace more than ever in this crazy city.'

'I can understand that,' she said genuinely. 'And thank you for your invitation this evening. And for my drink. It's very refreshing.'

'As are you, Eleanor,' he replied without a hint of salacious-ness. 'Unpredictably so, I hope you don't mind my saying? After all, it's not just English politeness that's stopping you, I'd wager, if I was a betting man. Which I'm not, by the way.'

'Stopping me from what?'

'Mentioning Ogden straight out of the saddle.'

She hesitated. 'I meant to offer my condolences as you greeted me, but I feared it might spoil your evening.' She crossed her fingers. 'You seemed like good friends.'

His calm tone didn't waver. 'Our "friendship" was merely an act of convenience.'

'Really? Well, it was very convincing.'

He nodded. 'Eleanor, not every death is a tragedy. Ogden was all mustard and no steak.'

She kept her expression neutral. 'I'm sorry to hear that. I thought you and Ogden had a lot in common? Like your business interests, perhaps? Do they lie in Broadway like Ogden's?'

Maybe you can find out about this 'Why Marry?' play from Atticus while you're probing him about Dellaney, Ellie?

He laughed. 'Everybody in this city has something to do with Broadway. It's like back home in Texas, everybody has something to do with cattle.'

'Would you enlighten me then? The theatre is a world I know nothing about. Not in England, and certainly not here. I haven't had a moment to see a production yet.'

'Why sure.' A waiter appeared with an oval two-tiered silver trolley. 'But first, dinner.'

The Lobster Newburg, as it turned out to be, was precisely the irresistible sauce-drenched distraction she didn't need. And so good, she had to wait until she'd finished it to continue the conversation.

'That was simply splendid!'

Wyatt put down his fork and dabbed at his mouth with a fine linen napkin. 'I think it's the madeira and cream that makes the sauce too good to resist. Or maybe it's how the nutmeg adds that little kick to the lobster.'

Madeira wine, Ellie? How does that work for a self-professed teetotaller? Maybe Mrs Vanderdale was right about it all being an act?

'I can't think I'll eat anything else while I'm here,' she said, trying to hide her puzzlement.

Their bowls cleared, Wyatt sat back. After the waiter had served the next course, she looked up from the succulently grilled fish, served unusually on a bed of melon slices, to see Atticus eyeing her intently. He put down his fork.

'Eleanor, let me tell you something. You need to be looking elsewhere.'

She frowned. 'You've lost me?'

'No, I haven't.' His slow drawl suddenly sounded a hint intimidating to her ears. 'You think Ogden was murdered.'

'I've no idea where you've got that notion from,' she said as airily as she could. *This is getting ridiculous, Ellie. How is it everyone in this city seems to be keeping tabs on you?*

'It's no notion, Eleanor. So let me spare you any more wasted time trying to be tactful.' He gave her a knowing smile. 'Then you can tie up the reins on my being involved and simply enjoy the view and the food. And hopefully, the company.'

She shrugged. 'Genuinely, I've had no thought at all that you might be involved in anything untoward, Atticus. But Ogden's accident does seem to have happened somewhere rather odd.'

'I agree. I know where it happened, and Ogden wouldn't normally be seen dead in an area like that.' He glanced up sharply. 'Sorry. Bad choice of words. And to save you trying to ask politely, I have no alibi for the time that vehicle struck him.'

Flummoxed by all these revelations, she waited to see what else he might offer.

'I was driving from here to a business meeting. Way uptown.'

She leaned forward. 'Perfect!'

His brow furrowed. 'Now you've lost me?'

'No, I haven't. The police will be able to check the timing from here to wherever your meeting was.'

'Sure won't.' He waved a hand up at the fiery orange band of the sunset. 'Weather's been so much like back home of late, I took a detour to reminisce on the feel of hot wind in my face.'

Her tone turned cold. 'Then I hope for you it turns out you have no motive for dispatching Ogden?'

'I have the biggest motive.' With an effort, she kept her face neutral as he sat back, crossing one exquisitely tailored trouser leg over the other. 'But, Eleanor, as Ogden's no more, I've no bones about keeping it buried any longer. Least not from you.'

'As you wish,' she said, trying not to sound eager.

'I think you know I'm a widower.' At her nod, he continued. 'My wife died in childbirth. And nine months before that, Ogden was deep in having an affair with her.'

She gasped. 'Oh my! So... oh, forgive me.'

'So, yes, she probably died having his baby. Not mine.'

She winced. 'Atticus. Genuinely, I am so sorry.'

'Thank you.' His jaw tightened. 'But, you see, I'm not glad Ogden's dead.'

She frowned in confusion. 'Really? But what with what you've just told me, no wonder you two were fighting and—'

'Actually, we weren't. Ogden thought I knew nothing about it right up until he died. Which I didn't, at first. Not until after my wife died, that is. Then a little birdy told me.'

Mrs Vanderdale, I'd wager, Ellie

Wyatt smiled cruelly as he stared out into space. 'You see, I'm not glad Ogden is dead because I promised myself I'd bring him to his knees for what he did. Broadway is... *was* a large part of his business. He owned many theatres and had the major share in all the plays put on in them.' She jumped as he slapped the table. 'But while he was busy playing stallion to other people's wives, behind the scenes I was slowly pushing him out of business. I systematically bought out his theatres. Under another name, naturally. And I secured the rights to the most in-demand upcoming plays, which meant those theatres he did hang onto were forced to put on second-rate shows.'

So it was Atticus who bought the Lyceum Theatre and the play Why Marry? *And who was taking Dellaney to the cleaners!*

'I'm sure your planning was very thorough,' was all she could think to say.

'Of course it was! Once I'd done that, my next step was to

ruin him socially. Only now someone has done me the worst disservice imaginable! They killed Ogden before I could bring him down like a wailing, wounded coyote. How can I have my revenge now?'

While talking, he'd leaned further and further out of his chair, his whole body tensed up. He seemed to realise this and sat back, closing his eyes. After a few deep breaths, he opened them. To her surprise, he was... laughing!

'Eleanor?' She nodded in confusion. He smiled genially and waved his glass. 'You don't happen to know of anyone who wants to buy a bunch of theatres, do you?'

28

Eleanor sighed into her breakfast coffee. It was the morning after her talk with Wyatt, Mrs Vanderdale and, most memorably, a couple of thugs in a diner.

'Honestly, I'm in two minds, Clifford.'

'Really, my lady,' he said drily. 'Being in two minds might be an error for a certain lady of the house.'

'Because?'

His eyes twinkled. 'Because, surely one alone has consistently proved sufficiently problematic?'

She laughed. 'You are a terrible man! I meant, I'm in two minds because of that mystery man who accosted us after those thugs left the diner. Was he just trying to put us off? Or was he actually trying to help us? And what did he mean, exactly, by his parting remark?'

Clifford nodded. 'The gentleman's words were unsettling. How, indeed, do so many people seem to know our every move? And, most disconcertingly, your whereabouts at any moment? Even if that is, ahem, inelegantly straddling a lamp post.'

'Yes, yes! The point is, we need to talk to him again. But how? We've no idea who he is or where to find him.'

He held out a silver salver and tapped the lid with a white gloved finger.

'Actually, I'm quite full...' She caught his look. Whipping off the lid, she cheered as she scooped up a simple business card. 'Clifford, you clever bean! So you just made it look as if he had knocked your parcels off the table in the diner yesterday so you could pick his pocket. Marvellous ruse.' She turned back to the card. '"F. Newkirk. Private Detective."' She looked thoughtful. 'So, he's a detective. And he said his client has an interest in a "related matter". Which can only be Marty or Dellaney's murder, surely?' She glanced down at the card again. 'There's an address! Excellent. Let's go!'

Clifford paused in clearing away the remains of breakfast. 'The address is the other side of Central Park. Perhaps I might be so bold as to suggest we walk and talk the case down on the way?'

'A splendid idea!'

Swiftly heading to her bedroom, she changed, grabbed her large-brimmed olive-green hat and escaped out into the sunshine.

Once in Central Park, Clifford deftly steered Gladstone away from eagerly advancing on a small child mid-sandwich.

'This way, I feel, might be safer for anyone wishing to picnic in peace, my lady.'

He led her onto a wide avenue, grandly signed as The Mall. It was peppered with horse-drawn carriages, mostly occupied by courting couples, it seemed.

She paused, wishing it could be her and her beau. No, her fiancé, she corrected herself, with a wistful sigh.

Clifford scanned her face. 'Patience, my lady. A lifetime of heart-warming memories awaits.'

'I hope so!'

He cleared his throat. 'I am sure so.' He pulled a small, gift-wrapped package from his inner pocket. 'A certain chief inspector asked me to give you this when I felt the moment right.' He passed it to her.

Her fingers fumbled to slide off the velvet ribbon, not wanting to spoil the beautiful emerald-green bow. Inside was a darling little wooden box, the intricately carved top offering a tantalising peep that something special waited inside. She lifted the lid slowly and smiled. Set on a bed of rose petals lay a candle, and a note. *'To wish you goodnight, every night, my love.'* Without a word, Clifford turned the box in her hand so the carved top faced the dark front of his jacket and shone his torch through the carving.

'I love you, Eleanor,' she read. 'Oh, Clifford! And look, there's a little drawer at the bottom.' Opening it, her heart skipped at the tiny rolls of paper, each tied by another green ribbon and offering glimpses of Hugh's writing. 'It's too perfect.'

He nodded. 'Very special indeed, my lady.'

After he'd returned Seldon's present to his inner pocket for safe keeping, he pulled her trusty investigations notebook from his inside pocket. Checking no one was within earshot and, with one eye on Gladstone, he cleared his throat. 'Perhaps summarising where we are up to regarding our suspects is a good idea, my lady? I am mindful that it was too late when you'd returned from Mr Wyatt's residence to discuss developments then.'

She nodded. 'I know, and we – I – need to be a lot more circumspect. Lecture from last night accepted. Anyway, I haven't filled you in on my chat with Atticus either. But let's tackle Temples the chauffeur first. He seems to have had the motive, means and opportunity in both murders.'

He nodded. 'Mr Temples seemingly had a feud with Mr Morales and had access to the car that killed him. Mmm.

Perhaps, then, Mr Morales caught Mr Temples stealing off Mr Dellaney, as the police alleged?'

She nodded. 'And perhaps Marty didn't want to, er...'

'"Rat out" a colleague, as the phrase is, I believe, my lady?'

'Exactly. But Temples was worried Marty would end up exposing him at some point anyway, so he got him sacked. And maybe then Marty threatened to tell Dellaney in revenge, and Temples silenced him for good?' She shook her head. 'It's all supposition at the moment. Temples might have been framed for stealing as Balowski suggested.' She sighed. 'We need to arrange another meeting with Temples which, given he is in jail, will be tricky.'

Clifford intervened in a disagreement between Gladstone and a fluffy Pekingese sporting a pink bow, who seemed to object to her bulldog's presence in its park. Having averted a showdown, he turned back to her.

'Actually, my lady, I believe that can be arranged.'

She peered at him sideways. 'I won't ask how now, but we'll pencil that delight in as soon as possible.'

He nodded and returned to the notebook. 'The next suspect on our list is Mr Morales.'

'Earl? I've nothing new on him. He threatened to make whoever killed his brother pay, so he had a motive to kill Dellaney if he suspected Dellaney was responsible. But we still haven't got a motive for him killing his own brother. Which would mean, if he didn't, we are looking for two killers. And at the moment, we have our hands full looking for one! So, let's keep moving.'

'Mrs Dellaney, then?'

'Ah! And not just because, sadly, one always suspects the spouse, especially one who very publicly declares that they are tired of their husband's affairs as she admitted she was. But she also told me when I bumped into her last night that she wouldn't have been surprised if her husband *had* been murdered. And that, even though she didn't kill him, she was actually out at the time of the hit-and-run "getting her revenge".'

'Interesting. Revenge for?'

'His infidelity, I assume.'

He straightened his tie. 'Perhaps by indulging in the same, my lady? Tit for tat, as it were.'

She nodded. 'Of course! And there's more, actually.' She peered sideways at him again. 'However, pretend I've told you more decorously than it's bound to come out. You see, Mrs Vanderdale declared that Ogden's affairs were not only with women. He enjoyed liaisons with men as well, apparently.'

Clifford merely nodded.

'That's it?' she said in surprise.

'My lady, the proclivities of another are not such which require my opinion or comment. Be and let be, I believe.'

'I wholeheartedly agree.' She paused at the impressive fountain. 'But it does have a bearing on the case.'

'Indeed. If, that is, you are suggesting Mr Dellaney was involved... intimately with Mr Morales. What stronger motive might a wife have for murdering her husband than the embarrassment of him "carrying on" with their chauffeur, as it were?'

'It's a possibility, isn't it? Especially as Mrs Morales and Earl each mentioned that Marty never once breathed so much as a word about having a girl he was sweet on? He certainly never brought one home, even though Mrs Morales did say she thought he once had girl problems. But maybe it was boy problems! Anyway, Mrs Dellaney might have first eliminated her husband's—'

'Paramour?'

'That. And then dealt with her embarrassing situation once and for all by eliminating her husband.'

'Disconcertingly, it is always easier to kill the second time.'

They walked on in sombre silence. She broke it first.

'This new information might also explain some other parts

of the puzzle. For instance, why Ogden sacked Marty. Perhaps Marty was actually an unwilling party to his attentions?'

'Excellent point, my lady. And it might further explain Mr Morales' assertion that his brother, Marty, suddenly seemed unhappy in his chauffeuring post with Mr Dellaney.'

'Although, if we're taking that tack, the rolls of banknotes I found under Marty's floorboards might have been payment for—'

'Extra-curricular services rendered on Marty's part?' he said hastily.

'Yes, decorously put. So maybe Ogden's advances weren't that unwelcome?' She sighed. 'With Marty and Ogden dead, I don't suppose there's much chance of finding out. However, we now come to last night's chat with Atticus. Well, to put it simply, he told me he should be our number one suspect for Ogden's murder.'

For one of the very few times she could remember, both of her butler's eyebrows rose simultaneously. 'Interesting.'

'I'd say! Atticus insisted that Ogden had an affair with his wife. And then to rub salt into Atticus' already open wound,' she winced, 'she died in childbirth...'

A pained expression passed over her butler's features. 'Please tell me it wasn't?'

'I wish I could,' she said glumly. 'But Atticus is convinced it was almost certainly Ogden's child she lost her life trying to bring into the world.'

'Revenge most ardent one might plausibly conjecture as a likely motive for Mr Wyatt, then?'

'There's no conjecture about it.' She shrugged. 'That's what was so odd, however. He volunteered the information unasked. He even went into detail about how carefully he'd planned to ruin Ogden in business which tallied exactly with what the theatre manager of the Lyceum told me about someone "taking Dellaney to the cleaners".'

'Hmm, as curious as it is confusing, my lady.'

She nodded. 'Atticus then told me he had intended to destroy Ogden's personal life as well.' She frowned. 'His personal life! Why didn't I think of it before? If you wanted to get your revenge on the man who had an affair with your wife, one way would be—'

'To return the favour?'

'Exactly! And if Atticus and Mrs Dellaney were having an affair, they might have arranged Ogden's demise together?'

Clifford nodded. 'An excellent deduction, my lady. Perhaps—'

'Oh cripes, Clifford, look at Mr Wilful now!'

They hurried over to her bulldog who was trying to out-growl a hissing swan on the shore of the ornamental lake. He was fast losing the battle, and his grip on the bank, as the swan advanced menacingly. Clifford coaxed the bulldog away from the water and the irate fowl with a selection of treats from his pocket. Back on the safety of the path, he shook his head at the bulldog.

'Master Gladstone, might an ounce of sense ever prevail?' His gaze slid to Eleanor's. 'My lady, why could it be that I am minded of the saying about pets growing similar in character to their owners?'

'I really couldn't say, Clifford,' she parried with a good-natured eye roll. 'Now, lead us somewhere fowl-free and some-where you'll be less of a mischievous monster where your mistress is concerned.'

He led her along a winding path occupied, like the carriages, mostly by courting couples, and then up a long run of steps to what appeared to be an open-air fortress.

'Belvedere Castle, my lady. Built in 1837 almost entirely of Manhattan schist, a crystalline rock of laterally layered minerals.'

'It's absolutely beautiful.' They wandered on to the expansive terrace and stared out over the oasis of green she hadn't realised could exist in a city as crowded as New York.

Having climbed back down, they were about to continue, when a familiar voice came from a few feet away. She froze and glanced at Clifford. He nodded imperceptibly and mouthed, 'Wyatt!' The voice came again.

'So, you show Temples this.' There was a pause and a slight rustling noise as if something were being handed over. 'And tell him he gets the charges dropped and then when he gets out, the money. That is, if he keeps his mouth shut. He's had a taste of this before, so he knows I keep my word. But remember to warn him, just for clarity, of the consequences if he doesn't play along.'

An unfamiliar voice replied. 'We got that, Mr... I mean, we got that. No problem, sir.'

Wyatt's voice came again. 'Good. And, boys, if you're thinking of getting light-fingered with any of that money...'

'No. Wouldn't think of it, sir.' Two voices came in unison, tinged with fear.

'Good. Now get out of here!'

She waited a moment and then risked a peep around the corner. No one was there. She scanned the area, but they'd gone. Her brow knitted.

'What was that about?'

Behind her, Clifford shook his head. 'I've no idea, but it's certainly something else to ask Mr Temples when we arrange that meeting. The two men Mr Wyatt were talking to seem to have access to Mr Temples even though he is in jail. That would suggest they are prison wardens or, more likely, police officers in Mr Wyatt's pay.'

She spun around. 'Gracious, Clifford! Now I realise what he meant!'

'He who, my lady?'

'Mr F. Newkirk, Private Detective.'

'Then please enlighten me?'

'Well, the sort of powerful people we... *I* might have ruffled enough to send their goons for me, don't leave anything to chance. In Ogden's case, they lured him to an area they knew they could control completely before dealing with him. But in Marty's, maybe he was too streetwise? Or was about to expose Dellaney, so they had to act quickly? So, being unable to make sure the "accident" took place in such an area, instead they sent a false witness, the chap from Coney Island, to cover themselves.'

He nodded. 'As we conjectured previously.'

'Yes, but the detective's words have just hit home. If you're going to leave nothing to chance, you plant not only a witness you can control but also—'

'A policeman! Of course. "Be careful whose company you're keeping!"'

'I gotta say,' a familiar belligerent drawl made them both freeze, 'I had a heck of a job trackin' you two down.'

29

'The Tombs!' Eleanor whispered to Clifford as they waited at a greasy, finger-streaked window. 'That's a shockingly macabre name for this place.'

'Indeed.' Her butler flicked a horrified gloved hand over each of his jacket sleeves. 'The original Halls of Justice, which included the city prison, was bizarrely designed to replicate an Egyptian mausoleum. Hence the unfortunate epithet, "The Tombs". It subsided into the unspeakable filth it was constructed upon some twenty years ago.'

She shook her head in wonder. 'When all this hideousness is over, please can I borrow you for a guided tour of New York? If only so I can admire just how much unnecessary information you manage to cram under your impeccable bowler hat.'

'Unnecessary, my lady? Tsk! It is history.'

'As Temples must believe he will be if he stays incarcerated in here much longer awaiting trial.'

'Let us hope, however, my lady, that Officer Balowski does not get wind of our actions this afternoon.'

They peered over their shoulders in unison.

She nodded. 'I know. It took us ages to shake him off after

he unnervingly appeared at the Belvedere Castle. Still, we had to drop Gladstone off at the apartment. I don't think Balowski believed me, though, when I said I hadn't learned anything from Mrs Vanderdale or Atticus.'

'Would that I could offer a contrary opinion, my lady.'

'So, I say we somehow have to exclude Balowski entirely from our investigations until we know for certain which side he is working for?'

He nodded emphatically. 'Agreed. Along with Mr Morales as we agreed previously.' His usual impassive expression fell grave.

She scanned his face in concern. 'Earl? I know. And we can't even talk to Mrs Morales in case she lets something slip.' She groaned. 'There's no way around it. We're getting more and more isolated.' The echo of officious boots finally returning from deep within the inner vaults made her lower her voice further. 'But don't fret if our plan here doesn't work. If feminine guile should fail...'

Clifford's lips pursed. 'Money will almost certainly prevail. Much to the further decimation of the household accounts.'

Seconds later, it was obvious the hard-bitten face scowling back at her through the smeared glass wouldn't be moved by feminine charms. Not even if she danced a fandango naked, purely for his singular enjoyment. The fact his nose had been broken at least once and poorly reset, strangely didn't imbue him with any extra sense of charity either. He rammed a slip of paper halfway underneath the hatch with a barked, 'Here's your bail notice, lady.'

'Oh marvellous, the judge agreed it. Thank you.' She winced as she read the amount. No wonder it had been granted without the need for any feminine charms! The sum listed sounded astronomical. She reached into her pocket but jumped as he rapped on the glass.

'You sure you wan'it, lady?'

'Er, yes. I'm certain.'

'Nah, see, that ain't no New York accent I ever heard.'

'That's because I'm from England.'

He wrenched the paper back out of her reach. 'Then you definitely ain't sure you wan'it. Lady, if you pay this, you gonna be responsible for that lowlife showing up to trial. And if he don't show, you don't get one bean of this back.'

From across the gloomy space, she caught Clifford's eye roll.

'I'm still sure, thank you.' She crossed both sets of fingers.

It seemed an age after she'd paid that they had to wait before the steel door before them opened.

'You!' The haggard face of Dellaney's chauffeur appeared. He twisted around as the door closed and banged on it. 'Let me back in!'

'Rather hasty, Mr Temples,' Clifford said.

The chauffeur turned and stared at Eleanor. 'Why would you—'

'I'll explain somewhere more private. Come on.'

Despite Clifford's chivvying, Temples dragged his feet all the way out of the Halls of Justice and into the street.

'You're making this more of a chore than it need be,' she said in confusion.

Clifford nodded. 'And a "thank you, Lady Swift," would not go amiss. Her ladyship has paid your' – he shuddered – 'not inconsiderable bail.'

'Thank you?' The chauffeur stared at Eleanor again. 'Do you just like actin' crazy or are you nuts for real?'

'Manners!' Clifford growled.

She stepped out onto the road but leaped back as a lorry swerved around a horse-drawn cart. Her eardrums winced as the driver blared the horn and shouted out the window. She felt the last of her patience evaporating. She turned to face the chauffeur.

'Look. What's your problem, Temples?'

He gawked at her. 'You seriously thought I'd be grateful you paid my bail-bond?' He gestured around. 'Now I'm out in the open, I've probably got a target painted on my back just for bein' seen with you two! I was safer in there!'

Clifford spun him to face the jail's entrance. 'Back we go then, Mr Temples.'

'To the gallows!' she added, and then remembered the offer Wyatt had told the two men to make to Temples at Belvedere Castle. 'And don't rely on the charges against you getting dropped either. That's not going to happen!' She fell into step beside Clifford as he frogmarched their unwilling charge forward. 'Hang on! Actually, I'm wrong, Temples. Clifford, you said something about it being death by electric...?'

'Chair, my lady. Yes, originally invented as a more humane method than hanging. Many executions by chair still fail, however, leaving the convicted man with horrifying—'

'Alright!' Temples cried. 'Alright. What do ya want from me?'

Eleanor held her hands up. 'I simply want you to walk and talk. Oh, but I wouldn't get any ideas about running.' Clifford flicked open his suit jacket to reveal his pistol. 'Which is it going to be?'

He eyed her sullenly. 'Like I got a choice. So, what's so important we got to talk about it, Lady Swift?'

'Marty Morales' murder. And Mr Dellaney's too.' She waved at the jittery chauffeur to keep walking. His eyes swung back and forth between her and Clifford.

'I... I didn't kill 'em. I swear. Not neither of 'em.' He buried his face in his hands. 'Who are you people? Really?'

'Really?' she said. 'Just two strangers to New York who don't believe murderers should get off scot-free.'

Clifford pulled out a silver case and offered a cigarette to Temples. 'Gitanes?'

The chauffeur scowled. 'No one smokes those things. Ain't you got nothin' normal, like Woodbines or Lucky Strikes?'

'Unfortunately, not.' He closed the case. 'Does Mrs Dellaney smoke foreign cigarettes?'

Temples shrugged. 'I ain't never seen her smoke.'

Clifford and Eleanor exchanged a glance.

It looks like that cigarette butt you found, Ellie, was a red herring after all. Mrs Vanderdale doesn't seem the type to smoke. And you've never seen Earl with a cigarette.

She fixed Temples with a firm look. 'Now, keep talking. Did you ever drive Mrs Dellaney over to see Mr Wyatt? Perhaps clandestinely?'

He shook his head. 'I know what you're thinkin'. Everybody knew Mrs Dellaney was fed up with Mr Dellaney foolin' around, so maybe she was doin' the same with Mr Wyatt? But I never drove her out to his place or anywhere else where they might have met.'

'Okay. So—'

He held up a finger. 'But she was messin' around with someone. I know 'cos she drove herself when Mr Dellaney weren't there. And she used to take the staff car and dress up like no one would recognise her.'

Her pulse quickened. 'Maybe with a hat and scarf?' She shared a look with Clifford.

'Sure, sometimes. And sometimes with a veil.'

'And you've no idea who she was seeing?'

He shrugged. 'Nope.'

'I see. Sticking with Mr Wyatt, why did he offer to arrange to have any charges against you dropped and a nice pay-off in exchange for keeping your mouth shut?' The chauffeur's mouth fell open. 'Don't bother to deny it! Now, come clean. Why was he paying you money in the first place?'

For a moment he hesitated, then groaned. 'Alright. He was

paying me for... for information. About... Mr Dellaney and...'
He shrugged. 'The kinds of stuff we just been talkin' about.'

The penny dropped. *Having ruined Dellaney's business life, Ellie, Atticus told you his next aim had been to destroy Dellaney's personal life.*

'You mean Wyatt had been paying you to pass on any dirt on Dellaney's private life? And let me guess, as Dellaney's now dead, the money he offered you was a final pay-off to keep quiet?'

The chauffeur's silence was all the confirmation she needed. 'Okay, let's move on to you and Mr Dellaney. Why did you steal from him?'

Temples jerked both his hands up. 'I wasn't stealin' off of Mr Dellaney, I swear it! I was set up. Why would I have done that?'

Clifford eyed him sharply. 'For the same mercenary reason you got Mr Morales fired. Because you wanted more. Including his job.'

'No, hold up, right there, Mr Clifford! Me and Marty had a spat, sure, 'cos he figured out I got him fired but I didn't got no choice.'

'Enlighten me as to why, then,' Eleanor said coldly.

Temples' eyes bulged. 'No can do, lady.'

'Oh dear, your playing ball hasn't lasted long. Now, you speak to me or it's back to jail and the elec—'

'Alright!' He flung his hands out. 'You win. I got pinned to the dirt in a back alley one day by two real mean fellas. They told me all I had to do was get Marty fired and everything else would be taken care of. I'd get his job, no questions asked.'

'Get him fired? How?'

'By squealin' to Mr Dellaney that Marty had been takin' "unauthorised bonuses", as in stealin' from him. They told me they'd already planted the "bonuses" in Marty's things in Mr

Dellaney's garage and in Marty's place where he lived with his brother and ma.'

The money under the floorboards, Ellie

'Then,' Temples continued, 'they rammed a fist of dollars in my face and told me to take the pay-off and do as I was told. Or else.'

'Or else what, Mr Temples?' Clifford said.

The chauffeur opened his mouth but then paused, glancing at Eleanor. He beckoned her butler closer and hissed in his ear. Clifford cleared his throat.

'Suffice to say, kneecaps and other more, ahem, vital parts of Mr Temples' anatomy, were threatened without recourse to mercy, my lady.'

'Mmm.' She see-sawed her head. 'So far, Temples, you've far from convinced me that the offer you say you were forced into didn't include killing Marty. Or Mr Dellaney.'

Temples sighed. 'Ain't you listenin', lady? No one said nothin' about killin' anyone. And I'd have been mad to try and kill someone as powerful as Mr Dellaney! You gotta believe me.'

'I'm trying,' she said.

'What I gotta do to make you see it's the truth, then?'

'Describe the two men who threatened your unmentionable body parts in the alleyway.'

As the chauffeur described them, she and Clifford nodded to each other.

'And the guy who did most of the talkin's got a scar, right from here to here.' Temples ran a line from his lip upwards.

She nodded. 'Yes. Nasty pieces of work. I took coffee with him and his companion, but they rather soured the already average roast.'

The chauffeur gasped. 'You *what*? You *are* nuts!'

'Probably. Now, Temples,' she said soothingly. 'We're nearly done. Last question. The two men who threatened you. Can you tell me anything more about them?'

'No, that's it. I ain't never seen 'em before they whacked me into the dirt.'

'Or after?'

Temples hesitated.

'Temples, I need the truth.'

She jerked around at the sound of screeching tyres.

'My lady!'

She dived into a doorway, landing on her stomach. She just had time to register Clifford shoving Temples down to the pavement before there was the sound of shooting, more tyre squeals, then another shot and shattering glass.

'Clifford!' she cried, scrambling up. 'Clifford!'

'Unharmed, my lady,' her butler's measured tone replied as he rose and dusted himself off. 'Unlike Temples, who has been hit.'

They both knelt beside the chauffeur, who was lying on one side, groaning, a stream of blood oozing from his lower thigh. Clifford motioned for her to turn away. She heard tearing trouser cloth. 'Flesh wound. Not as deep as it could have been.'

'Don't feel like it!' Temples wailed. 'It's burnin'.'

'We'll get you to medical attention as quickly as possible,' she said. We need a—'

'Policeman?' the gruff voice of Balowski interrupted. He stepped up from the road and glared at Clifford. 'And don't say a word, Suitsville. I came for one last crack at keepin' her safe.' He nodded in Eleanor's direction. 'On account of her cock and bull about goin' home to rest for the day stinkin' worse than the Lower East Side in July. But I gotta 'ave lost my mind, right, Lady Swift? 'Cos I thought we was workin' as a team and here you are springin' suspects from jail and takin' part in shoot-outs without so much as a nod in my direction?'

'Officer, I'm sorry. And I will explain, but not now because... look!' She pointed at Temples, who was swaying on one leg, leaning heavily on Clifford's shoulder. 'He needs to be treated urgently. And then taken back to jail. To the safest part possible.'

Balowski flagged down a taxi and manhandled a groaning Temples into the rear seat, before jumping in the front. Clifford leaned into the driver's window. 'The best hospital available in the vicinity. And charges to Lady Swift, if necessary.' He rapped the roof. They watched it shoot away.

'Are you alright, Clifford? Really?' She tried to read his expression.

'Aside from being greatly perturbed once more, yes, thank you, my lady.' He stared in the direction the taxi had gone.

'Balowski found us far too easily again, didn't he?'

He nodded. 'I was a little uneasy with him accompanying Mr Temples but could hardly have stopped him.'

'I'm sure it's perfectly safe with the taxi driver there.' She scrabbled for a positive. 'And anyway, maybe our suspicions are unfounded. Maybe he tracked us via information from other policemen. Other... good policemen.'

He arched a brow. 'Or through the two thugs who threatened you. And possibly just tried to kill you.'

'I think they were aiming for Temples.'

'Possibly. And next time?'

She grimaced. 'Things are going from bad to worse, Clifford. I feel we need to, somehow, go on the offensive!'

'Agreed, my lady. But' – he turned her respectfully by the shoulders with the tips of his gloved fingers – 'via the restorative of one of Mrs Trotman's finest home-cooked meals and a change of clothes first!'

30

The curtains of Mrs Melchum's apartment twitched as Eleanor and Clifford looked up.

'Earl's right,' she muttered as they trooped up the steps into the lobby. 'She really does need to get out more.'

'Speaking of Earl,' he whispered, gesturing around. 'The coast appears to be clear.'

'Phew! Let's scurry across to the lift then.'

He eyed her sideways. 'Scurry, my lady? If I might remind you again that I am a butler.'

'Yes, and I'm a lady of the manor, supposedly. But neither of us have a clue what to say to Earl about why we're avoiding him. Or his mother.'

As they reached the safety of the lift, Clifford opened and shut the door with only a slight scraping noise. On the seventh floor, she turned to Clifford as they stepped out. 'You know, I think you deserve a holiday after this supposed holiday! And I think I'll join you!'

'Lady Swift!'

She turned to see a vision of lilac taffeta glowering from Mrs

Melchum's doorway. 'Holidaying with your help! Outrageously improper. But why am I surprised?'

Catamina slunk out from underneath her mistress' voluminous skirts and twitched a haughty tail.

Catching Clifford's placating look, Eleanor slapped on her best smile. 'Actually, Mrs Melchum, holidays for my unwaveringly dedicated staff are something I delight in insisting on.'

The woman snorted in disapproval as she jerked around to march back inside her apartment. But whatever ailed her legs made her stumble. Shakily, she clung to the doorframe.

Eleanor winced in empathy. But before she could move to help, an overexcited bulldog appeared from across the hallway, dragging her young maid behind him. Catamina's ears flattened as she turned and hissed.

'Master Gladstone, stand down, sir!' Clifford called firmly, but instead the enraged bulldog surged forward, pulling his lead from Polly's grip.

'No, boy!' Eleanor cried.

She lunged for his collar, but missed as, hackles raised, Gladstone pursued the now spooked cat past her owner and into the apartment. Mrs Melchum shakily stuck out a foot to stop him, but her unsteady stance was no match for the bulldog's hurtling mass. As she fell, only Clifford's quick-thinking arms stopped her from hitting the floor.

'Mrs Melchum, please allow me to assist.'

Eleanor winced as her butler was slapped away. 'Unhand me, you... you—' The woman broke off into a debilitating coughing fit.

'Please take a seat and catch your breath,' Eleanor said as the old lady stumbled into her apartment and collapsed into an armchair.

'Pills,' Mrs Melchum wheezed. 'Beside my bed.' Eleanor dashed off in the direction her neighbour had flapped a faltering hand.

'Here,' she said softly a moment later, opening the mono-grammed china pill pot she'd found. Clifford appeared with a glass of water.

Lizzie darted in through the doorway. 'Polly mentioned as Mr Wilful had started a wee bit of bother... ach, what a mess!' the maid said in wide-eyed horror.

'Ah, Lizzie,' Clifford said calmly. 'I believe Master Gladstone might be retrieved from one of the other rooms.'

A minute later, an abashed bulldog was led from the apartment by a red-faced Lizzie, while Clifford finished setting the main room back to rights. He ended with a magician's touch, scooping up a scatter of calling cards strewn across the floor and seamlessly setting them in order on the mantelpiece.

Meanwhile, Eleanor offered calming words to Mrs Melchum on the antique settee. 'I'm so sorry. If Gladstone has broken anything, I'll have it repaired or replaced.' She looked around. 'You've a delightful apartment. It's... uniquely decorated.'

In truth, she was mesmerised by the sense of time long forgotten evoked by the antiquated furnishings and cloyingly dense patterned wallpaper. Not that much of the wallpaper was visible, however, for framed photographs were festooned everywhere. And in the centre of each, a beautiful creature frozen in time, surrounded by what was, Eleanor assumed by the expensive gowns and palatial surroundings, the cream of society of its day. They reminded her of the ones in Mrs Vanderdale's office, though hers were obviously more recent. And the photographs here, like the rest of the rooms, had the sad air of a long-stopped clock. It was almost as if they had been scattered around the walls in the hope someone would see them and restart the hands.

.   .   .

Back in her own apartment, Eleanor flopped into a kitchen chair which Clifford held out for her.

'So sorry Mr Wilful caused you trouble, m'lady,' said Mrs Butters.

Polly's bottom lip trembled as she stared at Clifford for permission to speak. Receiving his nod, she stammered, 'Oh, your ladyship, 'tis all my fault. I'm sorry, but you probably want to send me away on account...'

The rest of her words were lost in sobs. Clifford waved a pristine handkerchief at the maid.

'Waterworks not required, thank you, Polly. Her ladyship has made no mention of dismissing you, to my knowledge.'

'Really?' the young girl stuttered.

'Of course I wouldn't, Polly!' Eleanor patted the young girl's arm. 'It wasn't your fault Gladstone slipped his lead. Nor even Gladstone's really. Catamina has been taunting him since we arrived.'

'As readily as her owner has yourself, my lady,' Clifford said.

Mrs Trotman slid a delectable smelling fruit-filled pastry in front of Eleanor. 'Beg pardon for speaking out of turn, m'lady, but even if Master Gladstone hadn't chased her cat, that woman would still have a hive of bees in her bonnet about summat.'

Mrs Butters nodded. 'Anyways, there's no point telling off Mr Wilful at his age. Which he knows, I'm sure, seeing as how we all love him so much.'

All eyes turned to the bulldog, who stared back from his quilted bed as if butter wouldn't melt in his mouth. Mrs Trotman pointed at Eleanor's torn skirt.

'Gracious, m'lady, just look at the fine pickle Master Gladstone has made of your outdoor things.'

Eleanor flapped an airy hand in reply, not wanting to tell the ladies the truth about why she and her usually impeccably smart butler were looking rather dishevelled.

Clifford came to their rescue. 'Perhaps a collective cup of tea might be countenanced, my lady?'

'Oh absolutely!'

As the ladies busied themselves, Lizzie turned to Mrs Butters. 'Wasn't Mrs Morales ever so grateful earlier when we dropped by?'

The housekeeper nodded. 'She was, my girl. And she was brave enough to teach Trotters a thing or two about baking those little rice cake fellows and swapping to coconut milk.'

Mrs Trotman scoffed. 'Teach me? As if! It's called "sharing cooks' tips", I'll have you know.'

'How is Mrs Morales holding up, would you say?' Eleanor said.

Mrs Butters flapped her apron pocket. 'Up and down, in all honesty, m'lady. That's why we asked Mr Clifford if we could pop in and out regularly.' She looked awkward and bit her lip.

Eleanor frowned. 'What is it?'

The two women shared an uncomfortable look. Mrs Butters nudged Mrs Trotman. 'Speak up, Trotters, you said you would.'

But the cook shook her head.

Eleanor sighed. 'Whatever it is, I'd rather know, unless she asked you not to tell me.'

'No, m'lady, quite the reverse,' Mrs Trotman said. 'All she asked about the whole time was why... why you've been staying away?'

Eleanor leapt up. 'I'll be back presently.' As her butler opened his mouth, she held up her hand. 'And, yes, Clifford, I must before you respectfully suggest otherwise.'

But as she knocked on the faded blue door of the Morales' basement apartment, her doubts flooded in. She cupped Gladstone's chin as she whispered, 'What on earth can I give as an excuse, boy? Too busy sightseeing or attending cocktail parties to spare her fifteen minutes despite her terrible grief?'

His stumpy tail twitching hesitantly in reply only

convinced her she would probably make things worse. With a heavy heart, she waved him back towards the stairs. But as she turned, a husky voice called out.

'So, we still talkin' or not?'

31

At the sound of Mrs Morales' voice, Eleanor stepped back tentatively.

'I hope so.'

'Me too, honey.' Mrs Morales smiled. 'Now, you bring that beautiful face into my kitchen so I can see every inch of it properly.'

Eleanor waited for her hostess to turn her wheelchair in the tight space before following her into the diminutive room, Gladstone bounding in after them.

'Hello, Mr Wrinkles!' Mrs Morales said as the bulldog's top half landed in her lap. 'You're just like my Marty was. Always thinkin' the best is about to happen.'

Eleanor nodded. 'Marty did strike me as brimming with optimism.' She slid into the chair the other woman patted. 'I realise it must seem very quiet now. Unless, of course, Earl is equally exuberant at greeting the day?'

Mrs Morales shook her head slowly. 'If I hadn't carried the two of them into the world myself, I wouldn'a believed they was even brothers most days.'

Eleanor smiled wistfully as the voice she missed since she

was nine years old crept into her thoughts. She reminisced aloud. "'Remember, if the world wasn't filled with very different people, it would be awfully small in how it thought, darling girl.'"

'Your mama?' Mrs Morales said softly. 'She sounds like a beautiful and clever lady, too.' She smiled. 'But that weren't the end of that cricket of wisdom, was it?'

Eleanor shook her head, her cheeks colouring. 'No. It ended with, "So never be upset if someone just doesn't like you. Different does that sometimes."'

'Like Earl and Marty, you're thinkin'?' Mrs Morales wheeled herself backwards a foot and reached for a tin which sported a faded picture of rocky outcrops in an endless ocean on the lid. She opened it. 'Go ahead.'

Eleanor savoured the first mouthful. 'Oh my, that is delicious. Custardy, buttery, moreishly nutty and with a cheesy topping too. It's divine.'

'Cassava cake, in American speak. And kinda our Filipino version of your fancy English tea treat where I grew up.'

'Would it be awfully cheeky to ask you to share your recipe with Mrs Trotman?'

Mrs Morales clapped her hands. 'I spelled it out to her right this very afternoon. Along with a couple of others.'

'All of which she insisted on another, better, way of making, let me guess?'

The older woman laughed. 'Just as it should be. She's proud of her skills. And as fiery as the enormous range I bet you got in your castle's kitchen back in England.'

Eleanor laughed. 'Between you and me, I think whenever Clifford dares to "offer a contrary opinion" to Mrs Trotman about her cooking, he carries a miniature fire extinguisher about his suit's tails, just in case.'

Mrs Morales chuckled wheezily as she waved the tin again. Eleanor took another without needing to be asked twice. The older woman scrutinised her face. 'So, if we're really still talkin', why don't you go ahead and ask me now, child? You've had two pieces of cake. Whenever either of my boys had somethin' difficult to say, it would sweeten up their nerves enough to cough it out to their mama. So, has it worked for you, too?'

Eleanor nodded. 'It has. I want to wholeheartedly apologise for not coming to see you for a while—'

'For avoidin' me. Say what you mean.'

'Yes, that. But please don't ask me why.'

Mrs Morales slowly put down her cake. 'I don't gotta ask. I know why. You think that even though Earl and Marty fought like Mr Wilful and Mrs Grumpy's fancy cat, Earl might still a' upped and killed that Mr Dellaney in revenge for his brother's death.'

Eleanor groaned. 'Maybe. I'm so sorry. But it's not the only reason. I've also avoided you because I'm worried. Worried that the situation has got rather... darker than I imagined at the outset. I don't want you to be in danger because someone knows we've been talking.'

Mrs Morales shook her head slowly. 'Thank you. But, girl, you gotta learn how to lie better! You're really worried 'cos you think you're gonna find evidence that proves my Earl killed Mr Dellaney!'

Back in her apartment, Eleanor avoided her butler's questioning gaze. 'Dash it! What a terrible day! Has anything good come of it?'

'Very possibly.' He pulled a card from his jacket pocket and held it out to her.

She read it and shrugged. '"F. Newkirk. Private Detective". You've already shown me this. I know we need to go and see him, but we've hardly had time—'

'No, my lady. This is Mr Newkirk's calling card, yes. But it is not the one I picked from his pocket.'

Her brow furrowed. 'Then where?'

'I found it among the cards I collected from Mrs Melchum's floor after Master Gladstone had run riot.'

Her eyes widened. 'I remember seeing you pick them up.' She frowned. 'But why would she need a private detective? And it's rather an odd coincidence it's the same one.'

'I do not believe it is a coincidence, my lady.'

'Oh gracious!' She slapped her forehead. 'She's hired him to tail us. That's why he was in the diner!'

'That is my conclusion also.'

'But why on earth would she do that?'

'I am at a loss to present even a vaguely tangible suggestion. However, I fear—'

'There's only one way to find out. We'll pay him a visit today.'

He nodded. 'But first, that fine home-cooked meal of Mrs Trotman to offset the offal we have been forced to endure in this city's eating establishments?'

She nodded eagerly. 'Absolutely. And no arguing, we'll all eat together in the kitchen.'

At the table, her cook held a large tray, with her housekeeper standing beside her holding a smaller one.

'I thought as you'd like a special treat, m'lady, seein' as we're in New York, though I still can't believe it for the likes of us aprons and overalls. Especially as Mr Clifford said you'd insisted he break the rules and nibble at least a little something with us.'

She sniffed the air. 'And it smells wonderful. What New York delicacies have you conjured up, ladies?'

Mrs Trotman gave a reasonable impression of a drum roll which made Eleanor laugh. Even her butler failed to hide his amusement.

'The very finest this city's gour... gourmands demand, m'lady,' Mrs Trotman said proudly.

'Ahem.' Clifford waggled a finger. 'I believe you mean "connoisseur". A "gourmand" is one who eats excessively.' He caught Eleanor's eye. 'Mind you...'

'Ignore my scallywag butler, ladies, and please unveil your creations.'

'Tadah!' Mrs Trotman and Mrs Butters whipped the lids off the silver salvers. 'They call these "hot dogs" which had us all giggling,' Mrs Trotman said, pointing to the first salver. 'And these are "hamburgers", but there's no ham in 'em. And these little fellows are "Johnny cakes"!'

'Perfect!' Eleanor tried hard to hide a smile as her butler pinched the bridge of his nose in horror. 'It's just what Clifford was hoping for!'

32

Behind the narrow desk, a battered black typewriter was fighting with an overgrown potted fern for space. The navy-suited secretary sitting at it gestured at the door behind her. On the frosted glass was written *F. Newkirk. Private Detective.*

'He'll see you now.'

'Thank you.'

Eleanor walked into the back office with Clifford close behind. The room was small and basic. Two windows with wooden venetian blinds let in an equal amount of light and noise. Three framed certificates, an ugly metal bureau, two simple chairs and a baize-topped desk with a single brass lamp were the only other furnishings. Behind the desk sat the man who had warned them in the diner.

'Mr F. Newkirk, I presume?' Eleanor said, not waiting to be asked to sit.

'How'd you find me?' She recognised his nasal drawl from their last meeting.

'I didn't find you. My butler, Clifford, here did. How, I don't intend to elaborate. And I should probably let you know that my patience—'

'Has yet to be identified as ever existing,' Clifford said to the detective.

'Yes. That.'

A smile played around Newkirk's lips. 'No one's ever tracked me down before. I'm the one supposed to do the trackin'. So, I'll humour you. What'd you want to know?'

Eleanor leaned forward. 'First of all, I shan't ask who your client is because I already know.' At his startled look, she held up her hand. 'And I can't imagine they will be at all happy with you helping me.'

He looked back at her blankly. 'You lost me. Can't see why you think my client would care about that? Because they wouldn't.'

It was Eleanor's turn to look surprised. 'Really? Well, that's a relief. Now, what I do want to know is why you *really* warned me in the diner?'

Newkirk leaned back in his chair and steepled his fingers. 'Bottom line is, I was impressed with how you handled yourself with those two apes who pinned you into the booth as I said. And you too.' He nodded to Clifford. 'And also, because you're the greenest greenhorns to ever land in New York. Although, as you tracked me down and seem to know a few other details, maybe you're not as green as I took you for? You're certainly the boldest. Which is real bad. On account of you not knowin' the rules, that is.'

She sat back. 'Then, please enlighten me. What are the rules in New York?'

'There ain't any,' he said slowly. 'That's the only rule.'

She waved a disbelieving hand. 'Come come, now, this isn't actually the Wild West like the silver screen films portray.'

He laughed mirthlessly. 'No. It's way more lawless than that.'

A cold frisson travelled down her spine. 'I'm listening.'

'Right, then. See, in the good old days no one ran New York.

Sure, there were bad guys, but they were just lone schmucks who thought the law never applied to them. Then, some started gettin' smart and gettin' together in small gangs. And then bigger ones.'

She frowned. 'But that's not unique to New York. Even London has organised gangs.'

'Sure. But what it hasn't got is the one thing that makes even the average law-abidin' Joe born under a halo think the law is an ass.'

'Prohibition?'

'Exactly, Lady Swift. The best way to increase the demand, and price, for somethin' is to make it illegal. The crime bosses leaped on the bandwagon right at the pistol crack of prohibition comin' in. Soon enough, they were makin' so much money they needed accountants to keep track of it, banks to keep it in and lawyers to keep them out of jail.' Mr Newkirk tapped his desktop. 'And that's when the line between crooked and straight got less discernible than the Brooklyn Bridge on a foggy day. Anyone can be crooked now. Or straight.' He shrugged. 'And a lot of 'em are both.' He leaned forward. 'There are no lines between good and bad, moral and immoral, in this city any more. No black and white. Just an endless, murky grey.'

'Not quite, Mr Newkirk,' she said firmly. 'There is a line, even if it's an invisible one. And I, and my butler here, and...' She hesitated. *Who, Ellie? Balowski? Earl?* She shook her head. 'And plenty of other good people are firmly on one side. The side of law and justice.'

Newkirk leaned back in his chair again and applauded slowly. 'A nice speech, Lady Swift. But in my experience, law and justice haven't got that much in common.'

She sighed. *In your experience, too, maybe, Ellie.* She looked at the man across the desk from her. Was he one of the good guys? Or one of the bad? Or one of the grey brigade? She stared into his eyes, trying to gauge how honest he was.

He laughed, tapping his left cheek. 'Try the green one. Experts say green eyes are seen as more trustworthy than blue. Which is probably why you get along so well as yours are like emeralds in a china cat.' He shrugged. 'And, anyway, maybe I *am* one of the few real good guys.'

A knock on the door interrupted them. The secretary popped her head around and pointed to the clock.

'Next appointment'll be here in one minute, Mr Newkirk.'

'Thank you.' He rose. 'Looks like our time is up.'

She shook his hand while holding his gaze. 'Mr Newkirk. If you really are one of the good guys, help me bring a killer to justice.'

He pulled his hand away and glanced down at his desk, his brow furrowed. Glancing back up, he waved at his hovering secretary. 'That will be all.'

As she left the room, he turned back to Eleanor.

'Take heed of what I said, Lady Swift. I'd hate for tomorrow's papers to carry your obituary.'

She pursed her lips. 'The person I watched die had no obituary written about him in the society papers. Only in the hearts of his grieving family.'

For a moment she thought he hadn't heard her. Then he muttered, 'Eat the Moon,' to her retreating back.

She paused with her hand on the doorknob. Turning around, she shared a confused glance with her butler.

'I'm sorry, Mr Newkirk. Umm, is that an expletive?'

He let out a deep breath. 'No. It's the name of a speakeasy. But it's no place for any kinda lady.'

Her brow knitted. 'Then why mention it?'

'Because it's where you can find those two thugs from the diner. And' – he shook his head – 'if you live long enough, possibly some answers.'

In the street, Eleanor looked back up at the tall building, trying to pick out the private detective's windows.

'So, Clifford. Did Mrs Melchum hire Newkirk to keep track of me? Or of the two rogues from the diner?'

'An interesting question, my lady. Do you recall if Mr Newkirk was already in the diner when you were forced inside?'

'Dash it, no. I was rather caught up in wondering what I could grab to wallop both those brutes in the unmentionables with.'

Her butler flinched. 'Far from cricket, but an act eminently justified on that occasion had you succeeded. Unfortunately, however, as you are not sure if the gentleman was already present in the diner or not, it seems that question must go unanswered for the moment.'

She nodded. 'You're right. Come on, let's get home.'

Less than an hour after returning to the apartment, Eleanor was pacing the drawing room like a caged tiger, stumbling over Gladstone, who lumbered back and forth with her. Clifford intervened by setting down a small bowl of the bulldog's favourite liver treats in a corner.

'Thank you,' she said distractedly. 'But I really didn't commit that many faux pas at the formal events I've been to so far, I'm sure.'

'If you say so, my lady.'

'I do. And I didn't!' she said indignantly. 'Well, not serious ones. And yet suddenly I'm being given a universally cold shoulder. Talk about being the reluctant darling of New York society one minute and then her greatest outcast the next! Not one of society's elite on any of those telephone calls would give me the time of day. And they all retracted their invitations in a tone that suggested I should go jump in the Hudson River instead. It's really odd.'

'Or perhaps not, my lady,' Clifford said gravely.

'Oh, no,' she groaned. 'This doesn't sound good.'

He pulled an envelope from his jacket pocket and handed it to her.

Ripping out the letter from inside, she ignored the second sheet, which drifted to the floor.

'Oh! It's an eviction notice.'

'With immediate effect, my lady. Master Gladstone, drop!'

'It's probably just a slipper he's got. Focus, Clifford.'

Having wrestled with the bulldog, he stood up. 'Actually, my lady, it is in fact a now soggy treasury note repaying the advance rent you had paid.'

She threw her hands up. 'Well, that makes it official, then. Do you think that's why all those invitations were retracted so emphatically? Because I've been thrown out of here?'

He stroked his chin. 'Actually, no. I believe that the retractions, and the eviction, have been engineered to coincide as a double blow.'

'Because someone wants us to stop investigating? Someone who yields enough power, or fear, to have high society turn their back on us?' She collapsed into a chair. 'Oh, Clifford, I'm so sorry. For you and the ladies. Now, we all need to up sticks in a heartbeat and we've been so happy here.'

'Hardly the greatest hardship, my lady, but thank you. I shall inform the ladies and then arrange alternative accommodation as expeditiously as possible.'

Mrs Butters flustered in.

'Oh, your ladyship, beg pardon for interrupting. Only Earl is here, and he's in a fearful way.'

'Drunk?' Clifford queried, already striding out of the door.

'No. Just agitated like.'

Too intrigued to wait for her butler to report back, Eleanor hurried out after him. In the hallway, Earl stood facing the wall, striking the toe of his boot against the wainscoting.

'Mr Morales?' Clifford said. 'Something the matter?'

'Yeah. I got a message for Lady Sw— Oh you're here.' He rubbed his hands over his face.

'Earl, whatever is it? Your mother isn't—'

'No, she ain't sick. She sent me up to say she's sorry she won't be seein' you no more.'

Eleanor glanced at Clifford, but his uncharacteristically furrowed brow only fuelled her own worry. 'Because she's angry with me?'

'No. 'Cos we gotta leave the buildin'. No more maintenance job. No more apartment!'

'Leave when?' Eleanor breathed with a sinking feeling.

'Now! Door gets hammered on, letter gets shoved at my ma, and we're history!'

'Oh, Earl. Let me come down and reassure her I can help—'

'NO!'

She jumped back in surprise.

'We don't need no help. Certainly not from you. You've interfered enough. Our kind do things our way.'

'Understandably, Mr Morales,' Clifford said calmly, only Eleanor detecting the sadness in his tone. 'Out of concern for your mother's reduced mobility, however, will you be able to secure somewhere suitable?'

'Like that's any of your problem.'

The door closed loudly behind him.

Eleanor's heart clenched. 'Clifford, this is too terrible for words. And likely all my fault. We have to find a way to help.'

'And we shall, my lady. Rest assured,' he said gently.

The jangle of the telephone shot through her frayed nerves like an electric shock. Clifford picked up the receiver. 'Ah! Perhaps this is not the best time, Officer Balowski.'

She gestured for him to hand it over. 'Maybe he's got good news,' she hissed. 'We could do with some.' She prised Clifford's unwilling fingers off the handset and held it to her ear. 'Officer, how are you? I—'

'I said keep the investigation quiet, Lady Swift! QUIET! Even you gotta understand English that plain!'

She held the handset further from her ear. 'I did keep it quiet. I don't—'

'Oh yeah? Then why last time I found ya, Suitsville was shootin' the back window of a speedin' car out? And the guy about to stand trial for two murders was not only outta jail without me knowin', but also had a bullet hole in his leg?'

'Yes, yes. I admit and apologise. That wasn't so quiet of me. Is that why you're ringing, though? To rant at me?'

'No, Lady Swift. I got news.'

'Alright, fire away.'

'That supposed to be a joke? 'Cos it ain't funny when I just got called into the captain's office and fired. FIRED, YOU HEAR ME!'

The line went dead.

33

Eleanor stopped staring at her bare ring finger. 'Clifford, please stop fussing about our new apartment. It was only your ingenuity that secured us another so quickly. It's perfectly fine.'

He sniffed. 'For a builder and his family as your neighbour on this floor is, yes. But for a titled lady, it is far from fine.'

She shrugged. 'What's so special about me that I can't spend a few weeks living as they do?' She pointed to her bulldog, snoring contentedly on the small settee, his portly tummy rising and falling. 'Gladstone loves it. We survived the heat last night despite the lack of ventilation. We've space enough, albeit less than we had. The fittings might be a little simple, but they're clean and comfortable. And besides, whoever ensured we were evicted also appears to have made certain the owners of other apartment buildings you deem suitable all refuse to rent me one.'

'Indeed. However, if you would be gracious enough to consider this merely an interim measure, I am sure I can find—'

She held up her hand. 'What's really bothering you about this, Clifford? Is it Uncle Byron?'

He sighed. 'His lordship, your late uncle, wanted only the

best for his favourite niece and I vowed to make sure his wish was carried out. Most particularly after he confessed—'

'To feeling he failed to show me enough love and affection when my parents disappeared and he became my guardian? Well, he was wrong. He never failed in that or anything else. And neither have you.' She smiled fondly at him. 'And as you know perfectly well, I'm his *only* niece.'

Mrs Butters and Mrs Trotman appeared in the doorway, each with a small but loaded tray, one bearing coffee and the other a selection of delectable-smelling pastries.

Her cook smiled apologetically. 'M'lady, 'tis plainer china than you're used to, but the little range has taken to my recipes for your favourite savoury turnovers like a duck to water. And the grocer just along the way there has all sorts I can make into new dishes you'll love. Butters has worked her magic, too.'

Eleanor's housekeeper nodded. 'I've fixed up your bedchamber and bathroom with a few extra cosy touches as I managed to rustle up on a sewing machine I borrowed from them as next door. Lovely family, they are. And I'll work on round the apartment, brightening it up. It'll feel like home in no time, m'lady. Lizzie and Polly have some lovely ideas too.'

Clifford clapped approvingly. 'Well done, ladies. Commendations all around for your creativity and adaptability.'

'And I can't thank you enough, too. You're all wonderful,' Eleanor said. 'Truly.' Her features clouded over. Clifford arched a brow, clearly having read her thoughts.

'Ladies, have you heard how Earl and Mrs Morales have fared?'

'Yes, Mr Clifford,' Mrs Butters said. 'Young Polly and Lizzie told me only an hour or so ago.'

Eleanor's eyes lit up. 'Oh, please send them in.'

Before her two maids had even finished curtseying, she beckoned them closer. 'How did you hear first of all?'

Mrs Trotman nudged the hesitant young maid forward. 'Speak up, my girl.'

Polly swallowed hard. 'Lizzie and me were coming back from buying the cream and eggs and thought the gentleman chasing us along the pavement was up to no good, so we started running. Only he just went faster and started yelling too.'

Eleanor glanced at Clifford in horror. 'Gracious! It's not that sort of neighbourhood, is it?'

Lizzie grinned. 'Ach, no, m'lady.'

Polly stared up at the ceiling thoughtfully. 'He said his name was something funny like... like "Rover Dover".'

Lizzie giggled. '"Iver Driver", m'lady. Anyway, he said Mr Earl and his ma are staying with a friend and are not so bad off, given everything. But he dunnae know the address.'

Polly clapped her hands. 'But he'll chase us again when he's got it.'

Clifford shook his head, but Eleanor could tell he was as relieved as she was at the news.

At least they've a roof over their heads, Ellie. However temporarily.

As they trooped out, Mrs Butters paused in collecting Eleanor's empty coffee cup.

'Oh my stars, m'lady!' She laid a motherly hand on hers. 'Your beautiful engagement ring. 'Tis missing!'

'I know,' Eleanor groaned. 'It must have slipped off my finger last night when we were leaving the other apartment in such a hurry. I'll get it back, no question.'

Alone with Clifford, she shrugged. 'I was going to tell you.'

He arched a brow. 'Unnecessary as I was already aware that you had misplaced your engagement ring in the enforced move from your former residence, my lady. Why otherwise would you have been raking through the empty suitcases and trunks at four this morning?'

'Dash it, Clifford! Am I ever going to get away with anything?'

His eyes twinkled. 'It seems unlikely. However, I believe we can gain entrance to your original apartment in the morning. If you can muster sufficient patience?'

'Thank you. And, yes, I can.' She breathed a sigh of relief. 'We'll find it first thing tomorrow and Hugh need never know.'

Waiting until ten that evening to take their next step in the investigation almost finished Eleanor off. She sprang out of the modest front door of her new, red-brick apartment building and scooted down the steps. At the bottom, she looked up and down the street.

'I don't suppose Iver's around?'

'If you will forgive the suggestion, my lady,' Clifford said, scrutinising several passing taxis before hailing one. 'It might not be wise to engage Iver's services any longer, given the, ahem, problems that have plagued those who have associated with us.'

'You mean because he'll end up homeless and jobless, too? If not worse?' She groaned. 'You're right. I feel like the world's worst bad luck charm!'

The taxi pulled up. The driver seemed at first confused, and then downright reluctant to take them to the address Clifford gave.

'You're sure?' He nodded at Eleanor. 'Ain't the best area to escort a lady, pal. Just sayin' 'cos you seem from outta town.'

'Very astute of you,' Clifford said drily. 'But the lady will be fine.'

The driver shrugged. 'Okay. It's your funeral. But I ain't waitin'.'

As she climbed into the taxi, she grimaced. *Let's hope it's not your funeral, Ellie!*

Her trepidation increased as they sat in the back in the

stifling heat, stuck in street after street of congested cars, buses and, soon, mostly horse- and hand-drawn vehicles.

The driver half-turned to them. 'This is Harlem. So windows up! Doors locked!'

She gasped. 'But we're baking already!'

'Windows up or you get out!'

They reluctantly wound the windows up as they passed along streets lined with squalid tenement blocks similar to those where Dellaney had been killed. Only here, the pavements resembled the overflow from some dreadful refugee camp or plague hospital. They were crowded with people of every age and gender, all undernourished and under-clothed, many lying on what looked like torn bed sheets. She leaned forward to catch the driver's attention.

'Goodness! Have these people no homes to go to?'

'Sure they do. Of sorts. But in this heatwave, they know if they don't turn out onto the sidewalk and sleep there till it cools down, it'll be Hart Island for them.'

'Hart Island?'

'It is a mass burial ground for the poor, my lady.'

'Oh my!'

The driver nodded. 'Last heatwave took over a hundred of this lot in the first day.' The taxi screeched to a halt. 'Here you are. If you're sure?'

Clifford assured the driver they were, paid the fare, and he and Eleanor climbed out. He pointed across the road to a set of steps under a railroad arch.

'Are you sure about this, my lady? We can still—' The sound of the taxi speeding away interrupted him.

She shook her head. 'We're committed now. Or maybe we should be, I'm not sure. But let's go before common sense and self-preservation have the chance to persuade us otherwise.'

Crossing over, they hurried down the rough brick steps to a

door guarded by what Eleanor could only describe as a gorilla in a black suit two sizes too small.

Inside, she gasped for air, her eyes stinging from the blue pall of smoke, her nose wrinkling at the overpowering smell of strong liquor. She blinked in the gloom, only a few low-hanging lights offering any illumination in the underground room. At the long wooden bar, a throng of men were vying for the attention of a row of vividly made-up women perched on stools. Beyond them were high-sided booths set in each corner, the backrests of which were angled to shield whoever might be seated inside. It was only then she tuned in to the fact many of the drinkers were dressed surprisingly well and obviously monied.

'It's quite the party atmosphere, isn't it?' she said.

Clifford sniffed. 'If one craves illegal merrymaking in a bunker.'

'Well, we both need to look like we do enjoy partying illegally, otherwise we're going to stand out.'

'Like we don't already,' he muttered.

At the bar, Clifford ordered.

'Two what?' The white-jacketed bartender stared at him in disbelief. 'You want drinks without any hooch, pal?' Clifford placed a banknote on the counter. Without another word, the bartender took the money and slid two short tumblers at them.

'Look, Clifford!' she whispered. 'The two men we're looking for just slunk up from the far end of the bar. What do you think they were doing?'

'I really couldn't say, my lady. Perhaps they were checking the trapdoor or the sand below in the cellar? In the event of a police raid, which I would hazard is a rare occurrence in an area like this, the gentleman on the door—'

'The one built like a gorilla?'

'That is the gentleman to whom I refer. He would most likely press a hidden button, which would illuminate a warning lamp down here behind the bar. The barman would then press another button, or lever, which would release the floor below the barrels and bottles, sending them to an unbroken landing on the sand in the cellar where they would be hidden until the raid was over.'

'Ingenious.' She looked over to the table where the scar-faced man and his companion were now talking to a man with a swarthy complexion and slicked back hair. The man was surrounded by glamorous women and flanked by even bigger thugs than the two talking to him.

'He looks like the boss.' She rolled her shoulders back. 'Let's go introduce ourselves.'

And hope he doesn't do a nice line in concrete boots, Ellie!

34

'Well, well.' The man they assumed was the boss of the two ruffians who'd abducted Eleanor to the diner cracked his gold ring-covered knuckles. 'Now, why would a dame like you want to sit at my table?'

Eleanor shrugged. 'Oh, just to save your associates from having to trail me around New York.'

'Ah, so thoughtful,' he said sarcastically. 'Search 'em, boys.'

Once she and Clifford were patted down by the man's muscle, Eleanor smoothed out her dress and smiled. 'No concealed weapons, you see. Nothing more dangerous on either of us than a burning set of questions.'

The man grinned. 'Is that so? Well, ain't nobody ever gonna sit at my table without me getting them a drink. And since this is the finest establishment in all of New York, what moon juice'll it be?'

She waved at her half-finished glass. 'In that case, anything non-alcoholic, please.'

The man laughed but clicked his fingers at one of the hovering help. 'Okay. Bootsie, see to it.' As he left, their host gestured around the room. 'You're takin' one heck of a risk comin' here, ya know, Lady Swift?'

'Oh, I don't think so,' she said, far more confidently than she felt. 'I imagine it was your men who shot at Dellaney's chauffeur?' At his silence, she continued. 'I'll take that as a yes. But what I really want to know, is why they didn't shoot at me or Clifford?'

'Do you?' He seemed to think for a moment. 'Okay. It wasn't my brief to wing, or kill, you, so my boys aimed only for the mark. The chauffeur. But you' – he pointed a menacing finger at Clifford – 'you I should charge for a back window, seein' as it's now layin' all over the sidewalk.'

'Would you have preferred I swept it up and returned it to you?' Clifford said impassively. 'And I believe I should charge you for a bullet in return.'

'Wise guy, huh?'

He looked down as Eleanor slid a handful of coins across the table. 'That's for the window.' She added a bundle of banknotes. 'And that's for you telling me who paid you to have Dellaney's chauffeur shot.'

The man pocketed the coins, then sat back and shook his head at the notes. 'Lady, there ain't enough money in the Bank of England for me to tell you that. But I will tell you somethin' for nothin'. You're either dumber than a punch-drunk boxer or you got guts.' He scrutinised her face. 'And I think it's guts. So I'll cut you some slack. Here's your one and only piece of advice. Stop meddlin' or get out of town. Preferably both.'

'Oh, but I've hardly seen anything of New York yet!'

'You know, lady, seein' as you landed as an out-of-towner and a bit of a celebrity, we played nice, but now our patience is wearin' thinner than the kinda sheer underw—'

Her butler's overloud cough drowned out the man's words.

'It's alright. Let it pass,' she said to Clifford with a placating look. She turned back to their host. 'So tell me, what is it exactly I've done to test your patience?'

'Not mine, lady.' His eyes flicked to the right-hand corner booth and back to his drink. 'Not mine.'

Her eyes followed his. She couldn't see the occupant, but several tough-looking men stood close by, taking instructions, she guessed from their attentive faces. As they left, the man she'd seen talking to customers and behind the bar approached the booth. *Obviously the manager, Ellie.* Again, the man's deferential manner made Eleanor sure whoever was sitting in that booth owned the speakeasy, the manager, and the tough-looking men.

She rose and scooped up her glass. 'Then I shall go before I do. Thank you for the drinks.'

As they left, Clifford gathered up the banknotes on the table. 'To help repair some of the damage done to the household accounts of late. I'm sure you understand.'

Whether or not the man did, he waved for Clifford to take the money.

At the other end of the room, someone rose from the booth she was heading for. At the same time a mountain of a man stood up, blocking Eleanor's view.

Is that Mrs Dellaney's chauffeur-cum-bodyguard, Ellie?

In the dim, smoky light it was hard to tell and before she could get close enough to be sure, both of them had disappeared through an archway out back and two smart, burly men in suits were blocking her path.

Clifford quickly stepped up next to her. She smiled sweetly.

'Good evening, gentlemen. I was just hoping for a quick word with whoever is sitting—'

'Let the lady and her gentleman friend pass,' a relaxed Texan drawl commanded.

'Why, Atticus, what a pleasant surprise!'

He stood and gave her a gentlemanly bow. 'Welcome, Lady Swift. And it's Mr Clifford, I believe? Please, come join me both, won't you?'

She stared through the archway. 'I'm sorry if my arrival scared away your companion?'

Atticus shook his head. 'They were just leaving anyway.'

It was obvious he wasn't going to be drawn on who it was, so she settled into the seat he indicated, trying not to frown. It had definitely been a woman standing up. Mrs Dellaney? Maybe even Mrs Vanderdale?

Clifford remained standing, his eyes on the two burly men who, at a nod from Wyatt, sat back down.

She adjusted her dress. 'Forgive me, Atticus, but as a self-professed teetotaller, isn't this an odd place for you to be?'

He laughed easily. 'I'd have thought the same about you, Eleanor?' She raised her drink. He nodded. 'Ah! Non-alcoholic, I see.'

She held his gaze. 'I rather thought it would be sensible to keep my wits about me.'

'As well as your help.' He glanced at Clifford who was still keeping watch on where the two men had sat back down. 'Or is he your bodyguard tonight?' Before she could reply, his voice became colder. 'And very wise for you to have one too.'

Her smile faded. 'Why, Atticus?'

'Because it's reached my ears that you've been upsetting a lot of people.' He held his hands up. 'Not me, of course.'

She laughed. 'You don't seem the easily upset type. But New York has taught me that appearances can be very deceptive. Like yourself, investing in theatres. And now speakeasies too, is it?'

'No. Because, heck, that would be illegal.'

'As is being here at all, surely?'

Wyatt shrugged. 'So, as I asked before, what brings *you* here then, Lady Swift?'

'Just one thing. I don't like being shot at.'

Anger flashed across his face. He glared in the direction of the table she had come from. 'No one should have shot at you!'

So, he has got something to do with the man you just spoke to, Ellie.

His next words however, made her less sure.

'What I mean is, no one should shoot at *any* lady.' His genial smile was back in place.

'Quite!' Clifford growled.

'Atticus,' Eleanor said, 'why would those two men over there' – she pointed discreetly across the room – 'the one with the scar and the one next to him, have got Dellaney's original chauffeur, Marty Morales, sacked? And then tried to kill Temples, his replacement?'

He took a sip of his drink. 'You'd have to ask them. Or their boss.' He shook his head. 'Who isn't me.'

He's too in control, Ellie. Change tack.

'Why did you back the play *Why Marry?* and have it produced?'

His brow furrowed. 'An odd question. Because Ogden wanted it, so I outbid him. And I told you why before. But having bought the rights, I fancied actually putting it on to throw some more salt in his eyes. And make some money as a bonus. Apparently, it's doing okay.' He looked at her quizzically. 'Why the sudden interest?'

'What's the play like?'

He shrugged. 'I have no idea, having never read or seen it. I'm not much of a theatregoer myself.'

She stiffened. 'Really? Well, I appreciate you talking to me.' She tried to see through his still easy smile as she rose. 'As the rest of your high society circle have cut me dead.'

'An unlucky expression, Lady Swift.' He held out his hand. 'Let's hope New York herself is feeling benevolent soon enough.'

'I can't see that will help, actually, since it wasn't her who evicted me from my apartment, was it?'

He held her gaze. 'You'd have to go ask her, Lady Swift.'

'One last question before I leave.' He nodded. 'Were you having an affair with Mrs Dellaney as part of your revenge?'

A flicker of annoyance showed in his eyes, but then faded. 'Well, you've certainly learned to say what's on your mind. What happened to that good old English politeness?'

She shrugged. 'I don't know. I guess New York is rubbing off on me!'

In the taxi, she lowered her voice. 'Clifford, our main problem so far with Wyatt as a suspect is we couldn't work out his link to Marty, or his murder.'

Clifford arched a brow. 'Indeed not, but I feel you may now have an answer?'

She nodded. 'When Wyatt told me he had no interest in theatres and plays, I wondered if the reason he gave for buying them is genuine? I wonder if, in fact, he's really using them, including the Lyceum and *Why Marry?*, to launder his money from illegal speakeasies like the one we've just found him in?'

'Excellent thought, my lady. And if he was doing so in conjunction with Mr Dellaney before he found out about his wife's affair with the gentleman and subsequently tried to ruin him, then they may have involved Mr Morales.'

'Marty?'

'Indeed. And as we conjectured earlier, perhaps he refused to play ball and Mr Wyatt eliminated him? And then did the same with Mr Dellaney, either because he *was* having an affair with his wife—'

'Or because he wanted all the profit for himself? Or both? Either way, just like when we suspected Dellaney, we can't go to the police. So what do we do?'

He shook his head gravely. 'What indeed, my lady? Against a man so seemingly powerful, I fear whatever we decide to do' – he sighed deeply – 'will end badly. Very badly!'

35

'We can't just march in the front door, Clifford,' she hissed as they looked across at her original apartment building. 'Right, round the back and you can give me a leg-up through one of the storeroom windows in the basement.'

He gave her a withering look. 'Please forgive my respectful, but categorical, dissent to such an act, my lady. Manhandling my mistress in a rear alleyway of New York to aid and abet her in breaking and entering is not on my agenda for today. Nor any other.'

She sighed, but dutifully followed his lead and waited on the top step while he rang the concierge bell.

A young man Eleanor didn't recognise, in Marty's old doorman's uniform, hurried out from the tiny office.

'Good morning,' Clifford said smoothly. 'Mrs Melchum's visitors, thank you.'

The young man looked down at a sheet of paper. 'Is Mrs Melchum expectin' you?'

'Yes, of course.'

'Ah! Then she is—'

'Thank you, but we know where the lady resides.'

As they walked past, she turned to the young concierge. 'Have her new neighbours moved in yet?'

He checked his sheet again. 'No, ma'am, but there's a viewin' booked to come in half an hour, so it's likely the lady'll have new ones soon.'

'Half an hour, Clifford!' she hissed. Without another word, they shot up in the lift and hurried to the door of their old apartment. Clifford slid a familiar neat black-cloth roll from his inside jacket pocket and laid it open across her waiting palms, before adding a needle-thin file.

'And you packed those for a holiday in New York, why?' she whispered.

'Sober experience at "holidaying" with a certain lady of the manor.' He held up the file and ran his finger over its angled tip. 'On the day we took possession of the keys, I noticed from the "cuts and bittings" that the lock must be a seven-pin tumbler affair, designed to offer greater security. Hence last evening, I adapted this from my set.'

'Very forward thinking!' She held her breath, fearing any moment they would be discovered. Finally, she heard a click, and the door sprang open. Once inside, she cast her eye around the entrance hall and the doors and corridors leading off it.

'I don't suppose you've got a magic gadget to find my engagement ring as well, Clifford?'

He clicked his pocket watch closed. 'Regrettably not, my lady. However, we have but twenty-four minutes to do so.'

Twenty minutes later, she hurried back into the sitting room.

'We've scoured every inch. I've even searched through all the cupboards. Nothing!' She shook her head, her heart too filled with horror that she'd somehow been so careless. 'Oh, Clifford, this is too awful. All I can think of now is that I need to muster the courage to telephone Hugh and confess. But first I need to get my words right, for once. Especially since I can't even tell him in person.'

Clifford straightened up from searching under the last of the settees again. 'My lady, I am sure Chief Inspector Seldon will not imagine for one moment that you were careless with something that obviously means the world to you.'

She nodded, but grimaced. 'I know, I know. But I still feel terrible for losing it. Hugh and I agreed on a long engagement, partly to give us both time to adjust to the idea, and partly to ease his worries about wanting to build up some more savings. Bless him.' She sighed. 'I'm still reeling from the shock that he plucked up the courage to propose just before we docked.' Her cheeks flushed. 'And that he wants to spend the rest of his life with me. Or at least he did, until I tell him I've lost the engagement ring that probably took the last of the savings he never had to pay for!'

Clifford shook his head. 'There is no "think" in the gentleman's desire for such, my lady. Of that, we can both be entirely assured. And neither will the news of your lost ring engender any doubt he made the right decision. Now, we must leave.'

Out in the hallway, she closed the door behind her, only to turn around and find her path to the lift blocked.

'Mrs Melchum! How... how nice to see you again. We're, umm...'

'Looking for this?' The scowling woman held out a shaky fist before turning it over and opening her palm. 'I found it in the lift last evening.'

'My engagement ring! Oh gracious, I don't know how to thank you.' Eleanor scooped it back onto her finger. 'I've only just got engaged, you see. And my fiancé's had to return to England and—'

'And while he's gone, you should find someone significantly less cheap! I've never seen such a nasty—'

Eleanor glared at the woman, her voice shaking. 'Mrs Melchum! Not that it is any of your business, but Hugh is the least cheap man on the planet! Unlike everyone else, it seems, he couldn't be bought for all the crooked money in this wretched city. So, thank you again for returning my very precious ring. But I have heard quite enough of your scathing opinions on the most wonderful, decent and sincere man you have not even met! Now, your potential new neighbours will be here in a moment, so Clifford and I shall leave you to give them the pleasure of meeting you.' She stepped around her, but then turned back. 'Actually,' she said coldly, 'just before I go, kindly tell me why you hired Mr Newkirk to trail me as if I were a common criminal?'

Mrs Melchum reeled backwards, her hand over her mouth. 'How... how do you know about him?' She glanced down at the sound of the lift rising and then up at Eleanor. 'Please, come into my apartment.'

Eleanor hesitated, before nodding to Clifford and then following the older woman. Once inside, Clifford closed the door just as the sound of voices exiting the lift drifted down the hallway.

'Lady Swift, please sit.' Mrs Melchum gingerly lowered herself into an upright chair. She appeared almost contrite. 'I owe you an explanation. You see...' She looked up. 'I didn't hire Mr Newkirk to follow you.' She looked down again as she fiddled with her stick.

Eleanor leaned forward, her previous annoyance forgotten. 'Please don't distress yourself. But if you didn't hire him to follow me, why did you hire him?'

The older woman said nothing, seemingly struggling with some powerful emotion. Eleanor tried again. 'Mrs Melchum, my butler and I were just on our way home when the private detective you hired accosted us and—'

'I know what you were doing.'

Eleanor stared at the woman. 'You mean Mr Newkirk told you...?'

Mrs Melchum shook her head. 'I gave up, you see.'

What is she talking about, Ellie? She exchanged a confused glance with Clifford.

'Gave what up, Mrs Melchum?'

'Living.' She waved a disconsolate hand around the room. 'This museum of memories is all I have now.'

'It's not easy being a widow,' Eleanor said softly. She knew from painful personal experience, but had no wish to share the details of her disastrous first marriage at that moment.

Mrs Melchum nodded slowly. 'Henry Theodore D. Melchum, my husband, was a very wealthy and influential man, Lady Swift. And when he was alive, I achieved the pinnacle of elite society. But then he died suddenly, taken almost overnight by pneumonia.' Her voice became bitter. 'And it was then that *she* arrived!'

'She, who?'

'Mrs Lavinia Moira Vanderdale!'

Moira, Ellie. I never knew that was one of Mrs Vanderdale's middle names. Very unusual.

Mrs Melchum gritted her teeth. 'She was young, beautiful, and ambitious. And ruthless. She'd come to New York on a mission. To climb right up onto my throne in society! She isolated me from my peers. And then friends. They all joined her new club but she very publicly refused me an invitation.' She shook her head distraughtly. 'Within a year, I was... finished in society. An outcast in my own city.'

'No one likes to be ostracised,' Eleanor said gently.

Mrs Melchum's eyes flashed. 'If it hadn't been for Henry's death being so fresh... in my heart, I would have been stronger. I would have fought for my position. Instead, I became consumed by my own self-pity. To the point I... I had a breakdown and was incarcerated in a sanitorium. When I finally felt strong enough to emerge, everything was different. I couldn't have re-entered society, no matter my name or wealth. That woman Vanderdale had established her new guard so firmly, New York society was as unrecognisable as it was hostile. And beyond my ever being a part of once again.'

Eleanor reached out and patted the woman's arm. 'I'm so sorry. So you took this apartment away from it all?'

'Yes. I've hidden myself away here for nineteen long years, ever since I came out of the sanitorium with only memories for companions. Aside from darling Catamina, of course.' She ran a trembling hand along her cat's creamy silk fur.

Eleanor was torn. She felt sympathy for the woman, but she needed answers if she was ever going to get justice for Marty.

'Mrs Melchum. Again, I'm truly sorry for what you've gone through. And I really appreciate you sharing your story. But what has this to do with why you hired a private detective to follow me?'

She paled so completely, Eleanor instinctively reached for her hand.

'I didn't, Lady Swift, as I told you before.'

Eleanor bit her lip. 'Then why did you hire him?'

'I hired him... to find my son's killer.'

Eleanor gasped. 'Your son?'

Mrs Melchum nodded. 'Ogden Dellaney.'

36

'We're in the tightest spot ever over these hideous murders, Clifford. We need our sharpest wits. But it's too hot to think at all.' Eleanor fanned her face with her breakfast napkin. For once, she had little appetite for the wonderful fayre her staff had conjured up, the anxious churning of her stomach making her feel nauseous. 'New York really seems against us.'

Beside her chair, Gladstone stopped sniffing for crumbs and lumbered his top half up into her lap with a soft whine.

Clifford arched a brow. 'If you will forgive the observation, my lady, that is an uncharacteristic surrender to the native inhabitants' insistence that the city herself holds some sort of mystical sway over events. I believe it is due only to the mentally clouding effects of heat exhaustion. Hopefully, this might alleviate it.' He laid a large dish of ice cubes in front of her.

She stared at him and shrugged. 'Makes a change from you quietly wanting to boil my head when I've irritated the very starch from your collar, I suppose. But alright.' She flopped forward and buried her face in the ice.

'Ahem!'

She sat up. 'What?'

'The cooling remedy is to be applied to one's wrists. Not face.'

'Shame,' she spluttered airily, failing to disguise her embarrassment. Hiding her face in her napkin while surreptitiously drying it only seemed to add to her butler's amusement. She smiled sweetly. 'You know, Clifford, when I was cycling in the unspeakably hot and sticky parts of Asia, I'd find any fast-flowing stream and peel down to my—'

'You win, my lady,' he said hurriedly.

She laughed. 'Good. Because I haven't even got the energy to enjoy squabbling.'

He gasped in mock horror. 'Then it is worse than I feared!'

She shook her head and, mood restored, took a bite of her delicious bacon muffins and mysteriously named 'hominy gems', which were akin to Yorkshire puddings but made with irresistibly tangy sour milk and creamy corn.

As she ate, she slowly rubbed her wrists alternately over the ice. Breakfast finished, she sighed. 'Perhaps we need to get back to the matter in hand, as you would say?'

He nodded, and they both trooped out to the hallway where he passed her a sage-green silk headscarf, sunglasses and a large-brimmed straw hat. He left, only to return dressed in a light-grey summer suit by the time she'd arranged her headgear satisfactorily. In his hand, he twirled a matching homburg.

'It's a treat to see you in something so dapper.' She adjusted her hat brim again. 'Hopefully, we can escape from here unrecognised and then just fade into the crowds.'

'That is the general idea,' he said as she followed him out of the rear entrance of her new apartment building

'My lady!' Mrs Butters' voice floated out to them. 'Telephone. It's Mrs Melchum.'

Eleanor frowned. *What does she want, Ellie?* After their talk the day before, she'd given the old woman their new phone number, but didn't expect to hear from her so soon. If at all. She tuned into Mrs Butters waiting patiently. 'Coming!' As she headed back in, her brain whirled. So why *was* Mrs Melchum ringing?

A few minutes later, she returned. Clifford's brow furrowed.

'Are you alright, my lady? You look as if you have received bad news.'

She nodded. 'I thought everything bad that could happen *had* happened. That we couldn't get any more isolated. But that was Mrs Melchum on the phone. Newkirk just rang to tell her he's dropping the case. Without charge for his work to date. No explanation, only that no amount of money would change his mind. He apologised and hung up.'

Clifford said nothing.

She bit her lip. 'Not even a quip? Or platitude? Or quote from Voltaire or some fearfully ancient sage extolling how every adversity can be turned into an opportunity?'

He shook his head. 'Given our extreme circumstances, I fear it would be trite.' He gestured down the steps. 'Shall we?'

He led her a couple of blocks before opening the door of a stationary taxi.

'Thought you could avoid me again, lady?' a familiar voice said as she climbed in.

'Iver!' She stared at Clifford. 'But I thought we agreed...' She tailed off, not wanting to articulate in front of Iver that he might also fall prey to sudden homelessness and loss of job if seen with her.

Clifford nodded. 'We did. However, even I ran out of rebuttals this morning to his adamant insistence.'

'I'd say!' Iver said angrily. 'I seen Mrs Morales and Earl run outta their basement like flea-bitten strays, right when you were too. And that cop guy, he's been stalkin' the streets without no uniform outside the labour exchange, so I figured he got fired for the same reason.'

She groaned. 'I know! I feel so guilty.'

Iver shrugged. 'Ain't your fault, lady. Anyways, I says to myself, that crazy lady might a' upset the wrong kinda people, but she's the only one still tryin' to help Marty.' His head fell. 'Like I didn't when he was lyin' so broke up in the street.'

'Iver,' she said gently, 'feeling bad really won't help him.'

'No, but ridin' you around anywhere you need might. And yeah, before you start bleatin' that it ain't a good idea, or safe, my Sadie agreed somebody gotta have the courage to do somethin'. And, anyways, nobody gonna recognise the two of ya easily in those get-ups. So, where to, lady?'

She thought for a moment. 'How about you choose? All we want is a little movement and some time to think. Oh, and something to lift this awful shroud of despondency.'

'Then I know just the thing! A quick detour and then I'll show you the sights.' Iver started the engine and pulled away.

Wherever he was taking them, it involved criss-crossing the city and shouting, waving and cursing at every conceivable form of powered or hoofed transport they came across on the way.

She caught her butler glancing at her from under his unfamiliar hat brim. 'Feeling isolated and alone in a city of over five million is rather ironic, isn't it?'

He nodded. 'It is not something I was expecting, I confess, my lady.'

She sighed. 'No matter how positive I try and be...' She threw her hands out.

'The unpalatable truth is the murderer seems to be holding all the cards?'

At her nod he continued, 'However, my lady, I believe the word "seems" is accurate. I am confident we can find a way to turn the tables. Though, regrettably, I confess, the "how" totally eludes me at the moment.'

Iver waved a hand at them. 'That's because you ain't lettin' New York show ya her hand.'

Eleanor sighed. 'Honestly, I feel like she's not only shown it, but slapped me halfway back across the Atlantic with it.'

'Just relax. I got somethin' that'll turn those frowns around!'

He wasn't wrong.

'Oh, Clifford, look!' she cried a few minutes later, lifting her sunglasses up to properly take in the enchanting sight. The street in front of them was packed with half-naked children. Squealing in delight, they skipped and somersaulted in the arcs of water spraying high in the air from the fire hydrants dotted along the road. Her heart leaped as a rainbow shimmered in the water over the children's heads.

Iver nodded, a smile lighting his usually morose face. 'Heat's so fierce, the mayor's ordered the keys to the hydrants be given to the children in the worst tenement streets. They're watchin' the city's water level and will only shut 'em down when they need to.'

As they rode on, the image of the carefree children playing in the sun reminded her of Mrs Melchum. Alone, trapped inside a prison of her own making with nothing but faded memories. She shook her head at Clifford's quizzical look.

'I was just thinking about Mrs Melchum. It's so sad Ogden changed his name when she went into that sanitorium. Aren't children supposed to stand by you in difficult times? Not disown you and then announce to the world at large that they no longer want anything to do with you?'

'One would hope so. It was doubly unfortunate for the lady that Mr Dellaney failed to visit his mother in the sanitorium, or indeed, when she was discharged and moved into her current abode.'

Eleanor let out a long breath. 'I'm still amazed she hired Newkirk to find his killer after all that, but I suppose he was still her son.'

'I believe a mother cannot turn off the love for her child, no matter how much he may wound her. Though changing his surname to that of his godfather's must have felt like the blow of an axe.'

'Obviously. She still had that locket around her neck with a picture of him as a baby, though. She's never stopped wearing it.' Eleanor swallowed hard but failed to damp down the lump in her throat. Clifford glanced at her but said nothing.

'Yacht Club's coming up in a moment,' Iver called, turning sharp left. 'And then we're on to Carnegie Hall, home to the city's Philharmonic Orchestra, if you like that kind of thing.'

Their taxi continued on, weaving around overloaded wagons and trucks and dodging the incredible number of pedestrians milling around on every road they turned down.

'The Cooper Union Building on your left.' Iver pointed at a vast, brown brick monolith. 'It's a learnin' place. You know, like a college only it's "open and free to all". That's what their sign says, anyway.'

'Even women?'

'Yep! City Hall next, folks, then I've saved the best for last!'

Twenty minutes later, Iver stopped the taxi and spun around. 'No matter what you said earlier, lady, ain't nobody ever alone in New York. Not with her watching over 'em.'

'Goodness! The Statue of Liberty. I only glimpsed her on the way in as our cruise liner docked.'

He nodded. 'The torch is more than three hundred feet off the ground. You don't need glasses to see that. Not that you can go up it after those spies set off explosives there a few years back. Still being repaired. She's gone pretty green too lately.'

'Green? Why?'

'She is made of copper, my lady.' Clifford pointed to the torch. 'Which is why she is struck by lightning hundreds of times every year.'

Iver scoffed. 'Don't bother old Lady Liberty none. She can take it.'

'Wait!' Eleanor cried. 'Is that her name?'

'Yeah, what of it?'

Without explanation, she lunged across the back of the taxi and planted a kiss on his cheek.

37

Could there have been less warmth in those intense copper-brown eyes blinking back at her? Eleanor doubted it.

'I don't usually permit unexpected visitors, Lady Swift,' Mrs Vanderdale said coolly.

Eleanor didn't wait for the invitation so obviously not forthcoming and stepped smartly into the cream and silver office anyway.

'Then I am all the more honoured I made it past your secretary without having to resort to bribes or coercion.'

Mrs Vanderdale flounced her mahogany curls. 'The very idea! My staff, Florence especially, cannot be bought.'

'Ah! None of them can be from New York then, seeing as I've yet to meet anyone who can't be.' Eleanor stepped closer. 'Except one.'

The cupid bow lips in front of her pursed. 'I'm delighted for you, I'm sure, but I'm a busy woman.' She waved a hand over her Tuscan gold silk-suited shoulder at her desk. The papers on it were so precisely aligned either side of the silver-plated telephone, Eleanor found herself nodding approvingly on her absent butler's behalf.

'Do you see how much we have in common?' Eleanor said brightly. 'Such busy women, the pair of us. But I find myself all the more so now, which is odd, since the raft of invitations I was floundering under have all been withdrawn. Every one of them. New York high society has shunned me entirely, Mrs Vanderdale.'

She raised a perfectly manicured eyebrow. 'What can I say? You must have done something terribly gauche.'

'I did.' Eleanor held that copper-eyed gaze. 'I worked out who killed Ogden P. Dellaney and Marty Morales, my doorman.'

Mrs Vanderdale flinched almost imperceptibly. 'Then congratulations. So, I guess, you really are an anomaly among the English aristocracy who visit this city.' She walked over to her desk and leaned her shapely hip against the corner. 'Not just a touted, over-embellished newspaper heroine after all.'

'Not even,' Eleanor said firmly. She held her hands up. 'However, I've never set out to be anyone's heroine. I just seem to have a knack for getting caught up in these things.'

Mrs Vanderdale laughed mirthlessly. 'And for social faux pas. That I have seen first hand. On every occasion we have met, this one included.' Eleanor was confused. Even she couldn't have committed some heinous no-no in such a short space of time? 'However, Lady Swift, you are not shunned here, at the Ladies' Liberty Club. You have intuition and determination, at least. Two attributes essential for membership.'

The image of Clifford's often-repeated cautioning mime of tiptoeing on eggshells popped into her thoughts. *He's right, Ellie. You've only got a foot in the door. There's a long way to go.* She beamed at her hostess. 'Thank you, genuinely. That's very gracious of you. Just as I expected.'

Mrs Vanderdale's eyes narrowed. 'Flattery, Lady Swift, is not required. Remember, I told you coy has no place in New York. And certainly not with me.'

'I do. And it wasn't flattery. I meant what I said. I absolutely expected you to meet with me, even though I've arrived unannounced.'

Mrs Vanderdale seemed to ponder this for a moment. 'Then why did you believe so determinedly I would not spurn your presence like the rest of New York society apparently has?'

'For one simple reason. You are not part of it.' She held up a halting hand as those cupid bow lips pursed again. 'You are above it. Beyond it. Just as your impressive club here is. You, Mrs Vanderdale, control society, I realise. It doesn't control you.' She paused. *Mrs Melchum's story showed you that, Ellie.* 'But I suspect it isn't only society you control?'

Mrs Vanderdale's eyes lit up. At the same time, she seemed to be trying to keep a smug look off her face. 'You are correct, of course. And it is satisfying to hear, naturally. But as I said before, Lady Swift, my day is a busy one. I have no time for flattery, sincere or not. So, do tell me exactly what it is you want?'

Eleanor shrugged. 'Two things. I need your help. And your influence. Which is probably also terribly gauche, but there it is.'

Mrs Vanderdale slowly adjusted the edges of the papers on her desk, failing to hide her interest. She turned the pens in the engraved silver pot to stand up straight, but then gave in to her curiosity. 'Perhaps you'd better take a seat?'

Eleanor sat opposite her sole hope of catching Marty and Dellaney's murderer. And possibly her sole hope of making it through her supposed holiday alive. Without a bullet in her head. Or without succumbing to the depths of the Hudson River in those menacing-sounding 'concrete boots'. Suddenly, her mind went blank.

She blinked and licked her dry lips. *Think, Ellie, think!* 'May I trouble you for a drink? This heatwave is really taking it out of me.'

Her secretary was dispatched for two iced coffees, Mrs

Vanderdale turned to the nearest of the papers on her desk. She ran a pen down the end of each line, her eyes flicking over the page.

Sitting back quietly, Eleanor gratefully grabbed the few moments to recover. *Relax, Ellie, you can do this.* She calmed her breathing. The woman opposite was still hard to read, but she felt she'd come a long way since that first, uncomfortable meeting with this queen of New York society. As that thought struck, Eleanor's gaze darted along the run of framed photographs. Apart from the more modern setting and fashionable dress, and Mrs Vanderdale's ubiquitous presence, they could have been those in Mrs Melchum's apartment, casting painful memories of long-forgotten triumphs. She imagined what it must have felt like to be the most exalted member of such an elite clique of wealth and privilege. And how it must have felt to be toppled from that very throne and relegated to obscurity.

The click of efficient heels heralded the secretary bringing the refreshments.

Dash it, Ellie. You were supposed to be getting your words together, not wandering off on flights of fancy. But then again remember Mrs Dellaney's words: 'If the war Mrs Vanderdale is always waging with Atticus is being friends, I'll take enemies any day.'

'Will there be anything else, Mrs Vanderdale?' the secretary said, notebook at the ready.

Mrs Vanderdale waved her away. 'No thank you, Florence.' Once they were alone, she turned back to Eleanor. 'As I've repeatedly mentioned, Lady Swift, I'm a busy woman. You were asking for my help, and influence, I believe?'

Noting the pointed comment, Eleanor took a long sip of coffee for courage. 'Yes, but let me ask you this first. What have you got going on in your campaign suite right now?'

A hint of annoyance crossed Mrs Vanderdale's otherwise coolly composed features. 'I fail to see why you ask? But if your curiosity really needs to know, I am arranging the most prestigious charity ball to ever grace this island. Therefore, I have turned the campaign suite into a planning room to better lay out the details.'

'And in your debating chambers?'

Mrs Vanderdale's flawless brow creased. 'The members are currently debating refurbishment plans for the library. Lady Swift, where is this going?'

Eleanor raised her hand. 'Indulge me for a moment longer. And the project you are so deeply engrossed in on your desk?'

Mrs Vanderdale turned the papers face down defiantly. 'It is a private matter. Now, what exactly is your point?'

Eleanor shrugged, keeping her tone light. 'Oh, nothing, really. I just thought you might be interested in having an achievement truly worthwhile to announce at your next monthly meeting? More interesting than which of your members has married which wealthy Ivy Leaguer. Or how much of their husband's money, deceased or otherwise, each of your members has given to good causes, that only you decided are suitable.'

Mrs Vanderdale's eyes flashed. 'Forget gauche, and faux pas, Lady Swift! You have gone beyond the bounds of both! I suggest you leave. And do not return.'

'Shame. But as you wish.' Eleanor made a show of finishing her coffee. She collected her bag and retied her scarf before rising. All the while, her hostess' glare bore into her skull.

As she walked towards the door, she gestured around her.

'Mrs Vanderdale, your club building is as remarkable as it is impressive. And it will serve as a great legacy to your name. Until, that is, the next queen of society sees fit to have it demolished that she might build her larger, more awe-inspiring version. On this very spot, I imagine. How quickly people forget the original founder when that happens, don't you find?' Mrs Vanderdale opened her mouth, but Eleanor raised her hand. 'No need to answer. We both know it's true. And we know how painful it can be to spend the last of your days in insignificance, surrounded only by memories of past, but long-forgotten, achievements.' At the door, she reached out for the handle, but then spun around. 'Do you want to be that woman when you're old, Mrs Vanderdale? Or do you want the new guard to fall back respectfully when you appear and whisper about your past, but never-forgotten, triumphs? Triumphs that, with the passage of time, become *legends*?'

She held the other woman's gaze, the ticking of the mantel-piece clock the only sign time was still passing.

Finally, Mrs Vanderdale spoke. 'You have one minute to tell me precisely what you are suggesting and then I will have you thrown out.'

Eleanor stepped forward. 'What I am suggesting, Mrs Vanderdale, is that while you sit here in the ivory castle of your Ladies' Liberty Club, out there on the streets, the real Lady Liberty is on her knees. New York is rotten, Mrs Vanderdale. Rotten to its core. Everyone knows it, but everyone also agrees no one can do anything about it. And they are right. But the unified might of women of influence and power led by you can.' She took another step forward. 'What I'm suggesting is, next time someone asks you what you did last month, rather than telling them you refurbished your library yet again or arranged one more vainglorious charity ball, you did this. You helped a mad English lady bring one of the most powerful and evil men in New York to his knees. And to justice.' She let out a deep breath. 'And in doing so, helped the real Lady Liberty off her knees and back onto the pedestal where she belongs.'

Mrs Vanderdale ran her finger over her lips. Slowly, she walked past Eleanor to the door and opened it without a word.

Eleanor's heart sank as she called for her secretary. A moment later, she arrived, notebook in hand.

'Yes, Mrs Vanderdale?'

'Florence.' She glanced back at Eleanor. 'Lady Swift will be staying for lunch. We are not to be disturbed under any circumstances. We have something... of interest to discuss.'

38

'And Master Gladstone is assisting, how exactly, my lady?'
Clifford's voice floated across from the doorway. 'Since you
seem to have managed to destroy any sense of order single-
handedly?'

Eleanor reluctantly dragged her gaze away from the blanket
of open newspapers she was scouring on her lap and
outstretched legs where she sat on the floor. It was three long
weeks since she'd had her original meeting with Mrs
Vanderdale and each day the pile of newspapers and magazines
grew. She looked around the carpet of more papers scattered
across the sitting room floor.

'He was here about half an hour ago, but I haven't seen him
since.'

Clifford eyed her with a look she felt ought to be reserved
for a child who'd stolen the jam out of the fridge and was now
sick after eating the entire contents. 'What?' She shook two
halves of different newspapers at him. 'I'm trying to gauge if,
after three weeks, our plan is actually working and you're
fussing about an errant bulldog. Honestly, Clifford, he must be
in the apartment somewhere. He would never wander off even

if the front door and the one out into the street were both inadvertently left wide open.'

Her butler pursed his lips. 'Indeed, he would not. But mostly because the streets are not littered with the crumbs of misappropriated pastries, unlike the sitting room floor, disgracefully!'

She frowned. 'What crumbs? And anyway, if your butlering skills can't allow you to see through a slight scattering of—'

'Liberal blanketing of.'

'A slight scattering of newspapers,' she said firmly. 'You need to look for Gladstone elsewhere. And when you find him, I suggest you apologise for whatever misdeed you were inferring he's responsible for.'

'Ahem.' With a shudder, Clifford stepped around the edge of the room, lifting the newspaper sheets up by their corners so as not to walk on them. With a magician's flourish, he whipped a handful away in one corner, revealing a startled bulldog.

She stared at him in bemusement. 'Gladstone! What on earth are you hiding under there for, silly boy... oh, I see!' She winced as Clifford scooped up the empty plate from the floor beside her. He fixed the bulldog with a stern look.

'Master Gladstone. Mrs Trotman made that selection of savoury finger pastries especially for her ladyship's elevenses. Not for you.'

She smiled fondly as Gladstone, still licking his lips, rolled on his back, paws flopping on his chest as he tried to wag his stump of a tail. This only succeeded in propelling his portly frame from side to side like a lazy metronome. She laughed. 'Well, the half I had managed before I got too distracted were delicious. And it was my fault for putting the plate on the floor in the first place, so you can't blame him for eating the rest.'

Clifford's lips quirked. 'I wasn't. Discipline is instilled by example, according to conventional wisdom. But what does that know?'

'Very droll, you terror!' She gratefully accepted a top-up of home-made iced coffee, which had become something of a favourite with the still sweltering temperature. 'Now, tell me this heatwave is going to break in the next day or so.'

'It is forecast to, my lady. Very soon.'

'Thank heavens! Then, have you any more admonishments up your impeccable suit sleeves, or can I bring us back to the matter in hand?'

Her butler gave a conciliatory bow.

'Good, because listen to just a couple of the last few days' headlines. "Speakeasy raids on the rise." "Prohibition clamp-down on top-level joints." "Gin and ice, no dice!" "Broadway, a front for whitening up dirty-gotten dollars?" "Mayor promises to continue rooting out corruption in city council."' She looked up optimistically. 'What do you think?'

'That someone needs to introduce the basic principles of English grammar to the supposed wordsmiths of journalistic reporting. However, that aside, I believe a wholehearted bravo to you is most definitely in order, my lady. There is definitely an increase in reports of this type over the last three weeks.'

'I agree. I started to tally them up, and it feels very encouraging after what is such a short time. But it's no credit to me, really. All I did was talk Mrs Vanderdale into using her and her members' significant influence very discreetly behind the scenes to have Atticus' illegal business interests investigated and closed down. That part of the plan is obviously already working. The next part, as you know, is to wait until the pressure's too much and Atticus will do anything to find out who is responsible. At that point, Mrs Vanderdale will contact him and tell him she knows who is trying to ruin him and arrange a meeting. We'll set up a wiretap or whatever it's called with Balowski and the police and trick Atticus into making a confession. Then the police nab him, and justice is served!'

Clifford pursed his lips. 'If you say so.'

She scrambled up. 'Clifford? What barrel of iced water are you itching to hurl now? I agree, it's a long shot. But it's all we have and I'm willing to hold out for however long it takes.' She sighed. 'It has to work. For Marty's sake. And Mrs Morales.'

'But not Mr Dellaney's?'

She sighed. 'I don't mean to be uncharitable, Clifford. Particularly as he's deceased. But if he really was having an affair with Atticus Wyatt's wife and got her preg— Ah, yes, that thing you'd probably be more comfortable if I didn't articulate.'

'Decorous retraction noted. Thank you, my lady.'

'Yes, well, he seems to generally have slithered into various people's silky bedsheets irrespective of whether they were married or not. And irrespective of any distress he might have caused. Combined with the poor way I saw him treating everybody he encountered, it is making it a little tricky to feel equal sympathy for his passing as Marty's. Although, to be clear, everyone deserves justice, so I'm just as determined his killer will be brought before a judge, too.'

He tutted at her description of Dellaney's extramarital exploits but nodded.

'You too, Mr Ever-Even-handed?' she said in surprise.

'Unquestionably, my lady. I also find it hard to be equally sympathetic. Straying outside of one's vows can never be condoned. All the more so when it leaves one party caught so devastatingly unawares.'

'Agreed. But we don't actually know Atticus wasn't playing the field as well.'

'Also true.'

'Oh lawks!' Polly skipped in, wafting a flurry of newspaper sheets up in her wake. She curtseyed while staring at the maelstrom covering the floor and settees and then waited for Clifford's nod of permission to speak. 'Beg pardon, your ladyship, but didn't know you needed so much surface for makin' such a fearful mess. I could gather all the tables and little bureaus from around the apartment and put them together somewhere for you?'

Eleanor smiled at her maid. 'Too kind, Polly, but it's a little late for that.'

Clifford raised a gloved hand. 'I trust there was an important matter you needed resolving, Polly? Important enough to interrupt her ladyship in creating such disorder?' He caught Eleanor's eye and hurried on. 'Is there a problem among the ladies, perhaps?'

The young maid shook her head. 'Oh no. Mrs Trotman is dreaming up summat special for her ladyship's evening dinner. She's been down with that grocer man for ages choosing. And Mrs Butters is sewing her ladyship cooler underfril—' She clamped a hand over her mouth.

Clifford cocked his head. 'Then it is you and Lizzie who require something?'

Polly shook her head again. 'No, sir. Lizzie's fighting one of her headaches, so we're sitting quietly, working on my idea of stringing ice cubes together to make a bracelet for her ladyship. To help cool her down as you was saying she was getting overheated, Mr Clifford. We're drilling holes in the cubes with your corkscrew, but it's not as easy as we thought.'

Eleanor hid a smile as Clifford closed his eyes in disbelief.

'Most... ingenious, I am sure,' he said, opening them again. 'However, please enlighten me as to what necessitated this interruption, then?'

'Oh, the telephone is ringing, Mr Clifford, sir.' She curtseyed to Eleanor and skipped back out, tripping over Gladstone, who lumbered grumpily to his feet.

'I didn't hear it.' Eleanor cocked her head. 'I still can't, in fact.'

Clifford tutted as he started towards the door. 'A consequence of the inadequacy of the bell. Barely audible is too generous an accolade. And that only after I devised and installed an emergency amplification device.'

'You could have just given it that admonishing look you reserve for me instead. That would have stopped it misbehaving,' she called after him.

A moment later, he returned and respectfully beckoned her out to the entrance hall. 'It is Mrs Vanderdale, my lady.'

'Oh gracious, I wasn't expecting it to be her so soon. Fingers crossed.'

39

It was only a few minutes before Eleanor returned from taking the call but somehow, all the newspapers had been tidied into a perfectly aligned array along the narrow window seat. He laid the last one precisely so and then looked at her expectantly.

'You win.' Feeling breathless, she fumbled in her dress pockets and pulled out a dollar bill. 'Our quarry broke first. You were right.'

He took the note hesitantly. 'Dare I ask, a meeting arranged, perchance?'

'Yes, tomorrow. At eleven in the evening, so we don't have as much time as I hoped to contact Balowski and apologise and...' She winced.

'And convince him to help us persuade his still employed fellow police officers to set up that wiretap for us? Not to mention to actually arrest Mr Wyatt?'

Her face fell at his doubtful look. 'I know you had your reservations about the plan before, Clifford, but tell me now you believe it will work?'

His ever-impassive expression faltered. 'Perhaps, my lady. Back in England and on one's home turf as it were, certainly.

But in a foreign city, not to mention country? And against such a formidable opponent?'

She blanched. 'Clifford, please don't conjure up an encyclopaedia of cautions and reasons why we can't see this through. We've been over and over everything and agreed it's the only way.'

'And yet, in the final hour, it feels there must be another.'

'There is. We can walk away.' From behind his back, she caught the telltale tap of one of his gloved hands in the palm of the other, the only indication that he was thinking. Or stressed. She grimaced. 'But having said that, we can't actually walk away, you know that.'

'Because, my lady?'

'Because if we did, when we returned home to Henley Hall, together we'd have had to turn Uncle Byron's portrait at the top of the stairs to face the wall as neither of us could ever look him in the eye again.'

For a moment, he said nothing. Then he nodded solemnly. 'Agreed. Into the lions' den it is, then.'

She breathed out slowly. 'Thank you.' Then frowned. 'You know, I might ring Mrs Vanderdale back and check a few details. Just to make doubly sure we have everything for tomorrow night nailed.'

'A wise course, my lady.'

'She gave me her personal number when we last met.' She fumbled in her pockets. 'Drat! I think I may have... no, here it is!'

She pulled out the note and a scrap of paper. She frowned and dropped the scrap on a bread plate and unfolded the note with Mrs Vanderdale's telephone number written in bold, flowing strokes.

She stared up at Clifford, following his gaze to the scrap of paper.

'Sorry, Clifford. I found it in my pocket. I meant to put it in the waste bin. I picked it up in the street when I was examining the car that killed Ogden. And Marty, too, we're pretty sure. I should have just dropped it again, but I hate littering. Even if it's only paper.'

Clifford took out his pince-nez and uncrumpled the scrap. 'It appears not to be paper, but light card.'

She shrugged. 'Does it matter? I rather thought we had other, more important, things on our mind at the moment?' She raised a brow. 'Clifford?'

He stopped examining the scrap and took off his pince-nez. 'It might matter a great deal, my lady. Where *exactly* did you find this?'

She frowned. 'Well, it was among the broken windscreen glass. No, hang on, it was by the passenger door, so I suppose it was the glass from the broken side-window, if that matters.'

'And you didn't cut yourself?'

She shrugged again. 'No. I just picked it up... *off* the glass!'

He nodded slowly. 'So, it was most likely dropped *after* the accident.'

Her brow furrowed. 'So... maybe it isn't from the street? Maybe—'

'It came from the crashed car?'

'Or from the person, or belongings, of whoever was driving the car?'

'Certainly the driver would have been shaken, if not concussed after such an accident. Also, one assumes, the perpetrator would have been keen to leave the scene as quickly as possible.'

She looked at him in puzzlement. 'This is all very interesting, but why does it matter "a great deal"?'

This time they both caught the faint ringing of the telephone. She followed him out to the hall, where he handed her the scrap.

'Because, my lady, you will notice the card is blue. And a

very particular blue. In fact, I am fairly certain that this is from a packet of cigarettes. Gitanes, to be precise.'

She gasped. Turning it over in her hand she shook her head. 'Why anyone smokes those horrible Gitanes anyway, I'll never know!'

'Mrs Melchum, my lady.'

She looked up. 'I'm sure she doesn't smoke them, Clifford. I never—'

'Mrs Melchum *on the telephone* for you, m'lady,' he said firmly, holding the receiver out to her.

'Oh, golly. Sorry.'

What can she want this time, Ellie? Not more bad news, I hope?

She took the receiver from him. 'Mrs Melchum, this is a pleasant surprise. How can I help you?'

The old lady's voice crackled down the line.

'Your young maid left some unfinished mending or some such in my apartment after your hound visited. I just wanted to know if you intended to send one of your staff around to collect it?' There was a slight pause. 'Or... or I could have it posted to you?'

'That's very kind of you to let me know, Mrs Melchum, but I don't want to put you to any bother. I'll have my butler collect it tomorrow, if that's alright? And again, I'm so sorry about the incident with Gladstone.'

'No harm was done. Really,' the old woman said quickly.

Eleanor searched for something else to say. She sensed the left-behind mending had only been an excuse to ring.

Maybe she just wants someone to talk to, Ellie? Or she's trying to hold out an olive branch?

Before she could reply, the old woman's voice came back. 'And actually, Lady Swift, I agree with you. I don't know why anyone smokes those cigarettes either. They smell really quite obnoxious! A man smoking them is bad enough, but a woman!

Not,' she said hurriedly, 'that I was eavesdropping, I just happened to hear your remark to your help while I was waiting for you to come on the line.'

Eleanor laughed. 'Oh, I don't smoke them. In fact, I don't smoke at all.'

A sniff came down the line. 'I wasn't referring to you, Lady Swift. But to... *that* woman!'

The skin on Eleanor's forearms goosebumped. 'What woman, Mrs Melchum?'

'That Vanderdale woman!'

Eleanor frowned. 'But I've never seen her smoke?'

Mrs Melchum sniffed again. 'Neither have I. But one of her "admirers" who still considered me a friend at the time, told me a while after I was,' the old lady's voice cracked, 'outed from society, that Mrs Vanderdale smoked Gitanes in private with her "inner circle". To show off, I imagine, and convince her followers just how superior and special she is!'

A moment later as Eleanor put down the receiver, Clifford stepped forward, concern etched on his face. 'My lady, are you alright?'

She nodded slowly. 'Yes. But I fear we may have made a terrible mistake—'

The quiet jangle of the telephone interrupted them yet again. With a raised brow, Clifford picked it up.

Who can it possibly be this time, Ellie?

40

Eleanor stared out of the open taxi window in surprise. A distant rumble of thunder rolled around.

'Is this definitely the right place? I know Balowski said he was scared to meet anywhere too public, but...' She peered harder into the gloom. 'This feels a little too... *un-public*.'

In the opposite seat, Clifford's hand strayed to his inside pocket.

She shook her head. 'We've no reason now to mistrust Balowski. He lost his job because of me, remember? And he sounded genuine on the telephone. Besides, we still need his help so it was fortuitous he rang.'

Clifford sniffed. 'And why exactly could the gentleman not explain at the time why he needed to speak with you so urgently? Rather than dragging you out in the middle of the night to' – he sniffed – 'a forest!'

Iver spun around in the driver's seat with a wry grin. 'I think you might a' missed the point.'

'What point?'

He let out a wheezy cackle. 'It's not a forest. That big old mound of trees right there is Billycoo Hill. *Billycoo*. Like billin'' and cooin'? Surely even in prissy old England you got some outta the way places where couples go and—'

Clifford coughed. 'We can leave the rest to the imagination, thank you.'

She groaned. 'I came because Balowski said he had something vital to tell me.'

Iver shrugged. 'Bein' sweet on someone feels pretty vital, lady.'

Clifford tutted sharply and tugged on the brim of his bowler hat. 'Iver, please take her ladyship home immediately.'

'No, wait up, Suitsville!' Balowski's voice hissed from somewhere beyond Clifford's window. 'It ain't that at all. Over here... hurry!'

'Oh, thank heavens,' Eleanor muttered, following her butler out of the car. 'Officer, I mean, Balowski—'

She gasped as the former policeman, hands tied behind his back, stepped out from behind an enormous elm tree, a gun held to his head. The man holding the gun was the scar-faced thug from the diner. Out of the corner of her eye, she saw Clifford reach inside his jacket. But as he pulled out his ex-service revolver, two more people stepped out of the shadows. The first Eleanor recognised as scar-face's companion. The second...

'Mrs Vanderdale!'

The woman smiled as she pulled another gun from behind her back and aimed it at Eleanor's chest.

Stay calm, Ellie.

She held her hands up slowly. In her peripheral vision, she caught Clifford holding his gun steady, aimed at Mrs Vanderdale.

Behind her, she heard Iver's taxi roar off, his horrified words yelled out, 'Sorry, lady, I promised my Sadie I'd help but stay alive!'

Scar-face's companion let off a couple of shots after him, but they buried harmlessly into the taxi's bodywork.

'Ignore him!' Mrs Vanderdale barked. She turned to Clifford. 'Your weapon! Hand it over or I'll shoot your mistress without a second thought.'

'As I will you,' he replied calmly.

Mrs Vanderdale shrugged. 'Then I guess we'll both die. You have until three.' The second thug turned his gun on Eleanor as well. 'One... two...'

For a moment, Clifford hesitated, then lowered his revolver slowly. He stood there, allowing the thug to jerk it out of his hand. He regarded Balowski with disgust. 'You are the lowliest coward of a dog, sir!'

The policeman's eyes flashed. 'Like I had a choice in callin' the lady with the phoney message, Suitsville! This gun ain't left my head since they grabbed me. What was I supposed to have done?'

'Taken the bullet,' Clifford growled. 'Not the craven route of placing her ladyship in danger.' In the blink of an eye, he lunged forward and cracked his fist against Balowski's jaw so hard the thug behind him stumbled sideways. With a groan, Balowski reeled backwards, his eyes fluttering as he lost consciousness. He slumped to the ground.

'Men!' Mrs Vanderdale rolled her eyes. Eleanor cried out as one of the thugs brought a cosh down onto Clifford's head with a sickening thump.

Her butler's knees buckled. 'Apologies, my...'

He hit the ground. Like Balowski, he was out cold. Incomprehensible though she knew it was, that his always impeccable bowler rolled into a patch of dirt made her chest clench all the more.

Still your emotions, Ellie! There's no time. Mrs Vanderdale has unexpectedly seized the initiative. It's up to you now to get everyone out of this safely. You just need to stall her until Clifford or Balowski regains consciousness.

But that idea faded at Mrs Vanderdale's next words. 'Iron

bars are gauche but unwaveringly effective. Unlike you, Lady Swift. You are just gauche.'

She looked up from Clifford's slumped form. 'And you are just a fraud. Your real name is Lavinia *Moira* Vanderdale. Or "Mary" to your friends. If you have any!'

Mrs Vanderdale flinched. 'No one's called me that in twenty years.'

Not since Mrs Melchum's day, Ellie.

'No? Well, "Moira" is an Anglicised version of the Irish name, "Máire", isn't it? Which is also translated as "Mary".' She glanced down at her unconscious butler, whose encyclopaedic knowledge had furnished the information. It had made them more suspicious of Mrs Vanderdale for sure. But not until they'd discovered only an hour before that she smoked Gitanes, evidence of which they'd found at both murder scenes – a butt at Marty's and the scrap of blue carton at Dellaney's – had they realised they'd been wrong. Mrs Vanderdale was their killer, not Wyatt. But before they could come up with a new plan to ensnare her instead of Wyatt, she'd preempted it by kidnapping Balowski and luring them into her own trap.

Dash it, Ellie!

She tried to think of something to say while she regrouped. 'And "Moira" can also mean "Destiny" in Greek, I believe?'

Mrs Vanderdale nodded. 'Which is fitting, isn't it, Lady Swift, as I hold your destiny in my hand. I wonder what it will be?' She smiled cruelly, her finger tightening on the trigger.

Do something, Ellie!

'Wait!' The finger stopped. 'You... you at least owe me an explanation?'

For a moment, she was sure Mrs Vanderdale would just pull the trigger. Then the woman slowly lowered the gun.

'Actually, Lady Swift, I will explain because the truth is, I do owe you something for suggesting the idea that I bring Atticus down. You see, he was my main rival, but still wouldn't see me as his equal because I was a woman in a man's world. Your suggestion was perfect. Once I'd shown him just how strong I am, I arranged a meeting earlier this morning. At which, he was impressed enough to finally realise that together we could run this town. So, in exchange for me calling off my ladies, the police, and City Hall, he agreed to go into partnership with me.' She tutted. 'If you want a man to do what you need, get him on his knees. But it wasn't all one-sided. He had a contract out to find who was responsible for all those raids on his properties and so forth, so I told him.' She grimaced. 'I might just have let your name slip as the brains behind the idea.' She smiled sweetly. 'So sorry.'

Eleanor nodded grimly. 'So you're just one more gangster preying on the good people of this city? Corruption. Extortion. Murder!'

Mrs Vanderdale laughed. 'Well, what can I say? It runs in the family.'

'So your husband was a gangster, too?'

'Naturally. He was in construction. It's the most corrupt industry in this city. There's a building going up every minute and there are millions to be made legally, and illegally, every time.'

'So, the great founder of the Ladies' Liberty Club still owes her success to a man!'

Anger flashed in Mrs Vanderdale's eyes. 'Lies!'

'No, it isn't. You crawled to the top of your disgusting profession, if you can call it that, on the back of your husband's wealth and influence.'

Mrs Vanderdale's eyes narrowed. 'Okay, he might have gotten me halfway, initially. But I did it better, and bigger, without him. I expanded into new markets. Today, I've half of City Hall in one pocket and half the police in the other. Money talks, Lady Swift.'

'And then one of those new markets, prohibition, landed in your lap like a gift from above, didn't it?'

'Absolutely! The money-making possibilities are endless. And so are the offers that come my way. You see, in the beginning of prohibition, certain "businessmen" came to me with an irresistible proposal. They'd open speakeasies and gambling houses in all my suitable properties. "Suitable" being the ones where the governors and district attorneys and all the other top cats wouldn't feel out of place, or nervous, hanging out. So I'd no fear of my ever being prosecuted. I'd simply collect all the delicious money those fools spent.'

'So it was you leaving that speakeasy, Eat the Moon, when I went over and spoke with Atticus! You own it, not him. And you process the illegal profits from it, and all the other illegal operations you own, through your construction business as legitimate funds, don't you?'

'Of course. Prohibition has made me so many millions, I'm thinking of bribing those stupid, greedy senators to make it permanent. Smart girl for working that out, though. But no way smart enough. All I've got to do now is fulfil that contract that's on your head, and my deal with Atticus is signed and sealed.'

Eleanor's heart pounded in her chest, as much with anger for her struck-down butler as fear for her own situation. She tried to focus, but her brain was racing. Another rumble of thunder sounded, nearer this time.

Calm down, Ellie. Keep her talking.

She held Mrs Vanderdale's gaze. 'You know, I rather liked Atticus' way of describing Ogden. "All mustard and no steak," I think it was. But with you, it's all looks and no heart. All money and no—'

'Shut up!' she spat. 'Bullets are too good for you. I've a far better way to fulfil Atticus' contract. But we need to hurry. Do what I say. Now, move!'

Eleanor swallowed hard. Her mouth was so dry that had

any actual words penetrated her jumbled thoughts, she couldn't have articulated them. Her eyes roved over the woman opposite her, searching for a hint of mercy, a morsel of decency she might appeal to. Or even a crack in the callous creature's armour she might apply pressure to. But with an icy frisson, she realised the exquisite set of features before her had neither morals, nor pity. Nor any discernible weakness.

Except her vanity. Her need for recognition, Ellie. Could you play on that?

Mrs Vanderdale shook her head. 'Whatever you're thinking, forget it. You're out of lifelines, Lady Swift.'

A car lurched out of the trees and jerked to a halt in a cloud of dirt. She slapped the driver's face with her gun barrel as he got out. 'My shoes, you ape!' She grinned slyly at Eleanor. 'Good help is so hard to find. Oh, but you know that since you haven't any now, have you? Poor little Lady Swift. Helpless. All alone. Who will save her?' She laughed as she forced Eleanor to lie flat against the car with her gun. 'Now, let's see how you like what I've got in mind for you.'

The scar-faced thug waved his gun at the two bodies on the ground. 'What about these jokers, boss?'

Eleanor's heart stopped. Mrs Vanderdale let out an exasperated snort. She pointed at Eleanor.

'Just tie her hands up and get in before some disgusting courting couple turns up and we have to deal with them too. I want this nuisance dead above anything else. And we're running out of time.'

'Time, time, time,' Eleanor said, hoping to buy herself some. 'The lack of it has been the entire theme of my trip so far. Did you know that?'

She gasped as the scar-faced thug tightened the rope he'd wound around her wrists.

'Nope, we didn't. But after you, lady.' He shoved her onto the back seat and slid in tight beside her.

'Alright, alright.' She flinched at the jab of the gun barrel hard into her ribs. 'I'll behave. But didn't anyone ever teach you it's rude to poke a lady?'

'Yeah. But I like it all the same. So sit tight. And sit quiet.'

Mrs Vanderdale climbed into the front seat and slapped the dashboard. 'Grace's Peak. Go!'

As they sped away, Eleanor glanced in the rear-view mirror and sent the sprawled forms of Officer Balowski and her butler a silent apology.

41

The car shot left onto a surfaced road and kept going. Too fast for Eleanor to have any chance of getting her bearings.

'Maybe it's custom here too?' she said as airily as she could manage.

'What?' Mrs Vanderdale snapped, turning around in the front passenger seat.

'Car games on long journeys. I assume we're off on quite a jaunt? At least a few miles or so?'

Mrs Vanderdale's mahogany curls tossed as she turned back. 'Nice try, Lady Swift. But it wouldn't help if I told you the precise location of where I'm taking you. It would mean nothing. Nothing. Like you are in this city.'

Eleanor groaned to herself. She'd only asked to gauge how long she had to come up with some sort of plan. But that gun in her ribs felt horribly like it meant business. And three against one in a car hurtling through the dark was terrible odds. She shifted as best she could with bound wrists and the thug pressed close beside her.

Maybe, Ellie, these ropes will loosen with a bit of careful—

'Hold still, lady!' scar-face grunted. 'Another mile and a half and you'll be outta the car anyways.'

'She ain't gonna be any more comfortable though, right, boss?' scar-face's companion called from the driving seat.

'Shut up and focus,' Mrs Vanderdale snapped.

Eleanor's already tattered optimism took a sharp nosedive. A mile and a half at that speed? That was no time to conjure up an escape plan!

'Dashed time dictating everything again,' she muttered.

Mrs Vanderdale turned slowly around in her seat. 'Don't you believe it.' She reached over and ran the barrel of her gun down Eleanor's cheek. 'I'm dictating everything. Just as I always do.'

Eleanor saw her opening. 'Then at least sate the rest of my curiosity. You killed Marty because he recognised you, from when you used to be called "Moira", didn't he?'

Mrs Vanderdale shook her head. 'He recognised me from before that. When I was known as "Marenka". But I was told by other immigrants it was better to lose the accent and have a name that blended in. So, I changed it to "Moira" as I knew a lot of Irish at the time. But it was such a mouthful, I changed it again to "Mary".' Her voice was tinged with anger. 'I was penniless. And desperate. Home in Hungary was hell. So, I got myself out aged fifteen and did whatever it took to travel to America. And whatever it took wasn't pretty. But by the time I got to the United States, I'd done everything imaginable, so prostitution was easy. I met Marty when he was first chauffeuring for a rich man. Not Ogden. Marty's boss took a shine to me and made me his mistress. Slow-acting poison is such a gift of a tool for getting what you want, don't you find? He was at the end of his wits in the last week. Witless, in fact. And easy to manipulate. He died on our wedding night. So sad.'

'You murdered him!'

'Of course. And took his money. Then I reinvented myself as a rich grieving widow.'

The coldness of her tone made Eleanor wince. 'Let me guess, which is when you caught the attention of Ogden?' She didn't try to hide the disgust in her voice.

Mrs Vanderdale smirked. 'Men are so easily besotted with me. What can I say? He was just the ladder I needed to scale the elite of New York society.'

'Which you no doubt paid him handsomely for in kind, I imagine?'

And by forcing his mother, Mrs Melchum, out of society and into a sanitorium, Ellie.

Mrs Vanderdale shuddered. 'No! Ogden was repellent. I took his help and successfully batted off his advances until I was above him in society because I married a bigger, better, wealthier catch. Who, coincidentally, also died.'

'Again, at your hand, I assume.' Eleanor felt sick. 'As did Marty, because, I'm guessing, he was going to expose who you really were?'

'Yes. I was away out of town for the first few months after Marty got the job with Ogden. Then, when I returned, Marty recognised me. You see, he was as much besotted with me as my two husbands. Or Ogden.'

The 'girl trouble' Mrs Morales said she believed Marty had, Ellie.

Mrs Vanderdale tossed her curls. 'At first he promised, of course, not to reveal my past, but you can't trust a man, even one in love with you. So, I got him sacked. And can you believe it? The snivelling toad took his grudge to Ogden and blabbed! Mind you, it took him a few months to get up the courage, the worm!'

Which explains why she killed him when she did, Ellie.

'So Ogden then blackmailed you,' Eleanor said grimly.

'What was it? Be his mistress or he'd expose you? Maybe he'd guessed about your husbands, too?'

Mrs Vanderdale shuddered again. 'That odious wretch laid it out real clear. Either he got to slime his tentacles all over me whenever he wished or he'd ruin me by telling everyone where I'd come from. I'd have been finished!'

Eleanor swallowed hard. 'Which is why you killed him too. Using one of his cars in both murders so that you could then have Temples framed for his, and Marty's, murder.'

Of course, Ellie! Marty's dying words weren't 'Why Marry?' That was a red herring. They were 'Why, Mary?' He did recognise the driver of the car that killed him. The woman he loved who had ignored him, got him sacked, and then ran him down!

'What? No applause?' Mrs Vanderdale said sarcastically. 'You can't even acknowledge brilliance gracefully, Lady Swift. Mind you, you and graceful have yet to be introduced!'

Eleanor shook her head. 'Insult me all you like. It doesn't sting. Unlike seeing Marty breathing his last in my arms.'

'You're breaking my heart, Lady Swift.' The car slowed. 'As I'm about to break yours.'

Grace's Peak turned out not to be a place, but a boat, the name written in scrolling, gold lettering on the side. It was tied fast to a hidden jetty, alongside another smaller version. She shuddered. A boat could only mean one thing. A watery grave. It was then she spotted the concrete blocks with chains attached.

'Get in,' Mrs Vanderdale said.

'But I'm terrible on water,' Eleanor lied, digging her heels in.

'Throw her in!'

She landed awkwardly on the boat's deck thanks to her still tightly bound wrists. Her cheek felt raw with the vicious graze the non-slip decking had dealt her. She was about to shuffle herself upright when the collar of her dress jerked into her throat as she was yanked down against the base of the padded seating by scar-face. The craft's front end reared up out of the water.

'Who says women don't like speed?' Mrs Vanderdale cried at the wheel. 'It's almost as exhilarating as murder!'

Think, Ellie, think!

But the lurch of the boat slapping hard into the swell was jerking her up and down on the floor too much to think. And something was digging painfully into her side. She'd landed on the locker handle on the seat base and broken it!

Unobtrusively, she pushed herself against it, feeling for the sharp metal. With bated breath, she began to rub her rope bindings along it.

The lights of two small islands mid bay flashed into view with every wild roll the boat took to the left. After the fourth sighting, she settled on them likely being three quarters of a mile apart and likely a mile from where they were right now. Though calculating with any accuracy across inky black water, after years away from sailing and while trying to free her hands...

Not trying to, Ellie. Free!

She let out the breath burning in her chest and waited. She had one chance. And one chance only.

'Eight tenths of a mile,' she counted silently.

'Say, boss, ain't the channel right a bit?' the scar-faced thug called anxiously to Mrs Vanderdale.

'Don't question me!' He fell against the seat with the force of the woman's slap, the boat lurching momentarily until she had both hands on the wheel again.

Eleanor's stomach clenched, praying they wouldn't change course. 'Seven tenths,' she counted to herself. 'Six tenths.' In a single fluid motion, she pushed herself up off the floor and slid over the side of the boat.

42

Icy cold. Cruel undertow. That was all Eleanor could think of before she surfaced with a gasp. And then the heavy swell hit her. She struck out for what looked like the nearest of the two islands, failing to keep her mouth clear of the waves breaking over her head.

She heard a yell over the boat's engine. 'Say! Where'd she go?'

Never more grateful than now for her parents' insistence that she learned to swim strongly as a child, she willed herself to focus. Her father had repeated a mantra to her every time they'd raced each other across a stretch of azure ocean.

'Remember, darling, front crawl; body parallel, let it roll naturally, find your rhythm, breathe alternate sides every three to five strokes.'

'Five tenths.' She gurgled through a mouthful of foul water.

The roar of the boat turning forced her to surge on. She tried to ignore the sting of salt against her grazed face and the constant pain in her wrist from being thrown to the floor. As she swam, her technique held, but her out of practice muscles began to tire all too soon.

'Four tenths.'

Off to her right, she could see an arc of light swinging wildly across the water. If Mrs Vanderdale picked her out in the beam of the boat's searchlight, she was lost. There was no swimmer on earth who could outrun a motor like that. Focusing on the island, she struck out with all the force she could muster.

'Three tenths.'

'Ain't that her, boss? Right there!' The cry came from out of the dark above the constant sound of the circling speedboat.

She took the deepest breath she could and dived. Engulfed in black, freezing water, she ignored the burning in her lungs and exhausted arms and kept swimming. Something brushed against her body. The image of the concrete blocks with chains attached leapt into her mind.

How many people has that woman drowned down here before?

She gasped in horror, cursing her imagination as she headed for the surface as fast as she could.

'One and a half tenths,' she choked as she gulped a lungful of air, desperately hoping she hadn't come up near the speedboat.

The roar of an engine sounded terrifyingly close by. Before she could respond, the vicious swell carried her away. She dived again. The next time she came up, she knew she was near exhaustion.

'One tenth.'

Forget the boat, Ellie. Just swim.

How her muscles held out, she didn't know, but she finally reached shore. Dragging herself out by a drainage pipe, she sprawled on the ground, trying to get her breath. She listened for the boat's engine.

Nothing.

Bad. Very bad.

She scrambled up and set off. Behind her, a fork of lightning lit the sky. With no idea where she was, it didn't matter which direction she went in. She just needed to put as much distance between her and her pursuers as possible. A roll of thunder broke. Before she'd taken a dozen steps, she gasped.

'The Statue of Liberty! I'm on Bedloe's Island!'

She headed toward the monument with renewed hope. There had to be a park ranger. Or security. Or someone there.

'Please be open,' she begged as she reached the bottom of the enormous statue, its colossal form outlined against the dark sky. She ran along the towering wall of stone, her breath ragged.

The door has to be as you look at her face, Ellie.

She willed her legs on.

There it is!

She lunged for the handle.

'Stop!' Mrs Vanderdale's voice called through the dim lighting of the monument's pedestal.

'Say, lady. Statue's closed this time of night. I'm the park ranger. You shouldn't—'

Before Eleanor could cry out in warning, the man collapsed to the ground, scar-face standing over him with a cosh.

Where's the other goon, Ellie?

Mrs Vanderdale turned back to her. 'Move and I'll shoot you where you stand.'

Praying it wasn't locked, she wrenched the door open and ducked inside as a bullet ricocheted off the lintel above her head. She spun around, but even in the gloom, she could see there was no internal lock. But there was a torch. She clicked it on and ran as she heard the door being kicked ajar.

Having no idea what the layout could be, she stumbled up a wide run of stairs, trying not to panic at the sound of voices behind her.

'Stupid move, Lady Swift,' Mrs Vanderdale's voice echoed up to her in the gloom. 'There's no way out, don't you know that? Except for a fatal fall, of course!'

Fight to the end, Ellie. That's all you can do.

The sweep of another torch made her groan. So they had one too.

The cast iron stairs switchbacked dizzyingly, pushing her higher with every turn. Above, her torch's weak beam illuminated only more metal; bars, braces and rails, the framework Lady Liberty's copper sheets were nailed to.

She faltered momentarily. A bullet glanced off the rail by her hand. Turning off her torch, she clambered on and on upwards towards a seemingly inevitable end as the sound of her pursuers drew closer.

The staircase narrowed and spiralled at a sharper angle out of view. On the other side, she spied a shadowy second staircase. She considered risking a leap across the dark void and doubling back down. If she missed it, the fall would certainly kill her. But if she carried on to the top of the statue, what then? She shook her head. Even if she made the jump, one of the thugs could do the same and cut her off.

'You're almost in her crown, fool!' Mrs Vanderdale yelled from just below. 'Where do you intend to go from there?'

Eleanor hesitated. *She's right. It's suicide. You might as well give up now if you keep going.*

She caught sight of what looked like a barricaded exit to her left. Wherever it led, it was better than the crown. She turned and shouldered through it. The space on the other side was so narrow, she wondered if she was in one of the statue's arms? A ladder ran vertically upwards. The scores of rivets she could make out holding the statue's copper skin to its iron framework looked almost easier to climb than the ladder's rungs.

'She went that way!' scar-face's voice called from the other side of the barricaded exit.

She grabbed the first rung and scrambled up.

'She's just up there, boss.'

'Then kill her! She's trapped. It will be like shooting fish in a barrel!'

'We're all out,' scar-face's companion called. 'We gotta reload.'

'Well, I'm not.'

Instinctively, Eleanor swung off the ladder, hanging on with one arm. Bullets sent sparks flying all around her.

'Blast! I'm out too. Who's reloaded?' Mrs Vanderdale's voice came from below.

Swinging back onto the ladder, Eleanor wrenched herself on upwards until she reached a platform. Another ladder led further up. Another shot rang out.

'You've nowhere to go, Lady Swift,' Mrs Vanderdale's mocking voice called up to her.

Eleanor ran to the other ladder and started up. It stopped at a door after only a short distance. She crossed her fingers and pushed. The gust that greeted her almost knocked her off her feet. She gripped the doorframe and stepped out.

You're on the torch's balcony, Ellie!

She hunched down as lightning flashed and thunder rolled around the city and bay. The sound of someone else on the platform brought her back to her plight. She flattened herself against the far side of the torch's flame. A fork of lightning struck the island, the crack of thunder almost immediate.

The storm will be dead overhead in a moment, Ellie.

'You still think you can win?' Mrs Vanderdale shouted.

'Never underestimate a determined woman!' Eleanor yelled back.

'It's over, Lady Swift!' Mrs Vanderdale called chillingly into the increasing wind. 'Not even Lady Liberty can help you now.'

'What do you know about liberty?' Eleanor shouted bitterly. 'Your so-called Ladies' Liberty Club is a mockery.' She stared up at the statue. 'This is a monument to freedom. All you've built is a monument to evil.'

She frowned. Something's wrong. Where were her thugs? And why...

She's out of bullets!

Eleanor swung around and stopped dead. Mrs Vanderdale stood there, her gun pointing at her. She'd been too slow. She'd reloaded.

Mrs Vanderdale laughed maliciously. 'It's three hundred feet down, but the view on the way will be spectacular.'

A crackling noise filled the air and the hairs on Eleanor's arms stood up. The metal rail glowed blue. She stared up into the sky and then down into the barrel of Mrs Vanderdale's gun. Out of the corner of her eye, she saw she was level with the exit off the platform. She dived for it as Mrs Vanderdale looked around her in confusion. As Eleanor fell through it, she glimpsed a bolt of lightning hit the torch and run down to the balcony. A second later, she felt the most intense burning heat. And then everything spun into blackness.

43

'Welcome home, m'lady.' Mrs Butters' smile lit the room. 'I can't tell you how loud we all cheered when Mr Clifford sent word the doctors had released you so soon!'

Before Eleanor could reply, Gladstone assaulted her excitedly with his signature licky greeting. Clifford gently intercepted the bulldog as she held her bandaged arms out of harm's way.

'I love his new striped woollen neckerchief,' Eleanor said, letting Gladstone's wildly flailing tongue lick her nose at least. 'It's very fetching.'

Polly clapped excitedly. 'Mrs Butters knitted it 'specially.'

Mrs Trotman nodded. 'While Mr Clifford kept ringing the hospital for news.'

Mrs Butters laughed. 'Mostly to save us using up all his precious handkerchiefs.'

Clifford nodded while she glanced along the neat line of her staff.

'Thank you, all. Really. But the important thing is, I'm perfectly fine now.'

'Heartening news,' Clifford said. 'So the hospital convalescence has achieved its aim?'

She lowered her arms gingerly and shrugged. 'Mostly. Though, maybe things do still... smart a little.' She peered sideways at him. 'But I only agreed to stay in a few days longer to stop you fussing about pneumonia. Well, that and all the other ghastly scare stories you gave me about what I might have contracted from a quick dip in the Hudson River.'

Clifford tutted. 'Over half a mile in rough open water, swimming against the tide hardly constitutes "a quick dip" my lady. And as for the burns you suffered—'

She raised her hand carefully. 'But I mostly stayed so you could have a well-deserved break from me.'

His eyes twinkled. 'Too kind. Convalescence can be arranged for considerably longer, however?'

She laughed. 'You are a terrible man! Imagine if I had though. I was only gone a short time and you've decamped us all back across town, I see.'

He adjusted his tie. 'Sincere apologies for the significant overstepping in your absence. However, the second, smaller apartment was no place for a lady to recuperate. And the owner of this, our original apartment, wanted to show his deep appreciation for your courage and bravery.'

'By which, you heard "stubbornness" and "recklessness". And leaped at the offer of a reduced rent to repair some of the damage the household accounts sustained?'

'Perhaps. And perhaps. Though "reckless" and "impossible" I imagine might have been more the exasperated outpourings of a certain chief inspector?'

She sighed. 'Yes! But it was so good to hear Hugh's voice I didn't care. Three times a day he telephoned me at the hospital. And again to say goodnight.' Her shoulders rose with glee. 'And he didn't tell me off as much as he has on previous occasions, anyway. But I suspect that is because you entirely played down what happened?'

He adjusted his cuffs. 'I really couldn't say. But suffice to note we will need to get our joint story straight before the gentleman scoops you up as you dock in Southampton in three weeks' time.'

Eleanor nodded and turned back to the ladies. 'Well, as long as you are all happy back here, I'm happy too. You've had so much upheaval, though, for which I'm truly sorry.'

Mrs Trotman bustled forward, wiping her hands on her apron. 'Oh 'tis no bother at all, m'lady. Don't matter if it's Henley Hall, this apartment or t'other smaller one. Could be a cardboard box in the street and the six of us'd all be just fine.'

Gladstone let out an indignant woof.

'Seven,' Lizzie said. 'Ach! Where would we be without Mr Wilful?'

Mrs Butters sniffed as she pulled Lizzie and Polly into a hug. 'You'll be starting us all off again. And Mr Clifford doesn't need any more waterworks.'

'No, he doesn't,' Clifford said quickly. He caught Eleanor's look. 'Besides, her ladyship has been gracious enough to grant you the rest of the day to yourselves as a heartfelt thank you for having the apartment so welcoming upon her return.' He clamped his hand over his ears as the ladies cheered and bustled out, curtseying as they went.

Alone with her butler in the drawing room, Eleanor cocked her head questioningly as he checked his pocket watch again.

'Still fretting about time, Clifford? I rather thought we'd both beaten it hands down recently?'

'The mortal hour.' He looked at her earnestly. 'Perhaps. But only by avoiding a bullet by the skin of one's teeth and serious illness from contamination in the Hudson River by dint of a stubbornly robust constitution. Not to mention avoiding first-degree burns by a whisker of—'

'Clifford!'

'Or by not actually surrendering to the heart attack which threatened when one's mistress charged into grievous danger. Alone,' he ended quietly.

She wished just once she could show him the affection his loyalty always brought out in her. 'I wasn't alone,' she said gently. 'You arrived just in time. And with Balowski and Iver as reinforcements. Though how you found me, I still can't fathom.'

He examined his watch again. 'I am afraid there is no time to relay events. Your appointment calls.'

'But the weather broke with the storm, Clifford?' she said as she waited for the lift, still mystified as to where they were going. 'Why are you so insistent I need such a cool tea dress for this afternoon? Gladstone's still got his scarf on, after all.'

He merely pressed the lift call bell in enigmatic reply.

A minute later, she gasped. 'Oh, Clifford, tell me, are they back—'

The faded blue basement door opened to reveal a beaming Mrs Morales. 'Honey, get yourself and your good-lookin' butler in here so I can hug the life outta ya both.'

Clifford blanched. 'After you, my lady.'

The usually cramped Morales' kitchen was nothing like Eleanor's previous visits. Today, the old, worn table had been swapped for the long console from her own apartment, set with pretty napkins and sprigs of greenery. And, oddly, one of her upright dining chairs with sturdy arms. A run of tea chests had been perfectly aligned along the sides, each sporting a patch-work cushion, with space left at the head of the table for a wheelchair. And if the lovingly home-made decorations weren't enough, the throng of familiar faces packing the room made her heart skip.

'Balowski!' she cheered as Gladstone scrabbled up his leg.

'And Iver too! And, ladies, what a treat you all look!' Beside the taxi driver, her four staff curtseyed, showing off the home-made summer dresses they wore.

'Say, er, Lady Swift?' A figure stepped in from the adjoining corridor.

'Hello, Earl.' She was overcome with delight as he offered his hand for her to shake. He looked at the ground and then back at her.

'What you did for my brother Marty, Ma and me, well, we're real grateful.'

'So?' Balowski interjected before she could reply. 'What I did was no good then, huh? Takin' a gun to the head. Drivin' that boat so fast, like I'd done it my whole life. I ain't never driven a boat before!'

Earl see-sawed his head. 'Don't sound much.'

'Oh really? What about me then runnin' up the Statue of Liberty like I run races for a livin'? And then knockin' one of those clowns out that was tryin' to get to her?'

Clifford tutted. 'To Lady Swift, I believe you mean, Officer Balowski.'

'No, Suitsville. I meant *her*. Ain't no titled lady ever done, or gonna do, what she did. Not before now. And not after now. She is one crazy doll. But anyways, I owe you somethin'.'

Clifford shook his head, his lips quirking. 'Not all debts need be repaid, Officer Balowski. Besides, knocking me to the ground in the presence of ladies would be boorish in the extreme.'

Eleanor flinched as Balowski pushed past Iver to square up to her butler.

'Boys!' Eleanor slapped the table.

'Don't get your under-unmentionables in a twist, lady.' Balowski grinned. 'I was only gonna offer your help here thanks. I realised afterwards he only punched me to save my life.'

Clifford shook Balowski's hand. 'I confess, it was the only way I could think of to stop them shooting you on the spot.'

Iver folded his arms. 'So my caroonin' back to pick up Balowski who was laid out cold and Mr Clifford who was just pretendin' he was, ain't worth a bean. Is that what you're sayin'?'

'Iver, wait up!' Mrs Morales flapped both arms. 'Ya all killin' this old lady with all these little teasin' snippets of what happened. Now this is my kitchen, and my rules. So ya all gonna sit on your tea chests and tell your side in just a minute. First, I've got to show Trotters there what's what in the kitchen.'

Eleanor took the tea chest Clifford held out for her, too busy laughing to wonder why he hadn't insisted she take the dining chair.

Mrs Trotman let out a mock scoff. 'Well, tip number one had better be start by finding a grocer as looks as good in his little apron as the one I found along the way there. Otherwise I shan't be taking any notes, Mrs M.'

Amid the roar of laughter that filled the room, Eleanor caught Clifford shaking his head and tutting.

'I just meant as it shows a high level of professionalism, Mr Clifford,' Mrs Trotman said cheekily.

Mrs Morales laughed. 'No, ya didn't. But go on, tease him some more. Those good-lookin' cheeks of his look even better with those cute, red spots of colour. Ain't that right, Mr Wrinkles?' She stroked Gladstone's jowls where his front half lay sprawled in her lap. Eleanor shook her head as her butler glided out of the basement. Mrs Morales rolled on oblivious. 'But drink up your juice, everybody. Food's a way off. Us girls have plenty of squabblin' left yet. I—' She stopped and stared at the front door.

Everyone turned as Clifford walked slowly back in with an unexpected guest.

44

_____

'I hope I'm not intruding?' Leaning on Clifford's arm, Mrs Melchum looked around uncomfortably.

Mrs Morales smiled. 'Would I have sent you an invitation if you was intrudin'? Leave the door open for air, Mr Clifford, won't ya.' She wheeled herself down the narrow gap behind the tea chests and patted the other woman's hand. 'We both lost a precious son. And this lady, with some help' – she indicated the three men in the room – 'got justice for both our boys. So I figured you'd be itchin' to hear the tale too.'

'Thank you,' Mrs Melchum croaked. She sank her rose taffeta-clad form stiffly into the dining chair Clifford was holding out. 'And my gratitude to you, Lady Swift. And to your' – she waved a hand around the room – 'entourage.'

Clifford topped up everyone's iced juice, then dinged his glass with a spoon and bowed to Mrs Morales.

'Madam, shall we to the story?'

Her eyes twinkled. 'Oh, you are a keeper, fella! Lady Swift, you kick us off.'

She shook her head. 'I think first of all, I need to apologise to you all. I inadvertently caused you a lot of trouble.' She smiled at Clifford. 'And a lot of worry. Please forgive me.'

'After what you was so brave as to up and do, honey?' Mrs Morales reached over to cup Eleanor's cheeks. 'I'd forgive ya for takin' away the sun!'

Mrs Melchum nodded. 'So would I. And the moon and stars, too.'

'But, just what in the world were you thinkin'?' Mrs Morales exclaimed. 'Goin' out into the middle of nowhere like that?'

'Well, Officer Balowski's call sounded genuine.'

'It was.' He looked abashed. 'I didn't wanna make it, I swear. But—'

Eleanor raised her hand. 'You told me that day in the diner that no one in this city cared about "one more dead doorman". Well, you risked your job, and your life, from the moment you offered to help find out what happened to Marty, so I think you've earned your caring badge.'

Balowski shrugged. 'Whatever. But I got my real badge back, along with my job. And' – he stood and took a deep bow – 'a citation, too!'

'Congratulations!' Eleanor joined in with the collective applause. All eyes swivelled to Earl, who was the only one to abstain.

'What? One guy clappin' another guy for doin' what he's paid for? Yeah, right. I got promoted to building manager here. You gonna clap for me, cop?'

'Yeah, maybe. When oysters start growin' on the moon.'

Eleanor and Mrs Morales shared an amused eye roll. 'So, Balowski had a gun to his head, and...?' their hostess coaxed.

Iver nodded. 'And Lady Swift had one to her...' He waved an uncomfortable hand. 'Frontage.'

She laughed. 'So gallantly put. But well done for your quick thinking in speeding off as if running away. I confess, you fooled me.'

'Indeed,' Clifford said. 'The very moment after you were driven off, my lady, Iver's taxi reappeared from the other side of the hill.'

Iver shrugged. 'What can I say? Sadie and I were kids back in the day. Billycoo layout ain't no different today.'

'But, Clifford,' Eleanor said, 'that goon struck you so hard with that cosh. How come you recovered so quickly? With no injury?'

'A steel band added to the crown of my bowler hat, my lady.' He eyed her sideways. 'An addition I instigated after our last "holiday".'

'Sorry,' she groaned.

Balowski grunted. 'Suitsville here was able to slap me awake in Iver's taxi while you was swimmin' with the sharks. Luckily, I'm used to lowlife tryin' to knock me out, so I dropped to the ground when he made with the uppercut so it weren't so bad.'

Eleanor was staring at Balowski with an open mouth. 'Sharks! Clifford, tell me there aren't really sharks in the Hudson?'

'There aren't, my lady.'

Mrs Morales laughed. 'Fella, you gonna have to learn how to lie better! Just like my pride and joy, Earl, over there.'

'Ma!' Earl swallowed hard. 'Marty was your pride and joy.'

'No, son, it was always the both of ya. Ya just never heard me right. And maybe I never did tell ya right. But there ain't nothin more precious than sons. That so, Mrs Melchum?'

The older woman nodded. 'Amen to that.'

'So,' Eleanor frowned, 'Iver cleverly followed Mrs Vanderdale's car with the three of you in it. And you saw me being taken off in the boat?'

'To shorten the story, in essence, yes, my lady.'

'Suitsville jumped into the second smaller boat she'd got

hidden,' Balowski said. 'And somehow hot-wired the motor.' He paused and stared at Clifford. 'Say, I might get another citation for investigatin' just how you know stuff like that?'

'And how to pick the lock in your old apartment?' Mrs Melchum said questioningly.

'Oh, that would only make the story drag,' Eleanor said hurriedly. Clifford gave her a grateful look. 'But I still don't understand how you knew I was at the Statue of Liberty?'

'We saw Mrs Vanderdale's boat tied up on Bedloe's Island and came ashore, my lady.' Clifford shuddered. 'Terrifying though the thought is, I fear it was the consequence of constant exposure to feminine intuition that then led me to believe you might be found there.'

'At the very top of her!' Balowski and Iver chorused.

Iver chuckled. 'Lady, look at this face. And this body. When I told my Sadie how I'd run up all them stairs—'

'And still had punch left for Mrs Vanderdale's reprobates,' Clifford added appreciatively.

'Yeah.' Iver grinned. 'I did, didn't I?' He cocked his jaw at Eleanor. 'So, lady, you believe now that New York does just what the heck she fancies? 'Cos she brought that lightning down to save you, and teach that evil broad a lesson, I swear.'

Mrs Melchum twisted a handkerchief around her fingers. 'That terrible wretch who killed our sons? Was she struck by the lightning?'

'Yes,' Clifford said. 'And badly burned. But she will live.'

Mrs Morales gasped. 'You mean she's gonna pay for what she did to our boys?'

'Unquestionably, madam,' he said softly. 'Not that any punishment could ever be sufficient.' He glanced at Eleanor, who nodded.

'Mrs Morales, as Clifford said, nothing can pay you back for what Mrs Vanderdale has taken from you. We can only offer you justice for Marty and' – Clifford passed her a small parcel – 'this.'

Mrs Morales took it, confusion on her face. As she opened the parcel, her eyes widened. 'What... what is this?'

Eleanor smiled. 'It's the money Mrs Vanderdale had her thugs hide in Marty's room when she framed him for stealing so Dellaney would sack him. Temples told Dellaney Marty had been taking "unauthorised bonuses". Dellaney obviously found the ones Mrs Vanderdale's thugs had planted in Marty's things in his garage, but never bothered to have him arrested and his room searched. Probably, because he wanted the least publicity possible, given he was likely as crooked as everyone else in this town seems to be. Present company excepted, of course.'

Mrs Morales shook her head. 'I can't take this money.'

'Why not, Ma?' Earl shrugged. 'It's Mrs Vanderdale's money. And she took Marty. We could get you a new wheelchair, for a start, so you could get out more. That old one don't hardly wheel.'

Mrs Morales smiled gratefully at Eleanor. 'I guess Earl is right. Thank you. It'll be a great help.'

'So, what's next for everyone?' Balowski slapped a hand on the table. 'Me and Earl gonna be busy with our new jobs.'

'Important new jobs,' Earl grunted. 'Least mine is.'

'Oh, like fixing a tap is more important than savin' the city every night?'

'Give up, double buttons, I'm the building manager now, not the wrench monkey. And you needed a pretty lady with a fancy title to do all that savin' for ya.'

Mrs Morales raised her hand. 'Children!' She turned to Mrs Melchum. 'And what about you?'

The woman shifted uncomfortably. 'Me? Well, I rather thought I might venture out... to the theatre this evening.'

Eleanor's heart leaped at the woman's newfound spirit. 'That's wonderful!'

'Thank you, Lady Swift. Any suggestions?'

'Oh, we could try *Why Marry?* if you like.'

'*We?*' Mrs Melchum's face lit up. 'You and your... help would come with me?'

'If it's good with you?'

Mrs Melchum turned to her butler. 'I'd be honoured to be accompanied by Lady Swift and you, Mr Clifford. You both helped get justice for my son.'

'And what about you, Ma?' Earl put an arm around his mother's shoulder.

Mrs Morales beamed. 'Oh, son, I got the best treat waitin'. Soon as we done here, Lady Swift's gonna wheel ya mama round Central Park to see all the calamansi trees our Marty planted. If that's still on, honey?'

'I wouldn't miss it for all the world,' Eleanor croaked through her faltering emotions.

Mrs Melchum hesitated, then seemed to gather her courage. 'And after Lady Swift has returned to England, Mrs Morales, perhaps... perhaps you and I could go to Central Park together and see your son's trees?'

Mrs Morales' eyes teared up. 'I'd love that. I really would.'

Mrs Melchum smiled wanly. 'I'm so pleased. And we can go see Ogden's tree, too. I... I have asked the park authorities if they would plant one in his memory, and they agreed. With a donation on my part to the park fund, of course.'

Mrs Morales clapped her hands. 'Enough of all this before we all start blubbin'. It's cookin' time, Trotters.'

The two of them busied themselves around the table, with Polly and Lizzie acting as kitchen girls.

All was harmonious for five minutes until...

'But what ya doin'?' Mrs Morales tutted. 'Butter don't get rubbed inta the flour like that!'

'And the sugar doesn't get added before the fruit,' Eleanor's cook said huffily. 'Nor the cheese before the salt like you're doing!'

Mrs Morales rapped the table. 'Says the mare in the apron who puts herbs in after everythin' else for pastries!'

Eleanor's cook tapped her foot, hands on hips. 'Listen, dear. My mother always used to say—'

What she used to say, Eleanor never found out as Earl poked Balowski in the shoulder as he pushed past to get between the warring women.

'Say, watch it!'

'Watch what? You get one citation and suddenly you think you're somethin'.'

'Maybe it's just the heat in here?' Eleanor whispered to Clifford. But her butler seemed distracted. A haughty hiss made her realise he was staring at the front door in horror. Catamina had evidently followed her mistress and was now poised, ready to pounce in revenge on an unsuspecting Gladstone who was busy ogling the food preparations.

Clifford coughed discreetly. 'My lady, I suddenly feel an unrelenting urge to sample New York's finest cuisine... outside. Hot dogs with yellow sauce?'

She nodded eagerly. 'Johnny cakes in a greasy booth and no cutlery?'

'Permit me to race you!'

A LETTER FROM VERITY

Dear reader,

I want to say a huge thank you for choosing to read *Murder in Manhattan*. If you did enjoy it, and want to keep up to date with all my latest releases, just sign up at the following link. Your email address will never be shared and you can unsubscribe at any time.

www.bookouture.com/verity-bright

I hope you loved *Murder in Manhattan* and if you did I would be very grateful if you could write a review. I'd love to hear what you think, and it makes such a difference helping new readers to discover one of my books for the first time.

I love hearing from my readers – you can get in touch on my Facebook page, through Twitter, Goodreads or my website.

Thanks,

Verity

www.veritybright.com

facebook.com/veritybrightauthor
twitter.com/BrightVerity

HISTORICAL NOTES

PROHIBITION

The odd thing about prohibition is that it was never actually illegal to drink alcohol. It was generally illegal from 1920 to 1933 in the United States to import, make, distribute or sell alcohol, but not to drink it. Hence, when it was known the legislation was going to be introduced, many rich people simply bought up the entire stock of liquor stores and had it shipped to their cellars to keep them going. Others used medical prescriptions for alcohol – over ten million were written in the year Eleanor was in New York – or drank in illegal bars known as speakeasies. Not all states enforced prohibition either, New York being one of the most resistant, and some never ended it until way after 1933. Mississippi only repealed the law in its state in 2021!

ORGANISED CRIME

Prohibition made criminals throughout the US not only rich, but also legitimate. As Newkirk says, the line between criminal and non-criminal became so blurred it was almost invisible. In New York alone hundreds of agents from the Bureau of Prohibition tasked with enforcing the laws were sacked for corruption, while the bureau's boss resigned, stating the task was impossible. And boy, did it make criminals like Atticus Wyatt and Mrs Vanderdale rich. In the year Eleanor was in New York, the top crime bosses were estimated to be making around $1 to $1.5 billion a year.

FEMALE GANGSTERS

When anyone talks about American gangsters of the 1920s and 1930s, names like Al Capone, Charles Luciano and Dutch Schultz are mentioned. But as Mrs Vanderdale would delight in explaining, there were some women showing it wasn't just a man's world. One of the most famous, Stephanie St. Clair – nicknamed 'Queenie' – ruled Harlem and beyond, even making alliances with the likes of Luciano and defying Schultz. In fact, when Schultz tried to have her killed, Luciano had him killed instead. Defying convention again, Queenie later went straight and became a civil rights activist, something Mrs Vanderdale might have considered.

BROADWAY

Broadway in the 1920s and 1930s wasn't just the centre of theatreland Dellaney was so enamoured of, it was a place where gangsters and millionaires rubbed shoulders with movie and sports stars in speakeasies like the one Eleanor found Wyatt in. Charlie Chaplin and the Marx Brothers were frequent visitors, as was Babe Ruth who used to attend all-night poker games along with the likes of Al Jolson.

WOMEN AND SMOKING IN 1920s

Few women smoked in the US at the beginning of the 1920s. It was considered 'un-feminine', not only by men, but most women too. In fact, for a short period it was illegal for women to smoke in public in New York. The first real campaign by tobacco companies aimed at women was in 1917, but it wasn't until 1935 that it had a huge impact and women smokers became the norm. Of course, independent women like Mrs Vanderdale smoked, mainly in private. A habit of hers, like murder, that perhaps is best not copied!

NOTE: I have made Mrs Vanderdale smoke Gitanes as they were unusual being French imports and mostly smoked by the rich. However, I may have moved the date they were available in the US a trifle to marry up with the story :)

HEATWAVES IN NEW YORK

Heatwaves do occur in the Big Apple in April. In April 1896 and 1915 the temperature reached over ninety degrees Fahrenheit – 32 degrees Celsius. More usually they occur later in the year. Unfortunately, even though air conditioning had been invented by the 1920s, it was expensive, not very effective and few people had it. A heatwave some years before Eleanor arrived was estimated to have killed several thousand people. And when a storm finally brought the temperature down, five people were killed by lightning, something Mrs Vanderdale might have taken note of.

STATUE OF LIBERTY

This iconic landmark is so well known, there is little I can add you probably don't already know. Two facts Eleanor learns from Iver and Clifford, however, is that the torch was closed to visitors after a bomb blast on Black Tom Island on 30 July, 1916. It was believed to be the work of German spies trying to destroy the armament production on the island that the US were running to quietly supply Britain and France in WW1. The torch has never been reopened. And the statute's height, coupled, as Clifford says, with its outer structure being made of copper, makes it a perfect lightning conductor. It has been estimated that it has been struck by lightning over 6,000 times.

ACKNOWLEDGEMENTS

Thanks to my editor Kelsie for her stellar editing and support and to the rest of the Bookouture Team for their part in making *Murder in Manhattan* so much fun to work on.

Made in United States
Troutdale, OR
07/05/2023

11003058R00184